THE RANCHER MEETS HIS MATCH

She licked some ice cream off her spoon. "It's you."

"It's me, what?" Kaiden's gaze was riveted on her mouth.

"You unsettle me."

He sat back. "There's an easy fix for that, Julia. We just agree to keep out of each other's way for the next couple of weeks while you're here. It's not difficult."

"But, I don't want to do that."

Her words filled a silence he seemed unable or unwilling to end. Eventually, he stirred.

"What do you want then, Julia?"

She was equally slow to respond, and for once glad of the darkness and intimacy of the truck cab. Everything else—her job, her life, and her common sense—receded as she faced something far more instinctive and natural.

"You," she said. "I want you. . . ."

THE
RANCHER
MEETS HIS
MATCH

KATE PEARCE

ZEBRA BOOKS
KENSINGTON PUBLISHING CORP.
www.kensingtonbooks.com

ZEBRA BOOKS are published by

Kensington Publishing Corp.
119 West 40th Street
New York, NY 10018

All Kensington titles, imprints, and distributed lines are available at special quantity discounts for bulk purchases for sales promotion, premiums, fund-raising, educational, or institutional use.

Special book excerpts or customized printings can also be created to fit specific needs. For details, write or phone the office of the Kensington Sales Manager: Attn.: Sales Department. Kensington Publishing Corp., 119 West 40th Street, New York, NY 10018. Phone: 1-800-221-2647.

Zebra and the Z logo Reg. U.S. Pat. & TM Off.

First Printing: January 2021
ISBN-13: 978-1-4201-5255-5
ISBN-10: 1-4201-5255-6

ISBN-13: 978-1-4201-5256-2 (eBook)
ISBN-10: 1-4201-5256-4 (eBook)

10 9 8 7 6 5 4 3 2 1

Printed in the United States of America

This book is for my sister, Rachel, who inspires me in many ways and hopefully will finally forgive me for not dedicating the book with a heroine named 'Rachel' to her and accept this one instead.

ACKNOWLEDGMENTS

I have many people to thank for helping me with this book. Sian Kaley and Jerri Drennen for their critiques, and Meg Scales for ranch related questions. Elaine Torres-Pisio gave me some wonderful stories of growing up in a large Northern Californian family with Mexican roots, and Rachel Spall offered me her insights on living with MS.

Chapter One

Morgan Valley, California

"You still up there, Kaiden?"

Kaiden Miller took a second to remove the two long nails from between his teeth before squinting down through the haze of dust and wood shavings to the floor below. He was halfway up a ladder inside the gutted interior of what had once been the Morgantown movie theater attempting to repair a broken support beam.

"Yup, what do you need, Doc?"

He put the nails in the top pocket of his denim shirt and his hammer back in his tool belt before carefully climbing down.

"Sorry to interrupt you," Dr. Tio said. "But I wanted to check in before you headed home tonight."

Kaiden shook the sawdust off his battered old watch, and realized it was far later than he'd realized. He was supposed to be helping at the ranch while his brother Danny was away at some agricultural college thing. His father, who wasn't known for either his patience, or his good temper, would be yelling the moment Kaiden turned into the driveway to the ranch.

"Sure, how can I help, Doc?"

He was already late; he might as well enjoy the full Jeff Miller show with all the trimmings.

"I just had Juan Garcia in for an appointment."

"How's he doing?" Kaiden asked.

"Not too good. It looks like he's going to be using a wheelchair a lot more." Dr. Tio grimaced. "Which means his ranch house is going to need some adaptations."

"Do you want me to take a look at it?"

For some reason, even though technically he was just a carpenter, Kaiden was often asked to be the project manager for local jobs. Not that he minded. He got bored very quickly and appreciated some variety in his life.

"If you could, that would be great. I'd much rather someone local got the job." Dr. Tio looked relieved. "The family is willing to pay the going rate to get it done as quickly as possible."

"I'll have to check in with my dad as to my availability, and I can't do it all myself," Kaiden added. "But I know plenty of guys who would be happy to get the work."

"Thanks so much." Dr. Tio patted his shoulder. "I appreciate it."

Kaiden nodded. "Tell Mr. Garcia I'll drop in tomorrow morning, if that's okay."

"Will do." Dr. Tio paused to look up at the twenty-foot-high roof. "This place is coming along great. How many apartments do you think you'll get in here?"

"At least four, maybe six depending on what Chase Morgan's architect decides when we've finished checking out the structural integrity of the place."

Kaiden had fallen in love with the old building, which somehow, despite falling into disrepair, still retained the scent of popcorn, bubblegum, and anticipation from its movie theater days. Luckily, May Chang, the architect, was a big fan of keeping as much of the original spirit of the building as Kaiden was.

"Thanks again, Kaiden," Dr. Tio repeated. "I'll speak to you tomorrow."

He picked his way carefully through the debris and out onto the street. Kaiden took the time to make sure all the tools were locked away and the site was as secure as he could make it before locking the temporary door behind him and heading for his truck.

The sun hadn't quite gone down and cast a beam of light straight along Main Street illuminating the raised walkways, false shop fronts, and hitching posts that gave Morgantown its special Northern California gold rush town appeal. Even though he'd lived there his entire life, Kaiden wasn't immune either to its charm or its limitations.

His cell phone buzzed. He took it out to see at least ten messages with full-on caps and exclamation points and wished again that his sister Daisy hadn't taught their father how to text. He didn't bother to reply. He'd be home in fifteen minutes and then his father could give it to him straight.

As he approached his battered truck, Kaiden thumbed through his contacts checking to see if he had a number for the Garcia Ranch. As Juan's health had failed, a few of the local ranchers who matched boundaries with the Garcias had tried to help out mending fences and moving cattle when the valley had partially flooded. It wasn't as if they weren't busy enough, but out here in Morgan Valley, it was a tradition that neighbors helped neighbors.

Kaiden set his toolbox and belt in the passenger seat and stretched out his tired muscles. Working in the cramped roof space wasn't ideal for his six-foot frame, but there was no one else willing to get up close and personal with the hundred-year-old beams.

As the last of the sun disappeared behind the dark forbidding heights of the Sierra Nevada mountain range, Kaiden set off along the county road toward home, mentally cataloguing the chores he'd have to catch up on in order to escape his father's wrath.

"Who am I kidding?" Kaiden muttered. "He'll shout at me anyway. He just loves shouting."

Sure, Jeff Miller had mellowed a bit in the last year since the wife he'd divorced twenty years ago had reappeared. Not that Kaiden had a problem with that. His mom had put up with a lot before she'd finally lost it and walked out to teach their father a lesson he'd failed to learn. Coming back on her own terms to get to know her own kids took balls.

His cell buzzed constantly as he neared home. When he paused to punch in the gate code, he was tempted to throw it out the window. Hoping to avoid his father, he parked on the far side of the drive and took the back way to the barn where Danny usually fed the ranch horses and took care of any stray calves they were hand rearing.

Kaiden loved the calves with their long eyelashes and soft brown eyes. He could always pick out the ones he'd help rear in the herd for years afterward.

"Ha! There you are!"

He jumped like a guilty teenager as his father's voice boomed out from behind him. Jeff wasn't a particularly tall man, but for what he lacked in inches he made up in sheer cussedness.

"I got held up by Dr. Tio." Kaiden had already started on the feed. He knew the routine by heart. "I couldn't just walk away."

"Sure you could. We do have phones you know."

"Yeah, but—" Kaiden didn't bother to finish the sentence because one thing he knew was that he'd never win an argument with his father. "Excuse me." He pushed past Jeff and headed into the first two stalls, checking the water and hanging the feed buckets on the wall.

"What did he want?" his dad asked. "He was checking up on me again, wasn't he?"

"Dad, he only has to look at you to know you haven't listened to a word he said about lowering your cholesterol."

"I've been eating goddam salad!"

"Only when Mom's here, and only to impress her." Kaiden filled another two buckets and kept moving. He was taller than his dad now, and unlikely to get swatted, but you never knew what was coming. "You ate four slices of pizza yesterday."

"Because I work outside and burn up a lot of calories!" Jeff protested. "What does Dr. Tio know about that kind of work?"

"Seeing as he chose to practice in a town chock-full of ranchers you'd think he'd be quite knowledgeable."

By the time Kaiden got back with the third set of buckets, his dad had started on the other side of the barn, and they worked together in silence until all the horses were fed.

"How many calves do we have, right now?" Kaiden asked.

"Just the one." Jeff closed the lid of the feed bin and

locked it. "I was wondering whether young Roman would like to help rear him for the 4-H club."

"That's a great idea. Did you ask Adam and Lizzie?"

"Thought I'd run it by you first." Jeff studied his scuffed boots.

Kaiden stared hard at his dad. "Why's that?"

"Because I'm trying to check in with other people before I get stuff wrong."

"You are?" Kaiden fought a smile. "Good for you."

He received a scowl in return. "It's your mother's idea if you must know."

"I'd never have guessed that in a million years." Kaiden shook his head admiringly. "I was just wondering if you'd fallen and hit your head or something."

"Get on with you." Jeff's frown returned. "I don't know why I put up with your crap."

"Because I can run faster than you now, and you can't catch me?" Kaiden grinned at his dad. "Or is it that I could saw you in half with one hand tied behind my back?"

Jeff merely grunted and turned toward the exit. "Dinner will be ready in half an hour, so get a move on."

"Will do." Kaiden made up the milk formula and shook the bottle as he walked to the end of the barn where the calves were kept. The only occupant of the stall immediately came up to the bars and mooed like he hadn't been fed for a week.

"Here you go, youngster." Kaiden braced one booted foot against the bars, held the bottle with both hands, and offered the teat to the calf, who latched on immediately and sucked the whole meal down in minutes.

After cleaning out the empty bottle and checking all the horses were settled in, Kaiden turned out the lights, leaving the barn to the feral cats and the bird population. Darkness came quickly to Morgan Valley at this time of year, but he knew his way back to the ranch house blindfolded.

He went into his bedroom, painfully aware that his brother Ben, whom he'd shared a bathroom with his whole life, was no longer there. He'd moved out to manage the Gomez Ranch with his film star fiancée, Silver. Technically, Ben was only a couple of miles away, but Kaiden missed his messy brother more than he had anticipated. Even when they'd fought, they'd always forgiven each other and made up quickly.

At least his bathroom was clean now. Ben had tended to drop everything and leave it there while Kaiden liked stuff to be in its correct place. He stared at the immaculately lined up bottles and found himself missing the clutter, which was just weird.

"Get over yourself," Kaiden muttered as he turned on the shower. "Enjoy the space."

By the time he'd washed up and changed, he could already smell the heavenly aromas coming from the kitchen. His big brother Adam loved to cook and knew they all had healthy appetites, so he didn't stint on the portions.

When Kaiden reached the large open-plan kitchen, he paused to run his fingers over the work surface he had hand planed from wood salvaged from Miller land. He loved the ranch, but working with his hands to create his own unique furniture was sometimes even better.

"Hey," Adam called out to him as he set a big casserole dish on the table. "Can you grab some beverages from the refrigerator?"

"Sure." Kaiden got out the iced tea and lemonade and

placed them on the table with a selection of glasses. "Are Lizzie and Roman here?"

"No, she had to work late today." Adam frowned as he mashed the potatoes. "I'd like her to move up here permanently, but she's not keen on that."

"Give her some time, Bro," Kaiden advised. "She's got a lot on her plate right now."

"Yeah, I know."

Adam wasn't the most forthcoming of brothers at the best of times, and getting him to talk about the woman he loved was like pulling teeth. It wasn't because he didn't care or feel things deeply, it was just because he'd spent so many years bottling things up that it was still hard for him to open up even with his family.

Kaiden didn't push the conversation and, instead, went to call his father and brothers to the table. His sister Daisy was currently in Palo Alto working at her high-tech start-up, and Ben was living at the other ranch. Kaiden wasn't sure he liked all the absences around the table. It felt like his family was changing too fast while he somehow stood still.

"Where's Danny?" his father demanded as he came into the kitchen.

"He's probably on his way back right now." Adam handed his father a plate. "It's a long drive from Lake Tahoe."

"I don't know why he's bothering with that degree rubbish anyway." Jeff sat down, mumbled a quick prayer, and then helped himself to the pot of chicken. "I can teach him everything he needs to know about how to manage a ranch right here for free. I taught you guys everything."

"You sure did, Dad." Kaiden shared a wry glance with

his oldest brother, Adam, and his youngest brother, Evan. "And we all have the scars to prove it."

"No one dies from getting a clock in the head when they're being stupid, Son." Jeff chewed vigorously. "I didn't have time to consider whether I was hurting your feelings when a steer was running you down."

"You didn't even consider we had feelings." Kaiden took a huge portion of the creamy mashed potatoes and the rich chicken and red wine sauce. "Danny's degree will help keep this ranch in business. He's learning all new kinds of stuff that we've never even considered before."

Jeff made a face before continuing to eat. "Waste of money."

"He's paying his own way with what he makes here and working for me," Kaiden pointed out. "I think he's smart to do it. I wish I'd had the opportunity."

"You went to college, Son," Jeff pointed out. "I didn't like that, either, but at least you learned something practical, which saves me money."

"I learned a trade. That's different." Kaiden turned to Adam. "This food is awesome, by the way."

"Thanks." Adam nodded. "There's plenty more, so keep going."

By the time they got to dessert, even Kaiden was full, and decided to stick with coffee. While Jeff was busy trying to argue with Evan about something to do with the calves, Kaiden turned to Adam.

"Dr. Tio asked me to go out to the Garcia Ranch to see Juan tomorrow."

"Yeah? What for?" Adam frowned. "Don't tell me you're leaving to manage the ranch for him—although it could do with all the help it can get right now."

"The house needs adapting so that Juan can get around in his wheelchair."

"That sucks." Adam sipped his own coffee. "He's got multiple sclerosis, right?"

"Yeah. I said I'd check out what needs to be done—bathrooms, ramps, doorways, that kind of thing."

"Who's paying for that? I don't think Juan has taken any cattle to market the last two years, and the ranch is a mess."

"Dr. Tio said the family would take care of it." Kaiden shrugged. "Maybe Mr. Garcia got some kind of disability grant, or something. He's retired military."

"Maybe one of his kids is coughing up the cash. Miguel's in the military, right?"

"As far as I know." Kaiden kept his tone neutral.

"What about Julia?"

"I have no idea." Kaiden finished his coffee. "I guess I'll find out the answers tomorrow."

Julia Garcia turned a slow circle around her father's kitchen. Nothing had changed since she'd left ten years ago to attend college and never really come back. The coffeepot on the ancient stove was the same, as was the plastic covering on the table, and the loudly humming refrigerator. It was like time had stood still.

She pressed her hand over her heart and forced herself to take a deep breath as memories overwhelmed her. Miguel grinning and pulling her hair, her mom cooking at the stove, and her dad coming in the back door smelling like leather and cow shit.

"You okay in there?"

Her father's voice echoed down the hallway. She'd left

him settled in his recliner in front of the TV and offered to make some coffee.

"Yup! Do you have a coffee maker, Dad?" she called out.

"I thought that was you."

She smiled despite herself. "I mean like an electric one or a pod dispenser."

"Nope. Cowboy coffee made on the stove or over the fire is good enough for me."

Julia mentally added a coffee maker to her ever-increasing list of things she needed to survive in the boonies. "Right."

She approached the coffeepot like it was about to burst into flames and cast her mind back to how to make it. "Coffee in the bottom, add water, bring to the boil, easy," she murmured to herself as she opened the cupboard, found the scratched tin marked COFFEE, and added what she hoped was the appropriate amount before setting it on the stove.

She'd arrived last night when it was dark, greeted her father, fallen into her old bed, and slept for eight hours, which was unheard of. She'd forgotten how powerful the silence around the ranch could be. It felt like she was constantly holding her breath. She checked the refrigerator for cream and set out a couple of mugs. But wasn't that why she'd left in the first place? That silence? That sense that nothing would ever change if she didn't make it happen?

She went back to speak to her father. "What would you like for breakfast?"

"There's oatmeal. I like that." He smiled up at her.

"Do you have a microwave to make it?" Before he even

answered her, Julia held up her hand. "Scratch that. Of course you don't. I'll make you some."

"I don't want to put you to too much trouble, my love." Juan frowned. "I'm quite capable of feeding myself."

"I know that, but how about you let me pamper you my first morning back?" Julia kissed his cheek. "Just stay there, Dad, and enjoy your show. I'll be back."

The kitchen window still had the drapes she'd made with her mom about fifteen years ago. The lemon pattern looked like it hadn't been washed for years and was stiff with dirt and grease. For a horrible second, Julia wanted to rip the curtains down and scream at the unfairness of it all. But she was a different person now, a more controlled one, and she certainly wasn't going to let her current sense of helplessness beat her.

Even as she talked herself strong again, her gaze was caught by the endless vista through the smeared window, the vastness of the Sierra Nevadas in the distance, the rolling green foothills, and grasslands topped by a startlingly blue sky. Home: where you could run for miles without seeing another human being or hearing the sound of a car. Nothing like the city she lived in now with its endless sirens, people, and traffic.

She paused at the unexpected sound of a truck coming up the driveway. Did her dad still employ hands? She hadn't seen any sign of activity at the barn, and she'd been up since dawn. She watched as the truck drew up, and a cowboy got out and strolled toward the house.

Even though she couldn't see his face, she immediately knew who it was, and flew to open the front door.

When he saw her, he stopped as if surprised and angled his head to one side.

"*Julia*?"

"Who else?" She raised her chin. "What the hell are *you* doing here, Kaiden Miller?"

Chapter Two

Kaiden blinked at the accusatory tone and stared like a dumbass at Julia Garcia. She wore a skirt suit in blue with one of those soft, white lacy shirts underneath and heels that put her at his eye level. Her black hair was tied back in a high ponytail exposing the exquisite angles of her face. She was beautiful. She always had been.

The hackles on the back of his neck rose. "Nice to see you too, darlin'. How's it hanging?"

"Don't you darlin' me, Miller." She glared right back at him. "I asked you what you were doing here."

He raised an eyebrow, which had always infuriated her, and was glad to see it still worked. "I came to see your dad."

She crossed her arms over her chest. "He didn't mention anything about that to me."

Kaiden rubbed a hand over the back of his neck and sighed. "Look. Could you just go and check? If he's busy I'll come back another time."

"I'll go and talk to him."

"Great." He took a step toward the house and she shut the door in his face. "Really great."

Why couldn't it have been Miguel who'd come back? That would have been difficult in another way, but not the same. They might have settled things the old-fashioned way, but he'd almost welcome that. Why did it have to be Julia who had always rubbed him up the wrong way? Not that she'd ever let him actually touch her. She'd probably barf at the very idea.

She'd been one of the popular, brainiac kids at school, held a 4.2 GPA, and been a cheerleader, and class valedictorian. She'd wiped the dust from Morgantown off her feet, rode off to Stanford in a blaze of glory to study law, and hardly ever came back.

Even as he considered bolting for his truck, some part of him refused to budge. This wasn't high school anymore. He'd done okay at life and he wasn't afraid of anything, or anybody.

The door opened. "You can come in now."

"Thanks." He removed his Stetson as he went into the hallway and smoothed down his hair.

"Dad's through there." She pointed imperiously to the right. "I'm just making him some breakfast so don't be too long."

"Awesome, throw on a couple of eggs for me, will you, sweetheart?"

He walked away from her, his shoulders tensing as he anticipated a cast-iron pan being thrown at his head. Juan was watching one of the morning shows where all the women wore bright colors and everyone laughed a lot.

"Hey, Mr. Garcia." Kaiden crouched down beside the

chair and offered his hand. "Dr. Tio asked me to call and see what we could do to adapt your house."

"Kaiden." Juan shook his hand. "That would be great." He sighed. "When my MS is bad, I just can't do some things myself anymore."

"So Dr. Tio said. He gave me a general idea of what you need, but we can talk more after I've had a look around." Kaiden paused. "You okay if I do that while I'm here so I can get a sense of what needs doing?"

"That's fine by me." Juan's smile warmed Kaiden's heart. "I've got Julia home keeping an eye on me for a few days, so I'm good."

"That's awesome." Kaiden got to his feet and retrieved his phone from the back pocket of his jeans. "I'll take some pictures as I go."

"Isn't technology great? Miguel bought me one of those phones last time I talked to him." Juan grinned. "It's still in the box because I haven't worked out how to use it yet, but I will one day."

"Maybe Julia can help you with that. If not, you know our Daisy is a whiz with technical stuff." Kaiden took out his notebook. "I'll get started, then."

"Take your time, son, there's no rush."

Kaiden's smile faded as he left the room. Juan looked so damn frail. He remembered coming over to see Miguel when the ranch was thriving. Juan had been a much kinder, gentler father than Jeff had ever been.

"What are you doing now?"

He turned and looked back at Julia, who had stepped out of the kitchen, her hands on her hips.

"Just casing the joint." He retrieved his pencil from behind his ear. "How's my breakfast coming?"

Her indrawn breath was so extreme, he was surprised she didn't faint.

"I see that you haven't changed a bit."

"Oh, I have." He flexed his muscles. "Bigger, faster, leaner, and definitely harder." He finished with a wink, which made her press her lips together. He nodded at the door to the sitting room. "Maybe you should check in with your dad before you start making all these assumptions."

"I will."

She stalked past him, releasing a hint of starch and citrus perfume, and he continued on down the central hallway that led to the master bedroom. He paused at the door to appreciate the handmade quilt on the bed. Beneath the picture of the Sacred Heart sat a candle and a well-worn rosary. A collection of photos covered every other surface, military pictures of the three generations of Garcia men who had served their country, Miguel and Julia at every age smiling into the camera. Kaiden edged closer to the chest of drawers. There was even one of him when he and Miguel had played football together.

He swung around as Julia came into the bedroom.

"Okay, I understand you're the person Dr. Tio asked to look into making the ranch more accessible for my dad's needs."

"That's right." He nodded at the bathroom. "I'm going to start in there—if that's okay with you." He turned to the door, his nose wrinkling. "Is something burning?"

"Crap!" She rushed out, and he followed her down to the kitchen, where the smell of burned coffee was stinking up the space.

She went to grab the coffeepot and Kaiden thrust his arm in front of her outstretched hand.

"No."

"Don't tell me what to—"

He picked up the dishcloth and handed it to her. "Use this, or you'll burn your hands."

She did as he suggested, and he helpfully opened the back door as she went outside to dump the burned coffee. When she came back in, he had already gotten the coffee tin out and turned the faucet on.

"Rinse out the pot, check it's not leaking, and leave the coffee making to me." He glanced up at the ceiling. "You need smoke alarms in here."

Julia's cheeks were so hot she knew Kaiden must have noticed, but he didn't do anything more threatening than point out that they needed smoke alarms, which was the absolute truth. Although, not having one shrieking in her ear right now was something of a blessing.

She set the pot in the sink and cooled it down with the water. It didn't appear to be damaged so she meekly handed it over to Kaiden.

"You probably didn't put enough water in there. Easy to do."

She watched his large, capable hands add the scoops of coffee to the pot and fill it up with water, before setting it on a low heat. He glanced over his shoulder at her as he worked.

"Why don't you finish with your dad's breakfast? I'll keep an eye on the coffee."

Julia's legs were still shaking. For a moment, she wanted to sink down on one of the hard chairs and just bawl her eyes out. But doing that in front of Kaiden Miller would open her up to a lifetime of his so-called humor because he never forgot *anything*.

"Thank you." She at least managed to say that.

He had the nerve to grin. "See? That wasn't so hard, was it? Next time you see me maybe you'll just say hi instead of treating me like a criminal."

"I doubt it." So, she'd recovered to her sass. Good.

"So do I." He placed the dish towel on the counter. "I'll be back in ten minutes. I was just kidding about the breakfast."

Like she hadn't known that. Julia took a deep breath and tried to remember what her yoga instructor recommended for the stressful moments of a modern woman's life when running away wasn't an option. She'd added the last bit, but she really did need to get a grip. She was an accomplished and well-paid lawyer, for goodness' sake. This should be easy.

She checked the cupboards, found the instant oatmeal, and made it on the stove with milk rather than water, just as her dad had always liked it. When they'd been kids he'd kept a dairy cow for the milk, cheese, and butter her mother had loved to make.

There wasn't any fresh fruit, something she'd have to remedy, so she took the oatmeal through with a small bowl of brown sugar and a jug of cream on the side, just in case her father wanted it.

"Thank you, my love." Her father brought his recliner upright as she put the tray on his lap. "Isn't it nice to see Kaiden again?"

"Sure, although we were never really friends." Julia offered him a napkin.

"That's right, he hung out more with Miguel."

Until they'd had that big fight and never spoken to each other again, but Julia certainly wasn't going to bring that up. When Miguel had shared Kaiden's real opinion of her it had hurt so much she'd decided never to speak to Kaiden again. Yet, here she was, having to listen to him anyway . . .

"I'll go and check on the coffee."

She went back to the kitchen only to find that Kaiden had beaten her to it. She paused to assess his back view. He wasn't as tall and broad as his two older brothers but he certainly had muscles in all the right places and, if she was going to be completely honest, a very fine ass indeed.

"Like what you see?"

Julia glared at the back of his head. "Yes, until you open your big mouth and spoil it all."

He turned around. "I'll take that as a compliment."

"You would." She met his amused stare. "I . . . really do appreciate what you're doing here."

He pressed his hand to his heart. "Wow, I'm kind of touched. The great Julia Garcia is being nice to me."

"I want my dad to be comfortable in his own house, that's it." Her cell buzzed and she ignored it even as her stomach tightened. "Are you like some kind of a construction manager now?"

"No, I'm just the odd jobs guy." He dealt with the coffee, pouring it into the two mugs. "Do you take sugar with yours?"

"Of course not." She gestured stiffly at the pot. "Please help yourself while I take Dad's through."

"Thanks." He reached for another mug. "Seeing as I made it at least I know it's not poisoned."

Julia took her father's mug and went down the hall. Why did Kaiden have to make a joke about everything?

Was he really that shallow? Maybe he was. He was still living in Morgan Valley with his family, and, according to him, hadn't picked up any more education. Not that education was for everyone. Her dad had left school at sixteen to help his father and grandfather run the ranch, before going into the military, and he was as shrewd as anyone she'd ever met in the city.

Was she turning into the kind of snob she'd always secretly despised when she'd first gone to live in the affluent suburbs around Stanford? If Kaiden was happy and content with his life, and he sure looked happy, what he did had nothing to do with her. As she returned to the kitchen with her father's empty bowl she could hear Kaiden whistling as he walked around the house.

He'd always done that even as a kid.

She rinsed out the bowl and set it to dry, her gaze again distracted by the stupendous view. She shook her head.

"This could be so much better."

She took one of the kitchen chairs, climbed up on it, and then onto the worktop where she grabbed hold of the yellow drapes, sneezing as dust exploded in her face. To her annoyance the fabric clung stubbornly to the rail.

"Hold up there, Ms. Impatient."

Still sneezing, she glanced over her shoulder to see that Kaiden had reentered the kitchen. He drew up a second chair alongside hers and hopped up beside her.

"You need to unscrew the ends of the rail before you can slide the rings off. Hold on to the drapes, will you?"

He produced some kind of tool from the pocket of his shirt and set to work, his wide shoulder pressed against hers. Julia found she couldn't look away from the deft motions of his hands, and the faint whistling he seemed unaware of that still emanated from his mouth.

He leaned across her to reach the other end of the rail, and she eased backward, suddenly aware that her tight skirt had crept up to her ass, and that getting back down wasn't going to be as easy as getting up.

"Okay, you should be able to get the drapes off now." Kaiden released the tarnished brass rail and set it down on the countertop.

"Thank you." Even as Julia waited for him to descend, she knew she'd have to ask for his help, and was already dreading it. She waved vaguely at her skirt. "Could you . . . ?"

"Help you down?" He grinned at her, accentuating the fine lines around his mouth and gray eyes. "Sure. You might want to consider investing in a pair of jeans if you're going to stick around here for a while."

He placed his hands on her waist and lifted her down in one fluid motion, waited until she was stable, and immediately backed off.

"I have jeans." Julia made herself look him in the eye.

"Awesome." He gestured at the drapes. "Why did you suddenly decide they needed to come down?"

"Because they were obscuring the view."

"It certainly is a good one." Kaiden looked past her, his expression thoughtful. "You might need to clean the glass, too."

"I know that."

"Then, I'll leave you to it." He checked his cell phone and frowned. "I won't be able to get out here again until the weekend. Danny's on a course so I'm doing his ranch work as well as mine."

"That's fine." Julia nodded. "I've got a lot going on myself."

"You taking on the ranch work?"

"Hardly. I still have a job in San Francisco."

"You're a lawyer, right?"

"I am."

He hesitated. "If you need any help with anything—"

"I'll ask Dad," Julia said firmly.

"Okay, then." Kaiden held out his cell. "Can I have your number? I'd rather talk to you than bother Juan."

"Really?" Inwardly Julia winced as she relapsed into high school mode. What was it about Kaiden Miller that made her behave like a sarcastic teenager?

He rubbed his hand over his stubbled chin, probably to conceal a smile. "I can't believe I'm asking, either, but I guess we both want what's best for Juan."

She took his phone and punched in her number with one sharp fingertip. "We do."

"Thanks." He picked up his hat. "I'll call to let you know when I'd like to come up here again."

"Sure, it's not as if I'm planning on going anywhere."

Kaiden turned back to look at her. "Do you have transportation?"

"Dad's truck is still working, so yes. Are there any actual shops in Morgantown these days?"

"Plenty. You should come and check it out sometime." His smile was a thing of beauty. "I'm just going to say good-bye to your dad, then I'll see myself out."

"Fine."

He winked at her and strolled away. She heard her father's laugh and Kaiden's low-voiced murmur in reply, and then he was gone. His truck fired as he backed up and bumped down the pitted drive. She had the absurd idea of chasing after him and asking him what the hell she was supposed to do with her dad, with the ranch, with *everything*.

When had Kaiden Miller become the kind of guy people could depend on? He'd always been the outsider, the one too busy cracking jokes at everyone else's expense to ever be taken seriously. Or was she so desperate that the slightest hint of kindness had reduced her to rubble?

Her cell rang and she automatically picked up.

"Hey, Julie! Didn't you get my texts? I need to ask you some questions about the Mitan file."

She gripped the phone tightly as the coffee in her gut turned to acid.

"Blaine, I don't have access to any of the files right now. You're supposed to check in with Miley, not me, okay?"

"Miley's useless." Julia closed her eyes as her new boss's voice rose to its usual petulant whine. "She just tells me to sort it out myself."

"You are the lead negotiator on this now, Blaine," Julia pointed out, her gaze straying to the newly revealed window like it would save her soul. "You're supposed to be the one making the decisions."

"And, as your superior, I'm telling you to sort this shit out."

Julia breathed out slowly through her nose and imagined galloping her horse through the water meadows that led down to Morgan Creek.

"Julie? Are you still there?" Blaine was in full panicked meltdown mode now.

"Sorry, can't hear you too well." Julia held the phone away from her ear. "Signal's not great out here. I'll call you back."

"Don't you dare—"

She ended the call and spent a juvenile moment giving her own phone the finger before slipping it into her pocket.

Blaine Purvis wanted to be the big boss man? Then he could earn his paycheck for once. She was going to sit down with her father and find out exactly what was going on with the once thriving Garcia Ranch her great-grandfather had founded, and try to come up with a way to save it for the next generation.

Chapter Three

"So you just need to proceed carefully, shave off a little at a time, and . . ." Kaiden stopped speaking to stare at his companion. "Wes, are you even listening to me?"

"Sure!" His young apprentice jumped, shoved his phone in the pocket of his jeans, and looked Kaiden right in the eye. "Shave it all off, got it."

Kaiden held out his hand. "Give me your phone."

"What?" Wes squealed like a motherless calf. "You can't do that to me! Isn't it against the law or something?"

"You are supposed to be learning a trade, right? That's what you signed on for." Kaiden pointed up at the beams. "We're in an old building that needs a lot of love and tender care. We cannot afford to make stupid mistakes and bring it down around our ears."

"I get that." Wes nodded vigorously. "But what's it got to do with you taking my phone? It's my *life*."

"If you don't listen to my instructions because you're too busy looking at your phone neither of us might live much longer." Kaiden held Wes's gaze. "So, what's it going to be? You hand over your phone and work through till lunchtime when I'll give it back to you, or you go and tell Beth you've been fired?"

"Wow, that's harsh." Wes shook his head like he was disappointed in Kaiden. "You know she'll kill me if I blow this?"

"Not my problem." After four weeks of working with Wes, Kaiden had just about had it. "If you're not interested in doing the job, I'll find someone who is."

With a huge sigh, Wes handed over his phone.

"Thanks." Kaiden stowed it safely in his tool belt. "Now, let's get to this."

"Do you want me to get some coffee?"

"You've only been here for half an hour. You can't possibly need coffee." Kaiden walked over to his workbench trailed by Wes.

"I was thinking more for you. You look a bit stressed."

Kaiden reminded himself that Wes was only eighteen, and that after the upheavals of his childhood he deserved a chance. He concentrated on sorting through the tools and finding the right place on the structural plan.

"You see how this beam is anchored up here on the right?" He pointed it out on the plan and then at the actual beam itself. "We need to make sure that the joint is still secure so that it can hold up some of the weight of the roof."

"Okay." Wes squinted up at the roof. "So what do you want me to do? You know I don't do heights, right?"

"You'll be two foot off the ground, max," Kaiden reassured him as he handed over a screwdriver and sandpaper. "Get up there, examine the joint, test gently to see if there is any unstable or soft wood using the tip of the screwdriver, and tell me immediately if there is."

"Got it." Wes walked toward the post. He climbed awkwardly up onto the second step of the ladder, pretended to fall and waved his arms around like an idiot before he noticed Kaiden's measured stare and got to work. "It looks fine."

"Great, use the sandpaper to clean up the joint, and then you can do exactly the same thing to the other nineteen posts. Put a red tag on anything suspicious so I can check it out."

"*All* of them?"

"Yeah." Kaiden concentrated on the plans, reluctant to let Wes see he was fighting a smile at his apprentice's fake outrage. "That should take you through to lunchtime."

"When you'll give me my phone back?"

"If you do a good job." Kaiden used the calculator on his cell to check his math. "Every post has to be structurally sound, okay? It's important."

Wes muttered something under his breath and moved his ladder to the next post. Somewhere, someone was probably enjoying the spectacle of Kaiden having to be the tough, no-fun guy rather than the one making everyone laugh. Like most teenagers, Wes was a strange mixture of overconfidence and immaturity that Kaiden remembered all too well. Sometimes, he really wanted to laugh alongside his apprentice before he remembered he was supposed to be the boss.

While he had his phone out, he checked his messages, but there was nothing urgent. He scrolled through his contacts until he found Julia's, and paused before using his thumb to type.

Just checking in that you gave me the right number.

He waited a second, but she didn't reply, and why would she? She'd made it very clear that she didn't need his help even if her father did. The real question was, why did it bother him? Why was he determined to make a connection with a woman who had never given him a moment of her time without making it feel like she was doing him a favor?

"Because you want everyone to like you," Kaiden muttered to himself. "You're a people pleaser."

His cell buzzed and he picked it up.

Seems like I did. ☺

Encouraged by the smiley face, Kaiden kept typing.

What are you up to this fine morning?

I'm bringing Dad into town to see his doctor at 12.

Cool, I might see you around.

Kaiden grimaced. There he went again asking for her attention. She didn't reply, and he made himself put his phone away.

"How come you get to text, and I don't?" Wes called out.

"Because I'm the boss." Kaiden contemplated the climb up the ladder and made sure he had all the right tools with him before he ascended on high. "Now, stop yakking and get on with it."

Julia spent way too much time trying to work out how to collapse her dad's wheelchair so that she could put it in the back of his truck for their trip down to Morgantown. She had to wonder how he'd been managing by himself. A fresh pang of guilt ran through her as she finally shut the truck door. She'd taken his reassurances that everything was okay at face value, and used them as an excuse to work even harder, and not come back.

And where had that got her? A stomach full of acid, a full-time headache, and a new boss who hated her guts. Her cell rang, and she reluctantly answered it.

"Hi! Julia! It's Melanie."

Julia walked back inside the ranch house and paused in the kitchen, shutting the door so her dad couldn't hear the conversation.

"Hi!" she said brightly.

"Blaine said you hung up on him yesterday."

"The cell service here is very patchy." Julia made sure the coffeepot was safely away from the range.

"Look, I know you wanted that promotion, Julia, dear, but you do realize we all have to work as a team now?"

"Of course."

"Then why wouldn't you help Blaine?"

"Because I don't have access to the files he needs, Miley does," Julia said simply. "I explained that to him. Did he suggest something else?"

The senior partner went quiet for so long that Julia really began to believe the connection was lost. She was just about to give up when Melanie spoke again.

"I've patched Blaine into the call, Julia."

"Great!" Julia rolled her eyes and made gagging gestures. "Hi, Blaine."

"I didn't say you had the files, Julie. I just asked you where you'd put them when you'd left in such a hurry."

"That's a perfectly reasonable question, Julia," Melanie said.

But not the one he actually asked me. Julia wished she

had the nerve to say that, but as things were, she needed her paycheck more than ever right now.

"Miley has copies of every single file and project I was working on."

"But she doesn't have your experience." Blaine sighed. "All I'm asking for is a little help, Julie, while I get settled into my new job. As Melanie said, we all need to be team players for the greater glory of the firm."

Melanie's indulgent laugh set Julia's teeth on edge. "See, my dear? Blaine's got the right attitude. You're usually so conscientious, I can't imagine why you're not willing to help a fellow lawyer out."

"I can't help him from here. I don't have access to the files, and I'm currently trying to take care of my father who is sick," Julia said evenly.

"As to that, when do you think you'll be back?" Melanie asked. "You're missing a lot of billable hours."

Julia pressed her lips tightly together and fought a sudden urge to cry.

"I only just got here. There is a lot to sort out and set up before I can leave."

"Can't somebody else do it?"

"No." Julia gripped the phone so hard it was in danger of popping out of her hand like a cork. "It's my responsibility and my choice." She cleared her throat. "I'm sorry, but I have to go now. My father is due at the doctor's for an appointment he can't miss."

"I'll call you later, then, Julie." Blaine had to have the last word. "I'm sure we can work something out."

She hated him. It was that simple. The thought of having to go into the office for the rest of her life while he schmoozed his way up the corporate ladder made her feel physically sick. Her gaze settled on the ancient stove. But the ranch needed her and it wasn't going to be cheap to adapt it to fit her father's condition.

From what he'd told her last night, the place wasn't even really operating as a ranch right now. He had a few cattle and horses in the barn and two retired cowhands who had stayed on to help when Juan hadn't been able to get out of the house. She knew Miguel also sent money home, but it wasn't enough to affect the gradual decline of the once thriving business.

Maybe it was time to let it go. . . .

"Julia? Are you in there?"

She fixed on a smile and went to open the kitchen door.

"I'm right here, Dad. Do you want me to drive, or would you rather do it?"

"You drive." He tossed her the keys. "I taught you, so I know you're good."

"You haven't seen me in the city," Julia teased him. "I'm a demon on wheels."

She helped him to the truck, which she had parked as close to the back door as possible. "Your doctor's in town, yes?"

"In the building opposite Baker's gas station, and next door to the new pizza place."

"There's pizza?" Julia hoisted him up into the truck.

"Good pizza and gelato." Juan settled himself in the seat. "If you behave yourself, I might treat you to lunch."

Kaiden wouldn't say he'd deliberately suggested he and Wes should get a slice or two of pizza for lunch, but here they were, sitting outside despite the slight breeze while

Kaiden kept a close eye on Dr. Tio's. He'd checked the parking lot behind the building and spotted Juan's old truck in one of the disabled spaces. Wes was staring at his cell like he'd never seen it before, his eyes fixed on the screen as he typed with a speed Kaiden could only dream about.

A flash of movement made him look up to see the door into the clinic opening. He shot to his feet and walked over to take hold of it as Julia backed out with Juan in his wheelchair.

"Hey!" Juan looked genuinely pleased to see him.

"How's it going?" Kaiden smiled at them both. "Didn't want the door hitting you in the a— I mean rear."

"Thanks." Julia turned the chair around to face the front. Today she was wearing jeans, boots, and a peach-colored fleece that complemented her warm skin tones. She looked tired, as if all the cares of the world were on her shoulders. "Do I smell pizza?"

"You sure do." Kaiden pointed toward Wes, who seemed oblivious to the fact that Kaiden had moved away. "Do you want to come and sit with us, or, do you want to go inside?"

Even as Julia hesitated, Juan answered him. "We'll sit outside. It's good to feel the fresh air on my skin."

"I bet." Kaiden took over the wheelchair and maneuvered Juan toward the circular table so that his back was to the wind. "Wes, say hi to Mr. Garcia."

Wes didn't react and Kaiden leaned over and gently poked him on the arm. "Wes!"

"Don't take my phone!" Wes cradled his cell to his chest and cringed backward like some pitiful orphan child.

"It's lunchtime!" He suddenly noticed Julia and sat up straight. "Well, hi!"

Kaiden fought not to roll his eyes. "Julia, this is Wes Demoto."

Wes put out his hand and took Julia's. "Wes Baker, actually." He brought her gloved fingers to his lips. "A pleasure indeed, my lady."

Julia met Kaiden's gaze over Wes's head, her lips twitching with startled amusement.

Kaiden sighed. "Wes is my young apprentice."

"I hate the way you keep calling me that, it's so lame." Wes made a face. "Like *Star Wars* is so over."

"Do you work for Kaiden's father up at the ranch?" Julia asked.

"Nope, just for Kaiden. I got kicked out of culinary class, and electronics, and this was the only choice I had left."

Kaiden winced. "Thanks, Wes, you make working for me sound so appealing." He glanced down at Juan. "Shall I get you a menu, or do you know what you want?"

"Gina knows." He handed Julia a twenty-dollar bill. "Get whatever you want, my dear. It's on me."

"I'll give you a hand," Kaiden said. "Wes will be wanting a third slice, and a refill."

He followed Julia into the sparkling red-and-white interior of the pizza shop where Gina was standing behind the counter.

"Back for more?" She grinned at Kaiden. "I bet it's for Wes."

"You'd be right about that. I should half his wages the amount of food he eats." Kaiden handed over his debit card. "Can I have a coffee to go as well?"

Beside him, Julia tensed. "Are we keeping you from your work? We don't have to sit with you if you have to get back."

"We're good." Kaiden gestured at Gina. "This is Gina, the amazing woman who makes all the pizza dough."

"I'm Julia Garcia." Julia's smile was charming when it wasn't directed at him. "My dad says you know what he likes, and I'll take a chance, and have the same thing."

"Juan mentioned you might be coming home for a spell. How cool is that?" Gina put in the order and handed over two iced teas. "Your dad is such a lovely guy."

"He is." Julia smiled again. "I'm glad to be back here."

Gina went back to the kitchen and Kaiden glanced down at Julia. "Are you really glad to be back?"

She sighed. "It's complicated."

"I always got the sense that you couldn't wait to leave this place."

"I couldn't." She nodded at the door. "Shall we take these out?"

"You know, you can talk to me about stuff," Kaiden said as he held open the door for her.

Julia puffed out a laugh. "Kaiden, you are the last person in the world I'd share my secrets with."

"What's that supposed to mean?"

"You know." She eased past him. "Fool me once, and all that."

Kaiden stared after her as she headed toward Juan. What the hell was she getting at him for now?

Like she'd tell Kaiden Miller anything . . . They might not be in high school anymore, but she'd learned her lesson, and it had hurt enough to stick with her. She set the tea down on the table and took the only unoccupied seat, which left her between Kaiden and her father. Wes looked up briefly to acknowledge his drink, but rapidly returned his attention to his cell phone.

Juan took a sip of tea. "Wes was telling me about the old movie theater, Kaiden."

"It's certainly a project," Kaiden said. "Chase's architect has done a great job on the plans for its rehabilitation but it's slow work."

"What exactly do you do apart from being a rancher these days?" Julia had to ask.

"I'm a carpenter," Kaiden replied. "The original structure is mainly wood, so I've been stuck with the job of making sure it's structurally sound before anything else can go ahead." He sipped his coffee. "With all the earthquake activity over the past century, it's certainly moved around a bit."

"I remember going to that movie theater when I was a kid," Juan said. "It was run by Mr. Lopez who lived over the shop. He sold you your ticket, then your popcorn and candy. He ripped that ticket in half when you went into the theater, and said good-bye when you left." He chuckled. "I remember watching some cowboy show once and this rat ran over my boots."

"Ugh." Julia shuddered. "I guess that's why it closed."

"I think it was declared unsafe after some big earthquake in the seventies."

"I'm surprised no one tore it down," Julia said.

"No reason to do that when no one needed the land." Kaiden stretched out his long legs and crossed them at the ankle. "But things have changed around here. We're trying to use existing spaces to house incomers rather than building out into ranch territory."

"What's changed?" Julia asked.

Kaiden made a wide gesture. "All the stuff the Morgans are doing with their dude ranch and wedding business. It's creating employment opportunities for locals, and encourages the kids to stay rather than leave for the city."

"That's good, right?" Julia looked from her father to Kaiden, who nodded.

"Absolutely, but now we need affordable places for them to live. It's tough on the older families here when their own kids can't stick around. When it's finished, the movie theater will have at least four apartments to buy or rent." He laughed. "Sorry, I get quite passionate about this stuff. I didn't mean to bore you."

"That's really cool." Julia looked up as Gina approached with a loaded tray, and moved to one side so that she could place it on the table. "The pizza looks awesome."

"Try it first." Gina grinned as she handed out red napkins and pepper flakes. "Enjoy."

As Wes started on his third piece, Julia and her father dug in. Julia repressed a moan as the hot dough base and tangy tomato hit her taste buds.

"Good?" Kaiden asked

"Oh, yes," Julia breathed. "Almost as good as—" She caught herself before she finished the sentence, but Kaiden didn't look fooled. As Juan chatted to Wes, Kaiden lowered his voice so only Julia could hear him.

"If you equate the best sex of your life with a piece of pizza, someone hasn't been doing you right, my friend."

She snorted. "Like how would you know?"

His gaze lingered on her mouth and she unconsciously licked her lips.

"Jeez, don't do that," Kaiden breathed and she widened her eyes at him.

"What, this?" She did it again and added a breathy moan just for fun.

He let out his breath and sat back, one hand curved over the fly of his jeans. "You ready to go yet, Wes?"

"Sure!" Wes folded the pizza in four and stuck it all in his mouth at once followed by a huge glug of soda. "Nice to meet you, Ms. Julia." He stood up, shook off the crumbs, and belched loudly. "See ya, Mr. G."

"Charming." Kaiden winced as he also stood. "He's still something of a work in progress."

"I heard that," Wes said. "Even if I don't know what it means."

Kaiden patted his shoulder and turned him toward Main Street. "I'll explain it on the way back. Have a great rest of your day, guys."

Julia watched them walk away. Kaiden kept one arm around his apprentice and was obviously still talking to him.

"He's a good boy, that Kaiden," her father said.

"You didn't think that when we were at school," Julia reminded him.

"That's because he fell out with Miguel, and neither of them would tell me why." Juan sighed. "And, after he lost that friendship, I lost Miguel, too."

"Miguel made his own choices, Dad. I don't think you should blame yourself or Kaiden, and he's sorted himself out now, hasn't he?"

"The military did that," Juan said. "I just want him to come home, now."

"Have you asked him?" Julia held her father's gaze.

"Not in so many words." He shrugged. "I don't want him to worry about me. I want him to make his own decisions."

"But don't you think he'd rather know how things really are here, right now?" Julia persisted despite the firm set of her father's jaw. "Dr. Tio seemed really nice and knowledgeable, but he had some hard truths to share about your current condition."

"Dr. Tio is great, but you're here now, Daughter." Juan took her hand. "Maybe together we can hold on to things so that when Miguel does decide to come back there is something for him to come back to, eh?"

"Dad, we already talked about this." She gently disengaged her hand. "I have a job. I have to get back to it at some point."

"Then help me set things up so that I can go on without either of you," Juan said. "I'm not dead yet, and I'm certainly not ready to give up."

Julia stared at him as emotions and logic crashed into each other in her head making her feel like she was on a runaway horse. What Dr. Tio had told her about the likely progress of her father's MS now that he was out of remission had frightened her far more than she'd anticipated.

"I've only been here a couple of days. Can you give me more time to decide?" Julia asked.

"Of course, my love." Her father smiled at her. "I know that you'll do the right thing for everyone. You always do."

Julia wasn't so sure about that. She'd left Morgan Valley at the first opportunity and hadn't returned for years. Back then, her father had never suggested she owed the ranch anything. He'd been determined to pass it on to Miguel, and Julia's desertion had meant nothing. The fact that he needed her now was somewhat bittersweet.

She finished her pizza and allowed her gaze to drift to the bustling shops along Main Street. Kaiden had been right that the town was enjoying something of a renaissance. There were at least four tour buses parked up alongside her dad's truck and the through traffic was constant and loud.

"We almost lost the Cortez Ranch to developers last year," Juan said. "That's one of the reasons why the town started this infill project to make sure that all the historic buildings in Morgantown, and anything industrial, got a makeover and became useful. Chase Morgan is chairperson of the committee, and he's invested a lot of his own money into making the trust workable."

"He's a multimillionaire. He can afford it." Julia drank some tea, suddenly aware that Kaiden had left his coffee on the table. "It's probably some kind of tax break for him."

"So cynical." Juan chuckled. "Just like your mother." He pointed at the coffee. "Why don't you take that down to Kaiden while I sit here and enjoy the sun?"

"I don't know where he is." Julia felt herself blushing.

"Didn't you listen to a word he said? He's in the old movie theater." Juan pointed out onto the street. "It's right on the corner opposite the Red Dragon Bar. It's a five-minute walk at most."

It was hard not to stop and look at the shops that ran along both sides of Main Street. There were some familiar ones like Maureen's General Store, and Daisy's flower shop, and some newer places like a coffee shop that smelled divine. Aware that Kaiden's coffee was rapidly cooling down, Julia kept walking until she reached the crosswalk where the Red Dragon Bar sat on the corner. Even the bar looked in far better shape and had a new coat of paint.

She crossed the street and looked up at the unassuming façade of the old movie theater with its faded fake frontage, and the overhanging porch with spiral metal poles holding up what had once been an etched glass entryway. There was no open door in the front, so she walked around the back. She heard Kaiden whistling before she saw him and paused in the doorway to observe him until he looked up.

"Hey."

She held up the coffee. "You forgot this."

His smile brought out the dimple in his cheek. He'd always had a twinkle in his gray eyes and the kind of face that looked like he was inviting you to share a joke. She'd been one of the rare people not to fall for it because there had always been a watchfulness behind his gaze, as if he needed you to like him a little too much. And somehow, as if he'd known he didn't fool her, his comments to her had often been barbed.

"What?"

Julia blinked as he advanced toward her.

"You're staring at me." Kaiden angled his head and studied her. "Are you considering running off with my coffee after all?"

"I wouldn't do that." To avoid touching him, she set it down on his cluttered workbench. "I suspect there is much better coffee at that café a few doors down."

"Yeah, Yvonne's is great." Kaiden leaned back against the bench, his arms folded across his chest. He wore a tool belt low around his hips like a gunslinger. "If you like, we could have lunch there one day."

It was Julia's turn to stare. "Why are you being so nice to me?"

His brow creased. "Why wouldn't I be?"

"Because you've always disliked me, and I bet you have some opinions about daughters who don't come back to see their fathers very often."

He whistled. "Er, I think you're projecting here."

"I'm not—I'm just trying to work out what your game is."

"What game? You look stressed. I was just trying to be neighborly. There's no need to take everything the wrong way." He glanced down at his workbench and moved a screwdriver. "If you ask me, it looks like you just want someone to argue with right now."

"Why on earth would you think that?" Julia asked. "I don't know what to do about my dad, my brother isn't returning my calls, and I've got about a hundred problems with my day job." She shook her head. "Trust me, I really don't need to get into it with you right now, Kaiden Miller."

"Okay." He picked up his coffee and retreated to the other side of his workbench. "As I said, if you want to talk about any of this stuff, give me a call."

For some reason his calmness was fast becoming irritating.

"Is this amusing for you?" Julia asked slowly. "Because I'm not feeling it. But why should I be surprised? You've been making fun of me your whole life."

"Wow, that's some leap." Kaiden's smile abruptly disappeared. "Thanks for bringing the coffee, Julia. I'll be up to the ranch this weekend with some preliminary plans to discuss with Juan."

He took the pencil from behind his ear, bent his head, and started writing on the plans as if she no longer existed. She stared at his hair and swallowed hard.

"I'm sorry, Kaiden. That really wasn't fair."

He didn't reply, and she turned and walked away, her eyes stinging with tears. It wasn't his fault that everything was wrong with her life, and he certainly didn't deserve her anger. She *had* just been looking for someone to argue with, but why on earth had she chosen him?

"Hey, while you're being honest, would you care to explain why you don't think I'm trustworthy?" Kaiden called out.

His words made her stop and turn around. He met her gaze head-on. His usual easygoing smile was absent, making him look more like his terrifying father.

"I . . ." Julia made a helpless gesture. "It was a stupid thing to say."

"I'd still like to know what I'm supposed to have done."

"You *know* what you did." She sighed. She certainly wasn't going to talk about the awful things he'd said to Miguel about her, but there were plenty of other occasions to gripe about. "That ridiculous Valentine's Day thing when you grabbed that poem out of my hand and read it out loud just to make me look stupid."

"That's *it*?" He shook his head. "That's . . . all kinds of messed up."

"Why?" Julia demanded. "I was embarrassed not only for myself, but for the poor guy who wrote it. Why would you do that just to make everyone else laugh?"

His lips twitched, and she stared at him in frustration. "You still think it's funny?"

"Yeah, I do."

"*Why*?" She might have stamped her foot.

"Because I wrote the damn thing!"

She blinked at him. "Excuse me?"

"Seeing it in your hand, and watching you open it, I knew I'd made a terrible mistake, so I jumped in, and made fun of *myself* before you could rip me a new one."

"I don't believe you," Julia blurted out.

"Not my problem." He glanced down at the plans. "Wes is going to be back any minute now, so if you've finished doubting my every word, I'd like to get back to work."

This time she didn't stop to look back when she left.

She made her way along the raised walkway, aware that she'd messed up, and yet unable to think how to fix things. Kaiden had written the poem? She couldn't get her head around that at all. He'd always made fun of her. He'd never been one of the guys angling to ask her out. In fact, sometimes she'd thought he hated her.

"Julia?"

She looked up as someone called out her name, and she had to squint into the sun to see them.

"It's Nancy, Maureen's daughter. I just saw your dad down at Gina's. He was wondering where you'd gotten to, so I said I'd come and find you."

"Hi! It's good to see you again." Julia belatedly remembered her manners. "Are you still working at your mom's place?"

"Sometimes, but I mainly work at the bar. Jay's a good boss, and the pay is better because of the tips." Nancy frowned. "Hey, are you okay? You look like you're having a bad day."

Nancy had always cut straight to the point.

"I've had better," Julia admitted.

Nancy gently took her arm. "Look, I know you've got to get your dad home safely, but why don't you come and see me at the bar tonight? You can buy me a beer and share all your secrets. I'm really good at keeping confidences, ask anyone in Morgan Valley." She grinned. "If I ever want some extra income, I could set up a fantastic blackmailing business."

"That's really kind of you, but—"

Nancy held up a finger. "You either come see me at the Red Dragon, or I'll arrive on your doorstep with a six-pack of beer. Your choice."

Julia managed a smile. "Then I'll definitely come to the bar, if Dad's okay with it."

"Good." Nancy waggled her pierced eyebrows. Her short hair was dyed scarlet and styled into points like a hedgehog's spikes. "Remember, I know where you live, and I've got your dad's cell phone number, so you won't be able to avoid me for long."

"I hear you." Julia nodded. It was kind of nice to have someone telling her what to do. "Now, I'd better get back to Dad."

"So, if you and Ms. Julia aren't a thing, can I ask her out on a date?"

Kaiden looked up at Wes, who was propping up the doorframe. For a second he'd thought Julia had come back for round three. "What?"

"I heard you two arguing from the street, so I guess she's not that into you." Wes cocked his head to one side. "She's really pretty."

"And she's about ten years too old for you."

"I don't care about that. I've always preferred mature women." Wes eyed him carefully. "You're still mad."

"When do I ever get mad?" Kaiden prevaricated. "Even when you glued your fingers together I got you to Dr. Tio's without telling you what an idiot you were."

"You're definitely mad," Wes said smugly. "That means you still like her."

"I've always liked her. She's the sister of my best friend from high school." Kaiden scrubbed out the crooked line he'd drawn on the plan.

"No, you *really* like her." Wes paused. "Maybe you should apologize or something?"

"I'm not taking relationship advice from a teenager," Kaiden said as he misdrew the line again and gave up. "And, if anyone should be apologizing it should be her."

"Wow, that's harsh, dude." Wes shook his head. "You know that relationships take two people to make them work, right?"

Kaiden glared at him. "Who are you? Dear Abby?"

"I don't know who that is, but I do read the 'Am I the Ass?' boards online, and you're sure sounding like one right now."

"I don't care what kind of an ass I am," Kaiden said. "And crowdsourcing the answers to your problems on the Internet is why we're in this mess to start with." He glared at Wes. "Don't you have any work to do?"

"No, I'm waiting for you to tell me what to do next," Wes said with a shit-eating grin on his face.

"Oh, right." Kaiden let out a breath and consulted the schedule. "How about you clean up the floor?"

Wes groaned. "That's not teaching me anything at all!"

"I'm sure your uncle Ted and Beth will appreciate it."

"You know what I mean." Wes rolled his eyes. "Anyone can clean up, but you're supposed to be teaching me *skills*, man."

"I am. A clean workplace is a happy workplace." Kaiden handed Wes a broom. "Get on with it."

He checked his cell phone but there was nothing from his family, which was a relief. Danny was due back for the weekend, so Kaiden wouldn't have to handle two sets of chores for a couple of days. He stared at the back of Wes's head as his apprentice half-heartedly wielded the broom. Was he really the ass? Julia was obviously under a lot of stress, she'd needed to blow off at someone, and he'd just happened to be standing right there.

But it was more than that. He'd offered her the opportunity to tell him what was going on, and she'd suggested she didn't trust him enough to do so. Instead, she'd chosen to get annoyed because she didn't like him. She didn't damn well like him, and yet here he was, still dancing around trying to get her attention.

The thing was—maybe she had a reason? As a clueless teenage boy he'd tried so hard to conceal that he was attracted to his best friend's sister, that perhaps he'd gone too far the other way and convinced her that he didn't like her at all. The more he thought about it, the likelier it seemed. The incident with the Valentine's poem was a prime example of him screwing things up and giving totally the wrong impression.

Kaiden cleared a space on his workbench and picked

up his drawing pad. Maybe it would be better for everyone if he left Julia well alone. He'd finish off his plans for the Garcia remodel, get Juan's approval, and turn the whole project over to someone else so that he didn't have to go near Miss Julia Garcia ever again.

Chapter Four

"So come upstairs!" Nancy cleared away empty glasses with an efficiency Julia envied. "My shift is done and we still need to talk."

Julia had been sitting at the bar for an hour eating the excellent food, chatting to the locals who wandered over to reintroduce themselves to her, and drinking beer. As the evening progressed, the bar had taken on a rosy glow that shouted home to her, and she hadn't wanted to leave.

"But, my dad . . ."

Nancy waved away her objections. "Juan knows where you are, and that you're safe with me."

"Safe." There was a snort behind Nancy, and Jay, the bar owner, grinned at Julia. "Like, that's a terrifying thought."

Nancy poked him in the ribs. "Like you're scared of me."

"I am." Jay held up his hands like a hostage. "Really."

"Says the retired Navy SEAL who could kill me with one hand tied behind his back," Nancy scoffed.

Jay turned to Julia. "You will be safe with her as long as she's on your side, that's all I'm saying."

Nancy gave her boss the finger, came out from behind the bar, and smiled at Julia. "You coming?"

"Sure." Julia slid down from the barstool and took a moment to orient herself. She wasn't a big drinker and two beers had made her woozy. "Hang on—doesn't Jay live upstairs with his mom?"

"Not anymore," Jay said as he wiped down the bar. "I'm married now, and Mom is engaged to Billy Morgan. She spends way too much time up at his ranch these days if you ask me. Nancy's doing us all a favor living there."

"What he means is that if anyone breaks in, I'm the one who'll end up dead." Nancy winked at her boss as she linked arms with Julia and towed her toward the back of the bar. "Night, Jay. Come on, Julia."

Julia allowed herself to be maneuvered up the stairs and into the charming apartment above the bar that faced down Main Street. She tried to remember the last time she'd been there. Miguel and Jay had never been close, and she'd only visited briefly with her girlfriends when everyone was going out together.

"This is nice," Julia said as Nancy stuck her head in the refrigerator, pulled out two more beers, and held them up inquiringly toward Julia. "I think I'll stick to coffee if there is any, thanks."

"You always were a lightweight," Nancy joked as she rinsed the coffeepot. "Way too uptight to drink, smoke, and have a good time."

"Yeah, that's me. The perpetual party-pooper." Julia's tongue slid over the words and she almost giggled. "Try saying that ten times."

Nancy sat on the couch and patted the seat beside her. "So, what's going on? I know you've come back to help your dad, but how long are you planning on staying?"

"I'm supposed to have two weeks off, but you wouldn't know it." Julia sighed. "In my profession, you're not supposed to actually take your holidays or your sick days, because it makes you look weak and inefficient."

"That's stupid," Nancy said, shifting on the sofa. "How can you be at your best if you never take a day off for yourself?"

"My big boss and my new boss have been on my back since the moment I arrived. I'm almost ready to tell them to take a hike," Julia confessed. "Except I can't do that because I need my salary to pay for the remodel of the ranch house."

"That sucks." Nancy got up to tend to the coffee and then handed Julia a mug and assorted creamers in a bowl. "Help yourself."

"I didn't realize how bad things had gotten for my dad. It was a shock." Julia grimaced. "I should have known."

"Your dad's old-school. Those cowboys never admit they are sick or too old for anything. Look at Roy over at Morgan Ranch? How old is that guy? A hundred and fifty?"

Despite her woes, Julia couldn't help but smile in Nancy's bracing company.

"All I know is that Dad isn't capable of running the ranch by himself anymore, and he still won't admit it." Julia gripped her mug hard. "If I keep working, I can pay for the remodel and some continuing care, but I can't revitalize the ranch, and that's what he really wants."

Nancy tapped the rim of her beer bottle against her chin. "You should talk to Ben Miller."

"Why?"

"Because he and his fiancée have set up this charity thing for Morgan Valley, and they are looking for good ideas to fund in the local community."

"Since when has Ben Miller had any money?" Julia asked.

Nancy's grin was wicked. "Since he hooked up with Silver Meadows."

"*The* Silver Meadows?"

"Yup, the multimillionaire actress and producer who is also a really good person."

"You've met her?" Julia set her mug down on the cluttered coffee table.

"We've all met her." Nancy shrugged. "She even comes in the bar when it's quiet. I was quite prepared to hate her on sight but she's as nice as Ben, and they are perfect together."

Julia shook her head. "Wow. Who'd have thought Ben Miller would get it on with a movie star?"

"I know. If I'd taken a bet on any Miller getting a girl like that it would've been Kaiden."

Julia's smile slipped. "Kaiden?"

"You know the Miller I mean. Dark hair, gray eyes, dimples, and the kind of corny lines that ladies fall for every time."

"I suppose you've seen his finest work at the bar." Julia sniffed.

"He's no man ho if that's what you're thinking." Nancy set her bottle down. "But he's definitely never been short of a girlfriend. Have you seen him around yet?"

"You could say that." Julia let out a breath. "He came up to the ranch to quote on the repairs a few days ago, and Dad and I saw him in town at lunchtime."

"What did he do to put that expression on your face?"

"He . . . tried to be nice to me."

Nancy blinked at her. "And?"

"I was horrible to him."

To her surprise, Nancy gave a gurgle of laughter. "I bet that gave him a shock. I don't think he's ever met a woman since he was ten who wouldn't immediately succumb to his charms."

"I'm going to have to apologize to him at some point," Julia said gloomily.

"Oh, no, please don't. I'd love to see him running around trying to fix things for a change." Nancy tucked her feet up on the couch. "Talk to Ben Miller and ask him whether there's any way he could help preserve the ranch and keep it working. Ben, of all people, knows how important it is to keep the ranching community here thriving."

"I'll definitely sound him out." Julia nodded. "It can't hurt."

It was so nice to have someone to talk to who was on her side, and not her competition. She had friends, who weren't lawyers in the city, but they had their own work issues to deal with, and she never liked to bother anyone with her problems anyway. She'd been brought up to handle her own stuff without complaining.

"And you should definitely tell your work people to lay off you as well," Nancy said severely. "If you like, I can pretend to be your secretary, and tell them for you."

Julia shuddered at the thought. "I think I can handle them. I have no choice."

"You need a new job or a new boss, girl." Nancy nudged her in the ribs with her elbow. "Now, would you like some more coffee, or have you changed your mind about that beer?"

* * *

Kaiden cleared his throat and knocked on the front door of the Garcia Ranch. It didn't take long for Julia to open it and step out of his way. She'd tied her hair back, and wore a black sweater with dark jeans and brightly colored striped socks. He tried to catch her eye as he went past, but she wasn't having it.

"Thanks for letting me in this time." He took off his hat. "I'll go straight through."

"I'll make some coffee."

She turned her back on him and marched toward the kitchen while he headed to the family room where he could hear the TV blaring. He reminded himself that he was only there to see Juan, and that any interaction with Julia should be kept short and professional.

"Hey! Kaiden!" Juan greeted him with a smile and immediately turned down the TV. "How's your father?"

"Grumpy as ever." Kaiden took a seat on the couch and took out his phone. "Danny's back this weekend to help out, and Dad's still not happy."

Juan chuckled. "He's always been a tough nut, your dad."

"Tell me about it," Kaiden muttered.

When he'd informed his father that he was going to the Garcias, he'd only just managed to get out of the house without causing a minor riot. Only Danny's swift intervention to draw his father's ire had allowed Kaiden to escape. He definitely wasn't in the mood to be jerked around by anyone else this morning.

"I wrote out some ideas . . ." Kaiden started speaking, and Juan held up his hand.

"Let's wait for Julia so you don't have to repeat yourself twice."

Kaiden couldn't exactly tell him not to bother, so he

made small talk until Julia appeared with the coffee and then waited as she poured it out and sat opposite him next to her father. Keeping his gaze on Juan, Kaiden started speaking again.

"From what I can see, major alterations are needed in the bathrooms, the kitchen, and the entrance and exits to bring them up to code." He consulted his paperwork and passed a copy over to Juan so that he could follow along. "You'll need a good bathroom specialist and someone to at least resize some of the kitchen cupboards and sink to make them accessible. I've drawn up some basic plans for you to take a look at and amend if need be. I'd also recommend completely new appliances that can be easily used from a wheelchair, but that can get expensive."

Juan nodded as he turned the page over. Julia was examining the plans intently as her father passed the pages over to her.

"As for the outdoor access, that's probably the easiest fix because you're on a relatively flat surface with a straight run to the barn and parking area. We can simply pave those surfaces and lay a new slab," Kaiden finished up, and glanced over at Juan. "Anything in particular worrying you so far?"

"Only that it looks far more extensive than I imagined. I thought we could just redo the shower to allow me access in a chair, and we'd be done." Juan looked up at Kaiden.

"Unfortunately, it's not as simple as that," Kaiden said gently. "You've got to take the current pipe placement and drainage into account before you start bashing down walls. Do you know Mike Betts? He's a really good plumber. He'll see you right."

"I know Mike's father." Juan studied the kitchen plan.

"It does look nice with some of the countertops lowered, and the sink at chair level. Have you done one like this before?"

Kaiden handed over a photograph. "Yeah, I helped Sam Morgan do the kitchen in her new house on Morgan Ranch. She doesn't often use a wheelchair, but occasionally she needs one, and these adaptations helped a lot." Kaiden pointed at the wood. "I made the cabinets myself."

"*You* did?" Julia asked.

"Yeah." Kaiden briefly met her startled gaze. "That's my job."

"They're beautiful."

"Thanks." Kaiden reminded himself to keep things short and polite.

"Could you do that here?" Juan asked.

"It depends on the timeframe." Kaiden refused to commit himself. "I have quite a lot lined up right now with the Morgantown Preservation Society."

"But such beauty would be worth waiting for," Juan murmured. "Don't you think so, Daughter?"

"Sure, Dad, but if Kaiden is too busy then we'll have to do without, or get someone else just as skilled as he is."

"I can recommend a couple of guys from out near Bridgeport who do good work," Kaiden chimed in.

"I'd much rather it was you," Juan said firmly. "The less strangers in my house, the better."

"I understand." Kaiden nodded. He should really ask Juan how long Julia was planning on staying and arrange the work around that, but he couldn't do it in front of her. He'd much rather do the carpentry himself as he always enjoyed it.

"I'll leave you to think about it," Kaiden concluded. "I

included some cost estimates in the back, but they are pretty basic. You can probably expect to pay more for customization."

"Thank you." Juan looked up at Julia. "You'll take a look at those for me, won't you, my dear, and tell me what we can afford?"

"Of course I will." Julia patted his shoulder.

Kaiden stood up. "I'd better get on. I rode over so it's going to take me quite some time to get home."

He shook Juan's hand and stepped around Julia with a polite good-bye. He grabbed his hat and coat in the hallway, and was halfway along the path before he heard her shouting his name. This time he didn't make the mistake of looking back, and carried on into the dilapidated barn where he'd left Domino, his horse.

"Kaiden . . ."

He looked up from checking the girth. "What's up?"

"I need to apologize to you." Julia was now blocking his exit from the barn, which was just peachy.

He slid his fingers under the leather making sure he hadn't pinched the gelding's skin. "You already did, so we're good."

"I doubt that. I was out of line."

She paused as if waiting for a response he had no intention of giving her and kept right on speaking.

"Thanks for the plans. They really are great."

"You're welcome." He checked the reins, untied them from the hitching post, and started toward her.

"Kaiden . . ."

He had two choices. One, keep going and run her over, or two, stop and deal with her like an adult.

"Look, you apologized. I know you were having a bad day, so we're done, okay? Finished. End of story."

"But I hurt your feelings," Julia said earnestly.

Kaiden snorted. "Have you met my dad? I face him down on a regular basis, so your little temper tantrum barely registered."

"Temper tantrum?" She settled her hands on her hips. "*Really*?"

"You even stamped your foot," Kaiden added, and then remembered he wasn't supposed to be provoking her.

"I was . . . worried about everything, and you—well, you were just standing there smirking like you always do, knowing it sets me off, and—"

"So, now it's my fault?" He squared up to her.

"No!" She met his gaze. "I'm sorry!"

"You're welcome." He tried to fight the smile tugging at his lips, knowing it was going to infuriate her, and then let it go anyway. "Have a great day."

She stepped forward, poked him in the chest, and re-coiled, clutching her finger. "Ouch! Why are you so hard?"

"Can't help being fit and hot, Julia." He flexed his muscles and tried to look modest. "And please don't touch what you can't afford."

She started to splutter and he stood back to enjoy the moment until she finally ran out of steam.

"I shouldn't have touched you without your consent," Julia said firmly as she made herself meet Kaiden's amused gray gaze. She wasn't going to let him wind her up again and say things she really didn't mean. "If you truly are okay with my apology, and things are fine between us, then I'll get out of your way."

She stepped back and waited for him to walk the horse past her except he didn't move.

"Have you been out on the ranch yet?"

"What's that got to do with anything?" Julia asked suspiciously.

"I think you should saddle up a horse and walk me down to the boundary fence where you can make sure I get off your land."

"*Why*?"

"Because you're wound up tighter than a coiled spring. Sometimes things feel different from the back of a horse."

"I'm not—" She went to deny it, and then sighed. "Okay."

"Good woman."

Julia raised her chin. "Just because I am agreeing with you doesn't mean you've won or something."

"Why would I ever think that?" Kaiden murmured as he walked his horse out to the yard. "I'll wait for you out here."

She saddled her old horse, sent a text to her father to tell him what she was doing, and went out of the barn to find Kaiden already mounted while he texted on his phone with his thumb. He looked great on a horse. All the Miller boys did. Legend had it that Jeff had thrown them up on horseback before they could walk.

He glanced up as she mounted and ran his eye over her. "Looking good, Ms. Julia. You ready to go? I'll take it nice and slow."

"You'd better," Julia replied. "Or you'll be fishing my ass out of Morgan Creek."

His low laugh made her want to smile. How come he'd managed to talk her out of her anxieties so quickly? He specialized in making her spitting mad at one moment, and then disarmed her with his charm the next. The real question was why she was allowing herself to fall for it again?

Her attention was drawn to the ragged fence line along the drive up to the ranch.

"This all needs replacing."

"I guess it does." Kaiden cut across the sparsely graveled drive and out toward the open pasture. "Do you have any idea how many head of cattle your father has right now?"

"Not really," Julia confessed. "I've spent the last three days reorganizing the house."

"That's a job in itself." Kaiden angled his horse's head toward the longer grass and the downslope.

"I'm expecting a truckload of deliveries I've ordered online to turn up tomorrow," Julia added. "It was quite fun picking out all the new stuff."

"I bet."

They rode in companionable silence for a few minutes. Julia's shoulders lowered, and her breathing slowed as the familiar scenery rolled past her. She'd always loved riding and she missed it in the city. She'd tried to keep it up, but there was nowhere to really let go and just ride for miles.

"Has your dad been out on the property recently?" Kaiden asked as the ground sloped toward the gentle curves of Morgan Creek.

"Only in the truck. Jose and Andy, the retired hands, have been keeping an eye on what cattle there are left. From what they've told me, we don't have the manpower to round them up and make a proper count."

"If your dad decides to get rid of them, let me know. I'll tell Roy over at Morgan Ranch. He's usually the person who helps round up the strays and redistributes them to other ranches rather than your dad having to sell them to market off season or too young." Kaiden paused. "Or tell your dad to call Roy himself. I don't want to get in the way."

"Dad doesn't want to change anything right now. I asked him."

"Yeah?"

Julia waited for a follow-up question, but Kaiden seemed quite content to ride alongside her and study the view. She couldn't believe she was suddenly willing to confide in him, but he knew her family almost as well as she did, and that was a big plus. Maybe it really was time to let go of their past and move forward, and she desperately needed a friend.

"Dad's got this crazy idea that he can keep everything just as it is for Miguel," Julia said.

"Does Miguel know about this?"

"Why do you think he won't come home? He ran away for a reason. He's never wanted to be a rancher."

Kaiden nodded. "I can't see him coming back and settling here right now."

"Neither can I, which means my dad expects me to—" She abruptly stopped speaking and stared out at the ragged black line of the foothills below the Sierra Nevadas.

"Stay here until Miguel does come back?"

Julia glanced over at Kaiden, aware of the understanding on his face.

"It's hard when your family have expectations, isn't it?" Kaiden said softly. "After Ben crashed out of college, my dad expected me to stay on the ranch and work for him for the rest of my life. That didn't sit well with me, and we fought about it a lot. Eventually, even though I knew I couldn't go far from here, I at least made it to community college to study an outside trade."

"Dad was happy for me to leave as long as he had Miguel," Julia admitted. "Now that he's relapsed, he somehow expects me to make it all right for him. I don't think he's accepted his new reality yet." She made a hopeless gesture. "I don't know if I can help him see that things have changed forever, Kaiden."

"You can't. He's going to have to work it out for himself, and it'll be hard for him." Kaiden hesitated. "I talked a lot to Sam Morgan while I was building her new kitchen. She said it was really tough to learn how to walk again and adjust to a whole new world of limitations and endless expectations."

"But Dad's decided that if Miguel returns everything will suddenly be okay."

"I'd say he'd just be opening up a whole new barrel of problems." Kaiden grimaced. "What does he expect you to do in the meantime?"

"Live here full-time." Julia realized the horses had stopped moving, and that they were next to each other, their knees touching. "I have a job in San Francisco."

"A job that is probably going to be paying for all this work being done on the ranch." Kaiden sounded grim.

"Miguel does send Dad money every month, but it doesn't go far."

"Damn, I feel bad about even mentioning the upgrade now."

"Don't be. I have enough saved to pay for everything." Julia smiled. "And, I want to do it for Dad, not Miguel. He's the one who wants to live here."

It was Kaiden's turn to hesitate. "Forgive me for asking, but how long can your father physically continue to do that with MS?"

Julia bit her lip. "I'm only just understanding how serious his condition is right now. He was in remission for several years, and we all stupidly thought the illness wouldn't return to full strength." She straightened her back. "All I know is that Dad wants to live out the rest of his life here. I'm going to do everything in my power to make sure that happens."

Even if it meant dealing with Blaine and Melanie for the rest of her life . . . Just the thought of that depressed her, but what else could she do? Unless Chase Morgan suddenly decided he wanted a personal lawyer nobody in Morgantown could pay her the exorbitant salary she earned in San Francisco. And up until Blaine's appearance, she'd quite liked her job.

"You okay?"

She jumped as Kaiden snapped his fingers in front of her nose. "You disappeared for a minute."

"I was thinking."

"Whatever it was, it didn't seem to be making you very happy," Kaiden commented.

Julia gathered her reins. "Life can't always be one big joke, Kaiden."

"I get that." He clicked to his horse. "You ready to cross over the creek? It's not high at the moment so you shouldn't have any difficulty."

Prickly.

Kaiden glanced sideways at his companion, who was

staring resolutely ahead as they waded through the rocky creek. Like one of those hedgehogs Daisy had always wanted as a pet. But despite her obvious weapons, Julia's heart was in the right place, and she was willing to do whatever it took to keep her father happy. Kaiden could appreciate that. He could even admire it. He just wished he could get her to confide in him without having to fight it out. But maybe he was judging her wrong, and the spikes were just her armor, and the scars he got from fighting his way through were just part of the process. Why he was willing to put himself through such an ordeal was another conversation entirely.

"This ranch is a mess," Julia commented as the horses began to move uphill at a much slower pace.

"It certainly needs some TLC," Kaiden agreed. "We do our best to keep the boundary fences secure because it benefits us all, but none of the other ranchers have the bandwidth to take on the place full-time. You need someone like Rio Martinez to come in and buy the ranch."

"I don't think Dad would like that—although he is a big fan of Rio's."

"Rio and Yvonne bought the Cortez place from Ines with the proviso that she still gets to live there forever, and it seems to suit them well. My brother Ben's managing the Gomez place. He and Silver will probably buy it when Pablo dies, which means we've saved two of the local ranches from big land developers."

"Is that a problem around here?" Julia asked.

"It could be. And once a developer gets a foot in the valley you know what happens next. You're surrounded by housing developments."

Julia nodded. "I've seen it happen in the East Bay, so I

understand your concerns." She drew up her horse. "Is it true that Ben's developing some kind of Morgan Valley preservation trust thing?"

"Yeah. Who told you about that?"

"Nancy."

"How the hell does she know?" Kaiden raised his eyebrows. "It's supposed to be family only at this point."

"Then someone's been indiscreet. Maybe you should tell Ben."

"Nancy won't tell anyone," Kaiden said confidently.

"She told me."

"True," Kaiden considered. "I probably need to have a word with her, or I'll ask Ben to do it. It's his baby after all. Thanks for the heads-up." He pointed at the upcoming boundary fence that was in way better condition than the others surrounding the Garcia Ranch. "You can leave me right here."

"That's not your land."

"Nope, it's the Lymond place. I don't think Cauy and Jackson will mind if I cut across the bottom corner of their pastures. I'll be back home in no time."

He reached the fence, dismounted, and waited for Julia to join him. He watched her indecision as to whether to ride away, or get down and join him, and smiled invitingly.

With a sigh, she dismounted and immediately rocked back on her heels. Kaiden grabbed hold of her elbow to steady her.

"Hold on there. Riding's a bit like being on a ship. You need to find your sea legs."

She'd grabbed hold of his jacket and he looked down at her clenched fist.

"Speaking of touching me without my consent, I'm good with it, you know?"

He'd surprised her into looking up, and then he found he couldn't look away.

"Sorry." She uncurled her fingers and he took hold of them instead.

"It's fine. Really." He slowly bent his head, giving her plenty of time to exercise her own version of consent, and gently brushed his mouth against hers.

With a sigh, she kissed him back, and for a moment, he forgot everything but the taste of her. He was the first to draw back and smile.

"Wow, I've always wondered what it would be like to kiss Julia Garcia, and now I know."

She immediately bristled. "So, that was some kind of a dare for yourself?"

He fought a grin. "More like a promise." He stepped back. "Let me know when you've made a decision on the plans, and have a great weekend."

"I will."

She stomped off toward her horse looking so adorably confused that Kaiden had to pretend to be busy straightening his Stetson so she wouldn't see his triumphant grin. She'd let him kiss her, and he wasn't going to let anything spoil that moment—especially her.

She mounted and he went over to her side.

"You good on the way back?"

"I think I can manage." She nodded at the fence. "How are you going to get through that? There's no gate."

"Duh, how do you think? You've been living in the city for too long. Watch and learn, Ms. Garcia, watch and learn."

He mounted his horse Indian style, rode back in a

wide circle, set Domino in a lope straight toward the fence, and hopped over it. From the safety of the other side he hollered and waved his hat at Julia.

She gave him a slow handclap before turning away and riding off. Kaiden settled Domino down and set off home still smiling. Not bad for a morning's work, which somehow made the thought of seeing his father so much easier to bear.

Chapter Five

Julia was still thinking about her last exchange with Kaiden when she arrived back at the ranch. She'd confided in him, she'd let him tease her out of her bad mood, and then she'd let him kiss her.

"Way to go, Garcia," Julia muttered as she took Dolly's saddle and blanket off and rubbed her down. "You're a complete pushover."

But Kaiden understood her current situation better than anyone else in the world. He knew all the players and didn't have any qualms about speaking out about their particular issues. How could she *not* confide in him?

She lugged the saddle into the tack room, noting that everything in there needed to be cleaned, and mentally added it to her long to-do list. Her cell buzzed and she took it out of her pocket.

Hey! You around?

She typed back: **Yes, what's up?**

Her phone rang and she accepted the call. "Hey, Scott."

"Hey, babe. Are you available for dinner tonight?"

She grimaced. "Don't you remember me telling you that I was going to stay with my dad in Morgantown for the next two weeks?"

There was a rather long pause. "You must have forgotten to ask my admin to put it on my calendar."

Jeez, he was already sounding offended, and she really did not have the energy to deal with his hurt feelings right now.

"Maybe I'll see you when I get back?" Julia offered.

"I'm off to Japan for a month. That's actually why I wanted to see you."

"Oh, okay. Have a great trip."

"You don't sound very bothered."

Julia repressed a sigh. "Scott, you were the one who specified that we were just having fun with a no-commitment relationship. Why would you want me to be bothered?"

"Because I find that women usually do start to care for me despite their best intentions."

Wow, the conceit of the man. Julia tried to think how to reply, but he saved her the bother.

"It's okay, Julia, you don't have to pretend you don't mind. I was going to break up with you before I went away anyway. I thought I'd detected signs of you getting a *mite* too possessive of me last time we went out together."

"You mean when I introduced myself to your boss as your date?"

"Yes, that. It was very presumptuous of you."

"You're right, it was." Julia gave a fake sigh. "Oh, God, how am I ever going to live knowing that I am not your chosen one?"

"I'm sure you'll get over it and find someone else. You are quite attractive, and you have a very good job."

"But no one is as godlike as you, Scott. How will I survive?" she wailed. "My life is ruined!"

"Now, calm down, Julia . . ."

"How will I endure it?" Julia screeched. "My ovaries crumbling to dust, my skin to paper, my once straight limbs crooked and bent all because Scott Halton has rejected me!"

Her phone went dead and she laughed until her sides hurt. Who knew that bringing out her inner Kaiden Miller could be such fun? A text flashed on the screen.

I am blocking you now, Julia. Good-bye.

"Good riddance you jerk," Julia muttered as she returned to the house.

Why she'd ever gone out with Scott in the first place was a mystery. He'd seemed okay, not pushy, and not interested in anything more than the limited time she had to offer. With the hours she worked, and his frequent trips abroad, she'd barely seen him more than once every couple of months.

When her cell rang again, she held it to her ear.

"I thought you'd blocked me."

"I'd never do that while you continue to be useful to me, Julie."

Julia grimaced. "Hello, Blaine. How can I help you today?" It seemed like it was her day to deal with over-entitled men.

"Miley gave me those files."

"Great!" Julia opened the kitchen door and went inside enjoying the warmth and the sunlight streaming through the newly cleaned windows.

"But, I still can't make any sense of what you've done,

so I need you to walk me through everything before my presentation on Monday."

"Sorry, I can't do that." Julia set the new kettle on the stove. "As I've already stated, my father comes first, and the company is legally required to allow me to take my days off without interference from you or anyone at MZB."

"This is just sour grapes because you didn't get the job," Blaine whined.

"Everything you need to know is in those files. If you take the time to read through all my notes and make your own, you will be fine."

"I don't agree. Your work is shoddy."

Julia took a deep breath. "My work is fine. Ask anyone."

"That isn't good enough, Julie. I'm going to call you back in an hour, and you'd better be ready to help me, or I'll be taking my complaint to the senior partners."

He was definitely panicking. It would be the first time he'd be presenting a case without her and everyone on her team knew he wasn't up to it.

"I won't be here in an hour." She put a tea bag in her mug and made sure the coffee on the stove was still hot and plentiful for her father. "If you really are stuck, ask Miley to help you. She compiled the information, and she has a very good understanding of the case."

"Miley hates me."

That was true, but Julia wasn't going to confirm it, and get the paralegal into any kind of trouble.

"She's a professional, and she wants to advance in the firm. Give her a call." Julia poured her father's coffee into his favorite cup. "It was nice talking to you, Blaine. Good luck on Monday."

After four days at the ranch, the office seemed very far away and Blaine's hysterics ridiculous. Would she get some satisfaction at seeing him fail at the meeting on Monday? Sure she would, but she also knew he'd find a way to blame it on her, and the rest of the team, and that wasn't okay.

She scrolled through, found Miley's number, and called her.

Miley answered immediately. "Hey, boss. Aren't you supposed to be on vacation? How's your dad doing?"

It occurred to Julia that Blaine hadn't asked about her father once, but she wasn't surprised. He only cared about making himself look good.

"He's doing okay, thanks. How are you?"

Miley's sigh was long and loud. "Still dealing with that dickhead Purvis who is currently terrified because he has to present on Monday, and you're not there to hold his hand, and make him look good."

"So I gathered. He just called me."

"What an asshole." Miley snorted. "I told him to leave you alone. I even offered to go through the case with him, but he said he didn't need advice from the hired help."

Julia winced. "I'm sorry."

"It's not your fault. I'm doing my law degree the slow and cheap way, and that's just how it's going to be. At least I didn't get Mommy to pay my way through college like Blaine did."

"I'm worried that if he panics in the meeting he's going to start throwing blame around like confetti. I don't want you, Li Chang, or Smithy losing your jobs because of his incompetence." Julia stirred sugar into her dad's coffee.

"Damn, I was hoping he'd be the one leaving, but knowing how he operates, I'm fairly sure the door would be hitting *my* ass on the way out, and not his," Miley said.

"I told him to call you so that you could go through the file with him again." Julia braced herself for Miley's reply.

"I think that's the only way the team is going to get through this intact."

There was a long silence.

"Unfortunately, I think you're right, even though I hate his guts," Miley reluctantly said. "I'll call him right now."

"Thank you."

"You're welcome. You've stood up for me many times, and it's cool to be able to return the favor even if it helps that moron."

"I totally agree. When I get back, we'll think of a plan to get rid of him once and for all." Julia poured the boiling water into her mug.

"You promise?"

"Pinky swear."

"Cool. I'll bring the shovel."

Julia was still smiling as she took the coffee to her father. He had his new phone out, which was unusual, and was squinting at the screen.

"I had one of those texting things."

Julia took the phone and blinked at the all caps as she read the message.

WOULD YOU AND JULIA LIKE TO COME UP TO THE RANCH FOR LUNCH? ADAM'S COOKING A WHOLE PIG. J.

"Is this from Jeff Miller?" Julia asked. "Would you like to go?"

"If you're willing to drive, it would be nice. I haven't seen Jeff for quite a while."

"Then we'll go." It also meant she'd be out of the house where the cell reception was patchy if Blaine decided to call back in another panic. "Do you want to text Jeff back and say yes?"

Her father took the phone and frowned at the screen. "How do I make it all big like that?"

"You don't." Julia showed him how to use the keyboard. "Ask him what time he's expecting us, and I'll go and get ready."

She went into her old bedroom and thought about what to wear. She'd need pants and boots because it was another ranch, but they didn't have to be jeans. She opened her closet, appreciating the order she'd brought to it the previous day, and considered her options.

Her gaze caught on a box of old school stuff she'd sorted through the previous day and she took it off the shelf. Sitting on the side of the narrow bed, she sifted through the contents until she reached the diaries at the bottom. She extracted the one from her junior year and flipped through the pages until she reached February. Tucked into the crease of the page was a much-folded piece of pink paper cut in the shape of a heart.

She carefully opened the Valentine and tried to decipher the faded handwriting. She'd snatched it back out of Kaiden's hand after he'd mockingly read it out loud, and everyone had laughed. She'd read it several times later that same evening, wondering who had written it, never guessing that it had been her tormentor. Had he really thought she would make fun of it? She stared at the words.

Would she have laughed if she'd known it was from Kaiden? She hoped not, but she certainly would've been shocked he'd written it. No one had taken Valentine's Day very seriously at their small school. They'd all been friends and hung out together most of the time, and everyone had enjoyed guessing who'd written what to whom.

She replaced the Valentine in the page and shut the book. How strange that something she'd held against Kaiden had turned out to be so wrong. Who would ever have imagined that underneath his teasing exterior, Kaiden Miller had a sweet side?

But there was also the rift with Miguel, which had never properly been explained to her. . . . Suddenly aware of time slipping away in more ways than one, Julia shot to her feet. She'd put the box away, get changed as quickly as possible, and try and compose herself to meet her annoying friend again for lunch. The friend who had kissed her and she'd kissed back.

"You did what?" Kaiden stared at his father, who was sitting at the table drinking coffee. He'd stabled his horse, taken a quick shower, and come into the kitchen to find Adam cooking up a storm.

"I invited the Garcias to lunch," Jeff repeated. "What about it?"

"You never ask anyone over. You hate guests." Kaiden went to help himself to coffee.

"I don't hate guests. I just prefer to feed my own family and not hangers-on." Jeff shrugged. "But seeing as you're spending so much time over there, I guess I need to step in and make sure Juan doesn't get any funny ideas about poaching you to run his place, or anything. Look what happened with Ben!"

Danny, who was helping Adam in the kitchen, laughed. "I don't think it's Juan Kaiden is keen to see at the Garcia place."

Kaiden shot him a glare. "Thanks for nothing."

Danny just grinned and held up his hands.

"Are you after Julia again?" Jeff demanded.

"*Again?* What the hell is that supposed to mean?" Kaiden faced his dad.

"You always had a thing for her." Jeff studied him intently. "I think that's the only reason you continued to hang out with Miguel."

"That's not true." Kaiden had to defend herself. "And I'd hardly have been successful with Julia if I was hanging around with her brother, would I? He wouldn't have appreciated that at all."

"I bet he didn't."

Kaiden sipped his coffee. Sometimes his dad saw way too much. He'd hung around with Miguel to stop him even thinking of Julia as anything other than his best friend's sister. He found a smile somewhere. "If you'd told me you intended to invite them over, I could've asked them myself this morning."

"I didn't think about it until you'd left me in the lurch again." Jeff stood up. "Now, go help your brother."

"Will do." Kaiden sauntered over to Adam as if he didn't have a care in the world that Julia Garcia, whom he'd just kissed, would shortly be joining them for lunch. "What can I help you with?"

He was kept busy enough to stop him jumping every time the door opened, which seemed to be about every five seconds. Daisy and Ben were home with their partners, and Lizzie, Adam's girlfriend, turned up with her son, Roman, which meant they had almost a full house apart from their mother. Kaiden didn't have a problem with it. Seeing his siblings happy meant the world to him.

In the years when it had just been them and their father, life had been hard. They hadn't been encouraged to do much more than go to school, play sports, and work on the ranch.

Jeff had mellowed slightly since Leanne had returned on her own terms and, in his own gruff way, occasionally tried to make amends for his past behavior.

"Kaiden, did you see my calf?" Roman skipped up to him. "He's got such long eyelashes and when he drinks his milk I almost fall over he sucks so hard."

Kaiden lifted the hot pan deftly over Roman's head and set it on the table. "He certainly is cool."

"I wanted to take him home, but Mom says he can't live in our apartment."

"She's right, buddy. He wouldn't feel happy cooped up like that," Kaiden said.

Roman leaned in closer. "Mr. Jeff said something about clearing up all that cow shit, and Mom told him not to use that language in front of me, but I thought it was funny."

"I'd listen to your mom," Kaiden advised.

"And, then later, Adam said if we moved up here, I could take care of the calf all the time, and then Mom got all funny with him, and they made me go to bed." Roman sighed. "I hate it when that happens."

Kaiden put his hand on Roman's shoulder. "First thing to remember is that it's a good thing that Adam and your mom talk things out. Secondly, while I'm working in town, you can always hitch a ride up here after school to see your calf. What are you calling him?"

"Mr. Jeff says giving him a name will make him harder to kill and eat, but as I'm never ever doing that I've called him Buddy the Elf."

Kaiden took a moment to process that slice of harsh reality from the ever-tactful Jeff, and then nodded approvingly. "It's a great name."

"Thank you." Roman smiled up at him. "Now, I'd better go and help Mom, or she'll be after me."

As Kaiden straightened up he looked right into the eyes of Julia, who had just arrived with her dad. She wore a red fluffy sweater, black leggings, and her hair was down around her shoulders. His throat went dry at the luscious picture she presented and he hoped his tongue wasn't actually hanging out.

"Hey," he said.

"Hey, yourself." She came over to him. "Whose little boy is that?"

"That's Roman, Lizzie Taylor's son. Lizzie's engaged to Adam."

"She works at the coffee shop, right?"

"Yeah, she manages the everyday business while Yvonne concentrates on the baking."

Wow, look at him, putting words together into inane sentences while his gaze was fixed on her red lips—the lips he'd recently kissed. He hadn't meant to kiss her, but the devil inside him, that couldn't resist teasing her, hadn't wanted to stop.

"Are you okay?" Julia asked.

"I'm good." Kaiden looked over toward the kitchen. "I've got to help Adam."

Yeah, so he'd run away like an awestruck teenager with his first crush and leave her standing there. He was *so* smooth.

"I can help as well."

Jeez. She was right behind him, her body warming, the citrus tones of her perfume driving him to distraction. She put her hand on his arm, and he resisted the impulse to purr like a cat.

"It's okay. We don't expect our guests to work."

"That's not what your father said when we came in." She smiled and he returned the gesture.

Behind him someone coughed.

"Could you either help, or get out of the way, Bro? You're blocking the exit."

He half turned to see Danny with two pans of roasted potatoes in his well-protected hands and a patient expression on his face.

"Sorry." Kaiden moved out of the way, inadvertently colliding with Julia, who gasped as he trod on her foot. "Sorry."

She grabbed hold of his arm, and he helped her hobble over to the table and pulled out a chair. Wow, now he'd broken her foot. He crouched down beside her as she eased her boot off.

"I'm a clumsy ass," Kaiden said, frowning.

"It's okay, I should've moved quicker."

Julia felt down from her ankle to her foot. Trouble was she'd been too busy smiling at Kaiden to notice anything else in the entire universe. What was going on? Who *was* she? "I think it's okay. I'm glad I still had my boots on."

"Me too."

Kaiden wrapped his large, callused hand around her ankle and leaned in so close that his breath feathered against her skin. She looked down at his dark head and for a crazy second wanted to bury her hand in his thick hair and drag him even closer.

"I can't see any damage, but feel free to kick me if it makes you feel better."

"Wherever I want?" Julia rallied.

He winced. "If you must, but please think of my future children." He released her ankle and stood in one fluid motion. "Do you want to put some ice on that? I can get you some."

"I think I'm good." She put her boot back on and gingerly put some weight on her foot. "It's fine."

"Lunch should be ready soon. Do you want to come and meet everyone before it starts?" Kaiden glanced at her inquiringly.

Good, he'd gone back to being the perfect host and backed off a few feet. For some reason when he got close, he fried her brain, which she didn't appreciate.

"That would be nice." She glanced over at her father who was chatting with Jeff. "My dad seems to be having a great time without me."

Kaiden held out his hand and she took it, gently setting her foot on the floor and easing her weight onto it.

"See? I'm fine."

He nodded, and keeping hold of her hand, moved toward the tallest guy in the kitchen, Ben Miller, who stood with his arm around a diminutive blonde who even from the rear was instantly recognizable.

"Hey, Ben!" Kaiden called out. "Do you remember Julia?"

"Sure! Best-looking girl at our school and the smartest." Ben made a space for them and grinned across at his sister. "Apart from you, of course, Daisy."

He bent his head to the woman beside him. "Honey, this is Julia Garcia."

"Hey!" Silver Meadows, one of the most famous film stars in the universe, grinned at Julia. "Nice to meet you! The Garcia Ranch shares boundaries with our place, doesn't it?"

"Yes, that's right." Julia couldn't believe Silver knew that.

"Are you managing it now?"

"No, I've just come back to see my father for a couple of weeks. I have a full-time job in San Francisco."

"Really? What do you do?"

"I'm a lawyer."

"Gah." Silver pulled a funny face. "Not my favorite kind of people, but I bet you're one of the good ones."

"I try to be." Julia couldn't take offense at Silver's remarks. She knew her profession was a tough sell.

"Shame you're not into land management, we could do with some more female ranchers out here." Silver winked at Ben. "Way too many Miller and Morgan men strutting around like they own the place."

"Technically, the Morgans do own half the valley," Daisy mentioned. "But I take your point."

"Can't argue with Silver," Kaiden said. "Although Ruth Morgan *is* a badass."

"The original and best." Silver nodded. "I'm currently stealing all her recipes so I can impress Ben."

"You do that every day." Ben looked down at her so tenderly that Julia wanted to sigh. "Just by being here with me."

Kaiden made a gagging sound. "Dude. Stop that. You're in public." He punched his brother on the arm. "You two are way too happy together."

Silver went on tiptoe and planted a kiss on Ben's bearded cheek.

"Jealous, Bro?" Ben grinned at his brother.

"Damn straight, I am."

As he turned away, only Julia saw Kaiden's wistful expression. Didn't everyone want someone to love them like that? She knew she did, but in her world, it was as rare as hens' teeth. How Ben had managed to meet and fall in love with Silver was obviously a story for another day.

"Everyone take a seat!" Jeff Miller shouted. "Now!"

Kaiden again reached for her hand as if it was the most natural thing to do, and guided her to a seat between him and her father. She smoothed her fingers over the elaborate beveled edge of the table.

"Did you make this as well as the cabinets, Kaiden?"

"Yeah, I did."

"You really are very talented." Julia looked up at him. "If you lived in the Bay Area you could sell these hand-made items for a fortune."

"But then I'd have to live in the city." Kaiden made a face.

"Don't knock it if you've never tried it."

"You can't really say that you like it, can you?" Kaiden gestured at the window. "Compared to this?"

"I appreciate the energy there and the opportunities," Julia countered. "And I couldn't do what I love if I didn't live there."

"You love being a lawyer?"

"I do." She smiled at him. "Why are you looking at me like that?"

"Didn't you shout something at me about hating your job recently, or did I mishear you?"

"I said that sometimes the . . . people I have to work with are a problem," Julia tried to explain. "We've had a lot of upheaval at work recently. It'll take a while to get used to the changes in personnel."

That was lawyerspeak if ever she'd heard it. She hoped it would shut him up, but knowing Kaiden, he'd find another angle to explore until she finally lost her temper and told him everything.

Jeff loudly cleared his throat. "We say a prayer before we eat in this house. If you don't like it, then just keep quiet about it." He bent his head and pointed at Lizzie. "Do the honors, my dear."

Lizzie obliged, and everyone murmured "amen" at the end before the moment of peace was shattered as they all fell on the food. Julia was in danger of losing out before she regrouped and dug in, elbows out, to get her fair share as she fought off the marauding Millers, who had honed their hunting skills in a family of eight.

The roasted pork was delicious and came from Morgan Ranch; the vegetables were freshly dug up from the Miller garden or bought at Victor's organic farm on the other side of town. Julia sighed as she swallowed the last of the food on her plate and sat back.

"That was so good."

"Adam's a great cook," Kaiden said around a mouthful of food. "And, he loves doing it."

"I hate to cook," Julia confessed. "I had to do it when Mom used to go away, and I always resented it."

"Any news of your mom?" Kaiden very carefully didn't look at her when he asked the million-dollar question everyone in Morgan Valley usually tried to avoid.

"She's still alive and practicing medicine at her clinic in Guatemala." Julia kept her tone neutral like she was discussing the weather, but couldn't quite resist the urge to punch back. "How about yours?"

"Still based in New York, but she comes here four times a year now to see us and reconnect."

Julia searched his face. "Does that bother you?"

He offered her an easy smile that didn't quite reach his

eyes. "Why would it? She's free to do whatever the heck she wants."

"If my mom suddenly decided to come back, I don't think I'd be okay about it." Julia watched him closely. "And, she went on her own terms."

"Whereas mine got kicked out by my fool of a father who refused to let her come back, or have anything to do with us." Kaiden kept smiling. "She was brave to reach out when she had no idea how she'd be received."

"And everyone is just fine with it?" Julia asked curiously. "No hurt feelings or explanations needed?"

"Your lawyer is showing." Kaiden suddenly stood up. "Can I take your plate? There's definitely going to be some dessert."

Chapter Six

He'd let Julia rile him up, and that was not only irritating, but also unheard of. He was the king of avoidance, and he was usually able to deal with questions about his mom without even thinking about it. And, it was his own fault, he'd asked about her mother, and she'd immediately gone on the attack. She was probably just as sick of dealing with questions about Lupita as he was about his mom.

He rinsed off the plates and stacked them in the dishwasher while Adam gave instructions about the three kinds of pie he was currently about to put on the table. Kaiden obediently got the ice cream out of the freezer and set it beside the bowls on the long table. He gathered up a few more plates and took them over to the sink.

"Thanks, Kaiden." Adam briefly looked up from slicing the pies. "Lizzie loves custard on her pie so can you take that jug over to her?"

"What's wrong with cream or à la mode?" Kaiden asked. "Who wants to dump warm yellow goo on a good pie?"

"Don't worry, she likes them all." Adam looked over at

an oblivious Lizzie, who was busy talking to Roman. "And there are three different pies."

"I hear you two were getting into it about Lizzie moving up here again."

Adam stopped working. "Who told you that?"

"Roman." Kaiden held his brother's gaze. "He gets worried when you fight."

Adam grimaced. None of the brothers were big fans of marital fighting after having lived through the meltdown of their parents' marriage. "Jeez, I'm really sorry about him thinking that. I'll try and do better."

Kaiden just nodded and moved on. It wasn't really his place to interfere in his big brother's relationship, but he couldn't stand by and let Roman get unintentionally hurt. But, he'd said his piece, and he wasn't going to labor the point. Adam wasn't stupid and he truly cared for Lizzie's son.

Kaiden sat down again. Julia was chatting across the table to Silver about some kind of skin-care thing that was like listening to a foreign language. As soon as Adam took his seat, Ben got to his feet and everyone looked inquiringly up at him.

"I'm glad you're all here today because I want to share some news with you." Ben put his hand on Silver's shoulder. "We got married yesterday in Vegas."

As the whole table erupted in cheers and whistles, Kaiden's gaze was inevitably drawn to his father, who sat like a stone at the head of the table with his arms folded over his chest. Jeff definitely wasn't cheering and Kaiden braced himself for impact.

Ben was grinning like a fool and still talking, blissfully unaware of the little storm cloud hanging ominously over the brilliance of his day.

"Silver had some final scenes to shoot in Vegas last

week, and we just decided to get married one night without any fuss. We got a minister to come to our suite, and it was all over and done with in ten minutes." Ben chuckled. "We didn't even have to dress up."

"And you didn't think to tell your father about this important decision before you got married in front of strangers, or did you just tell the Meadows family?" Jeff asked.

Ben's smile dimmed. "We didn't tell anyone, Dad. We just didn't want all the fuss."

"The fuss." Jeff stood up. "Well, you've made your bed. I wish you well." He nodded at Juan. "Excuse me while I check the horses. One of my mares is likely to foal."

Kaiden glanced at Ben, who looked like someone had kicked his puppy, and immediately caught his brother Adam's eye. "We'll have to have a party for these guys, right? So that we can celebrate in style!"

"Yes, like we did for Jay Williams when he brought back his bride," Daisy joined in. "That was awesome. Would you like that? We can organize the whole thing, Silver. You won't have to lift a finger."

While his siblings were busy circling the wagons, Kaiden excused himself and went out into the yard, and on to the barn where he found his father leaning over the half-open door of the end stall. Jeff didn't turn around when he spoke.

"Still no sign of that foal."

Kaiden leaned up against the wall. "That's because it's not due for another month, Dad."

"They can still surprise you, Son."

"Just like people." Kaiden paused. "Why did you have to be so unpleasant to Ben and Silver?"

"I wasn't unpleasant. If they don't like it when I speak my mind, then that's on them."

"You were rude and ungracious, and you know it."

"Who made you the judge and jury?" Jeff swung around to glare at him. "I'm still your father, and I deserve your respect."

"You always told me respect was earned." Kaiden didn't look away from his father's irate gaze. "Ben's happy, Silver's happy, so what right do you have to blunder in and spoil it for them?"

"Spoil what?" Jeff looked affronted. "Am I supposed to be okay that my son, the first of my kids to get married, didn't ask me to his own wedding? I like Silver, I think she's a good match for Ben! I would very much have liked to see them stand up together in front of our family pastor, in our family church, and speak their vows to each other. Is that too much to ask?"

Kaiden winced as Jeff's words rose to a shout.

"What if the press had gotten wind of the information and the ceremony had been ruined by TV cameras, fans, and gawkers?" Kaiden countered. "Would you have enjoyed that, Dad? Because I can guarantee Silver and Ben wouldn't have, and it is supposed to be their day after all."

"Yeah, well." Jeff's gaze turned back to the horse. "Nothing I can do about it now, is there? It's done. I suppose I'd better call your mother, and let her know—unless Ben has already done that."

"You're hurt, aren't you?" Kaiden stared at his father.

"Don't be ridiculous, Son." Jeff avoided his gaze.

"I think I'm finally figuring you out. All this shouting is because you're actually upset, and the only way you know how to show it is by yelling and making everyone else miserable."

"Balderdash." Jeff slammed the upper door shut and

shot the bolt in place. "Don't tell me how I feel, Kaiden Miller. I have enough of that from your mother."

"Who would be extremely annoyed with you right now for going super negative on Ben, who is definitely her favorite kid."

"All right!" Jeff scowled at him. "If you'll just stop yapping your mouth off, I'll go and be nice to Ben, deal?"

"And Silver," Kaiden said firmly. "Don't forget her."

His father stomped off in the direction of the house muttering to himself, and Kaiden stayed where he was.

It occurred to him that Julia had a similar way of dealing with her problems. She got mad first, and offered more nuanced explanations later. Perhaps after all those years of dealing with his dad, he understood where she was coming from and didn't let it put him off. Whatever she said, things definitely weren't good at her job, and he wondered why. Not that it was any of his business, but he'd always been the curious type.

Just as he was about to go back in to make sure his dad was behaving himself, he heard Julia's voice coming toward him and instinctively went still.

"Look, Melanie, I assure you that I've done everything you asked me to do."

He eased himself back into the shadowy corner and realized she must be on the phone and walking toward him.

"No, that's not . . . No, I can't fly back for Monday. There's no one to look after my father."

There was another long pause.

"It isn't a question of money, Melanie. It's about my responsibility to care for the people I love. If you can't see that, I'm sorry, but I don't know what else I can say to you. Miley knows all about the case, she has offered to help, and that should solve any issues that might arise on Monday."

Kaiden tensed as Julia's voice grew louder. She was almost through the door now. He jumped as she kicked the doorframe hard.

"Sure, Melanie, you promoted him, so why are you in such a panic now? Regretting your decision? Afraid he'll make you look bad in front of the other senior partners when I'm not there to prop him up?"

Her gasp when she finally noticed him made him grin. He pointed at her phone.

"You didn't actually say that last bit to her, did you? Because if you did, you're probably going to need a new job. I hear the Garcia Ranch are looking for a manager."

She slammed a hand over her heart and gaped at him. "What the hell are you doing here?"

"Just checking out the horses."

"And spying on me?"

"Hey." He raised an eyebrow. "I was here first."

"You—" She shook her head. "You're right. I'm the one who is intruding. I'll turn around right now."

Kaiden frowned. "Backing down so fast? What's wrong with you? That Melanie lady must've really rattled you."

"She's one of the senior partners at my law firm."

"So not someone you want to piss off," Kaiden commented as Julia looked down the length of the barn and anywhere except at his face. "Are you going to fly back on Monday?"

She turned on him, her hands now on her hips. "Kaiden, has anyone ever told you it's rude to eavesdrop on other people's private conversations?"

"Sure, all the time," he said easily. "But sometimes

you hear such good stuff that you can't help but comment on it."

"You are . . ." She sighed. "So annoying."

He nodded gravely. "You're not the first person to mention that." He waited a beat before continuing. "What's going on?"

Her mouth settled into a now familiar stubborn line. "What if I just say it's none of your business?"

"I'll just keep bugging you until you tell me." He shrugged. "It's what I do."

"I am well aware of that." She took another turn around the barn before finally swinging around to face him. "My new boss has to present a case to the senior partners, and the clients on Monday, and he's panicking because I'm not there to hold his hand."

"What's that got to do with Melanie?" Kaiden asked.

"She's the one who promoted him, and she doesn't want to look bad at the meeting if he isn't sufficiently prepared."

"Makes sense I suppose." Kaiden nodded. "No one likes looking stupid."

"You think I'm at fault here? That I should get on that plane?" Julia asked.

Kaiden concealed a grin. There was his fighter coming back off the ropes.

"I didn't say that. If I was going with my gut here, I'd guess that you should've been the one doing the presentation in the first place."

She stared at him for a long moment. "Correct."

"He took your job?"

"He was given the promotion over my head, yes."

"Fools." Kaiden slowly shook his head. "They should have given it to you."

"How do you know?"

"Because I know you, and I know that you always strive to be the best. I bet you did all the work as well." He held her gaze. "Melanie should take a hike."

She walked slowly toward him and he tensed. "What's wrong?"

She framed his face with her hands, went up on tiptoe, and planted a smacking kiss right on his mouth.

"Thank you."

He blinked at her. "You're welcome. What did I do?"

"Validated my decisions."

"I did?" She went to step away and he curved an arm around her waist. "Not so fast. Now that you're here, right where I want you, how about you kiss me again?"

Julia gazed into his familiar laughing gray eyes and placed a hand on his chest.

"I don't think—"

"Then don't." He kissed her nose, his voice so low that she had to strain to hear it. "Just go with the flow."

"That's not who I am," she muttered even as she leaned into him, enjoying the hardness of his frame and the subtle curve of his lower lip. "I'm way too uptight for this."

"You seem to be doing just fine to me." He traced the seam of her lips with his tongue and her knees turned to Jell-O.

With a ragged sigh, she gave in to the physical, and pressed her lips to his, enjoying his growl of appreciation as their mouths met and clashed. Seconds later her hand was in his hair, and he was palming her ass, bringing her as close as possible to the hard bulge in his jeans.

Man, he was a good kisser . . . Julia let herself drown in the release of emotions, aware that she wasn't thinking straight, but too frustrated to care. There was no way she was getting on a plane tomorrow so that she could attend that meeting on Monday.

Her cell buzzed, and she tensed up and eased away from Kaiden, who groaned.

"Can't you ignore it?"

"Sorry." The fact that her whole body was humming and singing hallelujah was good enough reason to stop. She took out her phone and read the text.

"Melanie is not happy with me."

"What's new?" Kaiden leaned back against the stall door and rubbed his fingers across his mouth as if still tasting her. He held out his hand. "Come back here."

"I think we've done enough kissing for one day," Julia said.

"There's never a quota for kissing, honey." His smile was an invitation to sin.

"There should be one for you." Julia patted her hair. "And, don't call me that."

His smile widened into a grin. "Honey? Do you prefer darlin' or babe, or—"

She marched over and placed a finger over his mouth. "Stop talking, now."

His tongue snaked out and curled around the tip of her finger making her want to climb him like a tree.

"Stop that," Julia said severely.

"Are you sure, honeybun?" Kaiden kissed her hand and released it. "You look like you need a lot more kissing to me."

"But kissing leads to other things, and I am not, I mean, I *will* not be doing those things with you, Kaiden Miller."

He waggled his eyebrows at her. "Never say never, honey pie."

"Go away."

"I live here," Kaiden reminded her.

"Then I'll go."

She started for the door, and he gently took hold of her elbow and turned her around.

"Other way, unless you fancy walking home?"

She shook her arm free, and he let her escape him, enjoying the swing of her hips and the straightness of her spine as she marched away from him.

He liked kissing her. In fact, if she hadn't pulled away he might have been urging her into one of the empty stalls, and laying her down in the nice, fresh straw, and . . .

With a groan, he glanced down at the front of his jeans. He couldn't go back in to the house just yet. A slow stroll around the paddock into the gathering wind might help cool him off a little and remind him of all the reasons why getting involved with Julia Garcia was a bad idea.

But, whatever she said, she was in trouble, and something about that didn't sit well with him. If she needed his support, then how could he possibly not help her out?

"Jeez," Kaiden muttered to himself. "Wow, you're so noble, and this has nothing to do with the fact that you want her like crazy, and you always have."

She'd be going back to San Francisco in a week or so, and if she was her usual efficient self she wouldn't need to come home much again—because her dad would be well taken care of, and fully capable of getting on with his life in his newly adapted house. Did he want another fleeting physical relationship that never went anywhere? He'd done that before and, even if Julia wanted that, he wasn't sure he could give it to her.

Kaiden glanced back toward the house. He'd successfully talked his body back under his control without the need for a cold shower, so he might as well go back and make sure that his father had at least attempted to make things right with Ben.

When he entered the house, Julia was sitting talking to Lizzie and Daisy while the men cleared up. Adam glanced over as he came in and beckoned Kaiden to join him. Ben and Silver were standing with his dad and everyone was smiling.

"I'm not sure what you said to Dad, but thanks." Adam clapped him on the back. "He came in a different man."

"I told him he was being an ass." Kaiden shrugged. "You know, the usual."

"Don't underestimate yourself." Adam lowered his voice. "You're the only one of us apart from Daisy he ever really listens to."

"Lucky old me." Kaiden took the dishcloth out of his brother's hand. "How about you go and talk to Lizzie? You did all the cooking. I'll take it from here."

"You sure? Don't you want to get it on with Julia?"

"Don't even go there, Bro." Kaiden shuddered. "She's way out of my league. She always has been."

"Lizzie thinks Julia likes you."

"Yeah?" Kaiden perked up and Adam grinned at him.

"See? You do like her." His brother punched him gently on the arm. "Go for it, my man."

"Yeah, right." Kaiden cracked the dishcloth like a whip toward Adam's Wranglers. "Get out of here."

He went back to the sink where Danny was patiently washing and rinsing the huge pile of dishes. Kaiden took one look at him and held up his hand.

"Don't you start."

"Start what?"

"You know—that I'm panting after Julia Garcia."

"Are you?" Danny frowned. "Can't say I've noticed—except the way you keep tripping over your tongue because it's hanging so far out of your mouth every time you look at her."

"Sometimes this family just doesn't know when to stop," Kaiden grumbled as he picked up a dish and dried it vigorously.

"Says the biggest joker of them all." Danny grinned. "How does it feel to be on the other end of it for a change, Bro?"

"Just you wait until you meet a woman you like," Kaiden said. "I'll remind you of this moment."

His brother's smile dimmed. "Don't worry about me. I'm never going to put myself through that again."

Kaiden nudged him with his elbow. "You will, Danny. You're way too sweet to give up on love just yet."

Chapter Seven

Sunday morning started early because Juan wanted to go to church, and Julia offered to drive him. There wasn't a Catholic church in Morgantown, but the current pastor tried his best to appeal to all denominations, and Juan seemed to enjoy the sermons. Julia couldn't say she was a regular churchgoer, but she was finding it surprisingly soothing to participate in the service surrounded by people she'd known all her life.

She was also surprised to see that Kaiden and Danny had accompanied their father, who was uncharacteristically quiet and well behaved. After the service, she wheeled her father out into the spring sunshine, and waited as he spoke to the pastor about the Catholic priest who would be coming through Morgantown that afternoon to offer communion and confession to the faithful.

"Good morning, honey." She didn't have to turn around to know that Kaiden Miller had come up behind her. "Nice to see you getting your prayer on."

She finally looked up at him. He wore a blue shirt that

brought out the color in his eyes, and carried a white straw Stetson that he immediately slapped on his head.

"I'm surprised you didn't burn to a frazzle at the door," she retorted.

His wide, appreciative smile made her want to smile back at him. He leaned closer and murmured, "I figured that if they let my old man in, they wouldn't have a problem with me."

"Maybe your father is an undercover saint." Even Julia couldn't stop herself from smiling at that one.

"Saint Jeff. Patron saint of the perpetually angry?" Kaiden offered. "I kind of like it." He hesitated and looked down at her. "I was wondering if I might come over and see you today?"

"For what reason?"

He held up his hands. "Definitely not what you're thinking. I noticed you still have a chicken run at the back of the house. I thought I'd come over, patch it up, and fill it with some of our spare chickens."

She held his gaze. "Really?"

"Yeah, Juan said he missed having fresh eggs in the morning."

"He never mentioned it to me."

Kaiden shrugged. "Probably didn't want to bother you when you've got so much on your plate right now."

Julia glanced suspiciously back at her father, who was now talking to Jeff Miller.

"If you're sure you can spare the time."

"I'm sure." He stepped back and touched the brim of his hat. "I'll see you around two, then."

"With the chickens," Julia said sternly.

"Got it." He nodded. "Lots of clucking and definitely no—"

She cut across him. "Kaiden Miller! You just got out of church!"

He turned away laughing, and she returned to her father, aware that her cheeks were heated, and hoped that no one had overheard a word she'd shared with her rogue of a neighbor.

After they got back to the ranch, Juan decided to take a nap before lunch, and Julia went out to the barn to work up a sweat cleaning the old saddles and bridles. On her way, she took a look at the chicken house, which was in surprisingly good shape considering. If Kaiden could fix the fence and the hole in the roof of the wooden structure, she didn't see why the chickens wouldn't thrive in there again. Just to make sure, she swept out all the debris from the nesting boxes and perches, and replaced the ground soil.

Even though the sun was shining, it wasn't that warm, and Julia was glad of it. Midsummer in Morgan Valley, the temperatures could reach over a hundred degrees, and in the winter they usually had snow. Spring was always short, late, quite beautiful, and definitely Julia's favorite time of year.

As she filled a bucket with water and found the saddle soap, she considered what it would be like to live back at the ranch full-time. She knew she had the ability to run it just as well as Miguel could—maybe even better, but would she want that? And, more importantly, would her father ever trust her enough to let her take control?

After her mother had decided to go back to her home country to practice medicine, Juan's faith in women had diminished considerably. Until this week, he'd refused to allow Julia any access to the financial records of the ranch, or any say in how the place was run. It was as if he'd been worried that she'd use the information against him, which wasn't fair at all. She might have her mother's brains, but her loyalty was to the ranch and her remaining family.

It wasn't even that her father was unkind to her—he obviously loved her dearly, but he'd decided she didn't need to bother her head with such things, which wasn't helpful at all. She dropped the bridle in the bucket, picked up the brush, and started working on the straps. She could run the ranch and make it profitable, she was sure of it. All she needed was a good and reliable ranch manager who would respect her father.

Three hours later, she heaved the last saddle back onto its stand and looked around the tack room. Order and cleanliness had been restored and that made her happy. A good hot shower would easily remedy the fact that she now stank like old leather and was soaked to the skin. She was glad she'd borrowed an old pair of Miguel's denim overalls and hadn't ruined her only pair of jeans.

She emerged into the sunlight, groaning as she straightened her back, and walked toward the ranch house. It was weird not having dogs around the place. Her father had always had at least four working dogs as well as the occasional household pet. She shaded her eyes as she noticed a car parked up that definitely didn't belong to her or Kaiden.

Had the priest arrived early? She glanced down at her filthy clothing. She hoped not. Her father would have a fit if she received a man of God looking like this. She braced herself to apologize as the car door opened, and then went still.

"Julie? Is that you?"

Her apologetic smile froze in place as Blaine Purvis stared at her in horror.

"Blaine? What the heck are you doing here?"

Kaiden was whistling as he drew up outside the Garcia house. His dad had been more than amenable to his rebuilding the chicken house, and had even helped load the lumber into the back of Kaiden's truck before sending him off with a hearty slap on the back. Sometimes, catching his dad in his mellow mood right after church worked out well.

Kaiden checked out the fancy silver Lexus parked up alongside Juan's truck and wondered who on earth it belonged to. He'd sent Juan a couple of contractor names to consider bidding for the conversion, but neither of them were wealthy enough to own such a nice car. He surreptitiously peered inside and saw what looked like rental paperwork stuffed into the center console.

When no one answered his knock on the front door, he decided to walk around to the kitchen entrance, which came in through a mudroom. The door wasn't locked, but he used his manners and knocked again before entering. The smell of coffee and the sound of voices wafted toward him.

"Hey, Julia, I've brought the chickens," Kaiden called out as he came through the door. "Oh! Sorry, I didn't realize you had a visitor."

The man sitting opposite Julia at the kitchen table wore a fancy suit, had spiked, gelled, blond hair, and the discontented expression of a baby stuck in a wet diaper.

Julia turned to greet him, her expression unreadable.

"Hey, Kaiden." She nodded at the man sitting opposite

her. "This is Blaine from work. He decided to just turn up here and surprise me."

Blaine gave Kaiden the once-over and obviously dismissed him as unimportant. "Hi, now, as to what I was saying, Julie."

Julia rose from her seat. "Excuse me, Blaine. I really need to speak to Kaiden. Help yourself to more coffee if you want some."

"But—"

Julia maneuvered Kaiden out of the kitchen and into the yard. It occurred to him that he'd never seen her look so coldly furious before.

"He just turned up?" Kaiden asked.

"Yes." She kicked a rock so hard it ricocheted against the side of the house. "Demanding that I go through the damn presentation with him."

"Can you say no?"

"He says that seeing as he's here now, and his flight doesn't leave until six, I might as well capitulate and help him or he'll give me the worst employee evaluation report ever seen."

"Surely he can't do that?"

"Oh, he can." She made a face. "And I don't have the ability to tell him to stuff his job just yet because I need the money to get Dad set up."

Kaiden grimaced. "Jeez, I'm sorry, Julia. This sucks."

She straightened up. "If you want to go, that's fine. I'm sure you can sort the chickens out another day."

He gave her a pitying look. "I'm staying. I'm not the kind of guy to run out on a friend. Is there anything I can do to help while you deal with that asshole?"

The relief on her face was brief but unmistakable,

reminding him that she'd rarely had anyone to lean on her entire life, and had made the best of it.

"If you could keep an eye out for my dad, and maybe let the priest in if he turns up?"

"I can do that." Kaiden nodded. "Have you eaten yet?"

She picked at her filthy clothes. "Nope. I haven't even had a chance to take a shower. Blaine showed up just as I was coming back from cleaning out the tack room."

He'd never seen her so out of sorts. Kaiden grabbed her hand. "Come with me."

"What are you doing?" Julia asked as he towed her back through the kitchen door and faced the idiot at the table.

"Hey, Blaine, Julia's going to take a shower while I make some lunch for her and her father. Do you want anything?" Kaiden gave Julia a gentle shove in the direction of the door.

"He's right, Blaine. I can't concentrate when I'm damp and smell like a barn." Julia smiled sweetly at him and then looked back at Kaiden. "I won't be long."

"But—"

Blaine started to speak, but caught Kaiden's eye and subsided into his seat.

"Would you like some lunch?" Kaiden channeled his best Jeff Miller voice. "We've got ham, potatoes, and fried tomatoes on the menu."

"I don't, I mean, I prefer to eat plant-based meals."

"So eat the potato and tomato." Kaiden took out a large cast-iron skillet. "Or have nothing. It's entirely up to you."

He busied himself gathering the ingredients and ignored Blaine, who remained in his seat hunched over his phone reminding Kaiden of Wes, but far less likeable.

"Where did you fly in from, Blaine?" Kaiden asked as he sliced the thick ham.

"San Francisco."

"The big city, eh?"

"Yes, have you ever been there?"

"Once or twice. Not really my thing."

"You prefer riding the range, singing around the campfire, and all that stuff?"

"Yeah, especially the beans and the farting." Ignoring Blaine's condescending tone took some doing, but Kaiden just about managed it. "Much healthier way to live."

"Right, along with all that fat you're cooking up."

Kaiden turned to face Blaine and patted his flat stomach. "No fat on me, dude." He ran his eye over the other man. "You, on the other hand, look like you could do with losing a few pounds."

Blaine flushed red. "I work out. I just have a very busy and important job, which means I don't get a lot of leisure time."

"Oh, right. That makes sense." Kaiden turned back to the pan, which was heating up nicely. "I'll go and check up on Mr. Garcia."

He walked out, whistling, and checked that Juan was up from his nap and ready for his lunch. When he returned to the kitchen, Blaine was still hunched over his phone.

"I need to set the table." Kaiden said. "Unless you want to help?"

"I don't know where anything is." Blaine cast a dismissive glance around the kitchen. "I still can't believe Julie actually grew up here."

"I'll set the table." Julia came back in. Her wet hair was tied back in a severe bun and she wore all black, which from his intimate knowledge of women Kaiden knew was a bad sign. "Did you call Dad, Kaiden?"

"Yes, he's coming."

Kaiden turned back to the skillet and carefully placed the cooked potatoes in on one side and the ham on the other. The sizzling sound of the fat hitting the hot surface made his stomach growl. He flipped the ham, left the potatoes to brown up on the skin side, and put the halved tomatoes in. With the high heat radiating from the pan the meal wouldn't take long to cook.

Julia set four plates on the table and the silverware while Blaine just sat there like a sack of potatoes. If he took a wild guess, Kaiden imagined the guy had never done a thing to help anyone in his life. No wonder Julia didn't like him. Kaiden wasn't a fan, either. Juan wheeled himself through the door in his wheelchair and Julia smiled at him.

"Dad, this is Blaine Purvis. He works with me at MZB."

Juan held out his hand and Blaine shook it. "It's a pleasure to meet you, son. I'm sorry you had to come all this way to meet with my daughter."

"It's no bother, Mr. Garcia."

At least Blaine was being polite to Julia's father. If he hadn't been, Kaiden might have been wielding the skillet a bit too close to his head.

"Lunch is ready." He carried the heavy pan over to the table and set it in the center. "Why don't you go first, Juan?"

"No, that should be our guest." Juan smiled at Blaine, who was licking his lips at the sight of the ham.

"Nah, he only wants the potatoes and tomatoes." Kaiden leaned over and started dumping the ham on three plates. "He can wait until everyone else has got theirs."

* * *

Julia watched as Kaiden somehow managed to reduce Blaine to a mere inconvenience and wanted to hug him. Blaine had put her in an impossible situation. For a moment when he'd stared at her like she was trash, she'd thought of just quitting right there and to hell with the consequences. Kaiden's unexpected support was strengthening her resolve. She'd deal with Blaine in as short a time as possible and send him on his way. As soon as she got back to San Francisco, she would start looking for a new job.

Kaiden carried on a conversation with her and her father about the restoration of the chicken coop, the plumber who was coming to start on the bathroom renovations on Monday, and anything else that politely excluded Blaine from voicing his opinion. Of course he still did, but somehow he always ended up looking stupid, which was highly gratifying. Not that he realized he looked stupid, because he was far too conceited to notice.

It did help having someone pointing out how awful Blaine was, and she was grateful to Kaiden for making her take a step back and really look at her boss again. She'd gotten so tied up and tense dealing with his petty demands on a daily basis that she'd begun to think she was overreacting. But no, he really was that awful, and he didn't deserve the promotion that should have been hers.

At the end of the meal, Julia turned to Kaiden. "Thank you for cooking."

"You're welcome." He nodded at her dad. "I'll clear up and make Juan some coffee if you and Blaine want to go through to the farm office and get on with it."

"Thanks, we will."

She wanted to kiss him, but didn't want to do anything in front of Blaine that might get back to the office. He was incapable of keeping a secret, and implying that her focus was not on her work, but at home with a hot rancher, would be an excellent way to impede her forward progress in the law firm.

"I'll bring you some coffee, and then I'll get on with the chicken coop." He turned to Blaine. "Nice meeting you."

"Same," Blaine said without raising his eyes from his phone, which made Julia want to rip it out of his hand and throw it at the wall.

Kaiden rolled his eyes at Julia, walked Juan back into the family room, made sure he was settled, and returned to the kitchen just as Julia showed Blaine where the farm office was. She waited until Blaine went through the door and then turned back to Kaiden.

"I owe you."

"Yeah?" He gave her a slow wink. "I'll think about how you can repay me."

She kissed his cheek. "Please do."

She was still smiling as she went into the office where Blaine was setting up his laptop and shut the door. She'd keep her temper, be polite, answer all his inane questions, and wave him off with great pleasure in a few hours. Hopefully, that would be the last she'd see of him for the next two weeks.

Kaiden had just knocked the last fence post in and stood back to check that it was level with the others when the kitchen door opened and Blaine stepped out. He lit a cigarette, walked gingerly over to Kaiden, and stared at the chicken coop.

"I bet those eggs will taste good."

"They will." Kaiden put his hammer away in his tool belt. "Not sure if they qualify as plant-based though. Where's Julia?"

"She's just finishing up some tasks for me." Blaine exhaled a plume of smoke. "It's a shame that I had to come all this way. If she hadn't made so many mistakes in the initial documents, I wouldn't have had to chase her down. It's hard to manage people like her who are so sloppy."

"Julia's one of the hardest workers I've ever met," Kaiden said evenly. "I can't imagine her being anything but one hundred percent on task."

"And what's up with her dad? Is what he's got catching or anything?"

"He has MS." Kaiden measured the space between the posts. He did some mental math about how much wire fencing he'd need to surround the pen rather than calculating just how quickly he could dig a nice, quiet grave for Blaine.

"So he's been sick for a long time, which makes me wonder why Julie had to rush to his side right now. It's almost as if she timed it deliberately to make me look bad," Blaine said. "She's *so* not a team player."

"Her name is Julia, not Julie, and her dad's condition has gotten worse recently," Kaiden said. "He had a bad fall."

"But you're still keeping him on?"

"Excuse me?"

"This is your place, right?" Blaine gestured at the ranch house. "You rent it to them?"

Kaiden laughed. "One hundred percent wrong. I live on

my father's ranch about a mile away. The Garcia family have owned this land for almost a hundred years."

"They *own* it?" Blaine looked surprised.

"Yeah. Why would you think any differently?" Kaiden met his gaze head-on.

"I assumed they were recent immigrants." Blaine shrugged. "It's an easy mistake to make considering."

Kaiden measured and rejected several answers, which would not have helped Julia's career. "I don't see why. Several families in Morgan Valley settled here after the gold rush, and a second wave came in the twenties and thirties between the wars. Most of them are still here."

"How big is this place?"

Kaiden raised his eyebrows. "What's it to you?"

"I was just wondering." Blaine took another look at the pastures sweeping away from the house. "Can you see the boundary fence from here? I bet it reaches right to the edge of that cute little town."

"You'd have to ask the Garcias about that. I'm only a visitor just like you."

"It could be a nice place if it got a makeover."

"It is a nice place, and we're working on that." Kaiden headed for his truck. "Excuse me. I've got to get some wire."

By the time he returned, Blaine had gone back inside leaving only the remains of his smoldering cigarette behind. With one eye on the door, Kaiden took some pleasure in grinding the stub under the sole of his boot to make sure it was out. He decided he wouldn't repeat his conversation with Blaine to Julia because it would only make things worse. She didn't need him to tell her Blaine was a complete ass; she already knew.

Kaiden unwound the wire, attached the end to the first post, and hammered it into place. Normally, he liked to have someone else to work with because the wire could snap back, but he was so furious he was willing to tackle the job himself. The dismissive way Blaine had talked about Julia and her father had set his dander up. He wanted nothing more than to take the smug smile off the bastard's face with his fist.

He reminded himself that Julia was quite capable of taking care of herself, and that punching a lawyer was never a good idea. He rarely lost his temper, but when he did it was memorable. So today he'd pour that energy into the chicken coop and ignore the unusual impulse to step out of line.

Weirdly enough, the last time he'd lost his temper had been with Miguel in this very spot. They'd ended up on the ground punching each other's lights out until Juan had pulled them apart. He'd never forgotten Julia's stricken expression, and the way she'd rushed to comfort her brother, sending him a scathing look over her shoulder. They hadn't talked much after that, and Miguel had left town, something Julia probably blamed him for as well.

Kaiden let out a long, slow breath and steadied the coil of wire fencing. If he had any sense he'd listen to the signs pointing out that getting involved with the Garcias was never good for him. But maybe it was too late. He was already knee-deep in their concerns.

"Need a hand?"

He turned from his contemplation of the fence posts to find a man dressed in black with a clerical collar smiling at him.

"Hey."

"Hi! I'm Father Pascal. I've come to see Mr. Garcia."

"He's inside." Kaiden gestured at the wire. "Give me a minute to prop this up and I'll take you in to him."

The priest took off his jacket and set it on the back of the truck. "How about I help you finish this up first? It'll go much faster if I do."

Kaiden eyed him carefully. "You sure about that, Father? I wasn't expecting a Sunday miracle."

"Funny." Father Pascal chuckled. "I grew up on a farm in County Cork in Ireland. I quite miss the work."

"Then be my guest." Kaiden grinned at him. "Which end do you want to take?"

Chapter Eight

Blaine came back into the farm office smelling of smoke and chewing mint-flavored gum, which didn't make anything better. Julia looked up from the notes she was typing.

"Almost done."

"About time, too. In future, this is how I want you to prep me for all my presentations, okay?"

Julia looked at him. "Basically, you expect me to write them for you." She made it a statement rather than a question.

"Yeah, your job is to make me look good, and if you continue to do that, I'll make sure you continue to *have* a job."

God, she loathed him so much right now she was surprised she hadn't erupted into a ball of fire and taken him out. She couldn't even change the presentation to showcase his ignorance because the rest of her handpicked team would be in the room with him, and he'd have no hesitation in blaming them for any issues. She hated the fact that she'd promised them so much, and now Blaine had control of all their futures.

When she left MZB, she would make sure to take her protégés with her even if it took a while.

"So why is this place so run-down, Julie? What do you do with that huge salary we pay you?" Blaine sat opposite her and put his feet up on the desk.

"My father has MS and it's been hard for him to run the place."

"So why doesn't he sell it?"

"Because it's been in his family for generations, and it's his home." Julia stood to gather the final version of Blaine's presentation from the printer. "I'm currently working on how to adapt the house to suit his ongoing needs, and find someone to manage the ranching side of things."

"Sounds expensive."

"Then it's a good job I saved all that huge salary MZB pays me then, isn't it?" Julia offered him a bland smile.

"Stupid to pour good money after bad."

"Not on someone and something you love." She refused to look away and eventually he dropped his gaze to his phone. "Now, if you have everything you need, perhaps you'd better be getting back to the city before the country roads get too dark for you to drive on."

He held out his hand. "Give that to me."

She passed the completed presentation over and sat down again, hating having to wait on him, and yet having no choice. He read it through, pursing his lips as he sounded out some of the big words she knew he'd change to little ones when she wasn't looking. She'd tried to keep it as simple as possible, but there were depths she wasn't prepared to sink to.

"Looks good, Jules." He placed the papers in his folder,

zipped it up along with his laptop, and rose to his feet. "I'll leave you in peace, then."

"Great." Julia rose too. "Let me see you out."

She opened the door out into the hallway just as Kaiden came into the house with another man. The two of them were chuckling, which was a sight to behold.

"Hey!" Kaiden caught sight of her. "Julia, this is Father Pascal. He's come to see your father."

"A pleasure." The young priest shook Julia's hand. "I was just helping Kaiden here with a bit of yard work. He's promised me some fresh eggs for my trouble."

He had a rich, Irish brogue that made Julia want to smile.

"I didn't make him do it, Julia, he insisted," Kaiden said.

"It was nice to do something physical for a change." Father Pascal nodded. "Now, where is Mr. Garcia? I'm sure he's wondering where I've got to."

"I'll make some coffee," Kaiden offered.

"Do you have any tea?" the priest asked. "Sorry to be a bother."

"I'm sure I'll find you some," Kaiden said as he directed the priest toward the family room. "Do you and Blaine want coffee, Julia?"

"Blaine's just leaving." She turned around, but there was no sign of her unwanted visitor, and she frowned. "He must have gone to the bathroom."

"Why don't you go on through and get acquainted with Father Pascal while I sort out the coffee?" Kaiden suggested. "I'll keep an eye out for Blaine and make sure he leaves."

This time, Julia didn't hesitate to accept Kaiden's offer. She'd had quite enough of Blaine, and keeping her thoughts to herself, especially in her own home, was becoming increasingly difficult.

"Thank you, I'd appreciate that."

She went through to the family room, already certain that her dad was going to love Father Pascal, and more than willing to leave Blaine to Kaiden's tender mercies.

Kaiden kept an eye on the hallway as he set the coffeepot on the range and rummaged through the cupboards looking for tea, which he knew Julia would have somewhere. There was no sign of Blaine, and, eventually, Kaiden went to look for him. He found him in Juan's bedroom studying the group of family photographs and loudly cleared his throat, making Blaine jump.

"Julia said you were leaving."

"Yeah! That's right. I must have gone the wrong way after I exited from the bathroom." He pointed at a portrait of the Garcia family. "What happened to the mom and brother?"

"They're still around." Kaiden held the door open wide. "Have you got all your stuff? Julia's busy with her father right now so I offered to wave good-bye to you."

"You don't like me, do you?" Blaine stopped in the doorway alongside Kaiden. "I wonder what Julie's been telling you? I wouldn't believe anything she says. She's just a poor loser."

"Julia has never mentioned your name before today," Kaiden replied. "Why would she?"

"So, why are you so invested in this family, Kaiden? Are you hoping to take over the place if you get on the right side of Julie's father?"

"I know this might shock you, Blade, but not everyone thinks like you. In this valley, we look out for our neighbors, and don't expect anything in return."

"Yeah, right." Blaine sneered. "No one is that nice."

"Maybe not in your world." Kaiden looked down his nose at Blaine. "But some of us are better than that."

"Not when it comes down to money and inheritance." Blaine smiled. "I'm a lawyer, I know what happens. Everyone fights dirty."

"Not always. My dad left his ranch to my big brother. The other five of us are fine with it."

"Sure you are." Blaine started off down the hallway. "Which is why you're currently sniffing around the Garcias."

Kaiden stared after him, remembered his manners, and followed Blaine out into the yard.

"I hope you have a safe trip home." Kaiden stood at the open door of the car as Blaine slid into the leather seat. "Take care, now, Blade."

Blaine set his laptop carefully on the passenger seat and looked up at Kaiden.

"It's Blaine, and thanks for nothing, cowboy."

Kaiden might have offered a one-fingered salute as the car drove away, but he doubted Blaine noticed in all the dust he kicked up by driving too fast.

"Good riddance, asshole," Kaiden muttered as he went to take one last look at the chicken enclosure. "And, don't ever come back."

He was still contemplating his repairs when Father Pascal and Julia came out of the side door and headed straight for him.

"It looks great!" Julia admired the chicken coop. "Thanks so much to both of you."

"Ah, I did very little of it myself, Julia," Father Pascal said. "The credit should definitely go to Kaiden."

"I brought some laying hens, a cockerel, and some feed so if you want to do the honors and welcome them home, Julia?" Kaiden looked at her expectantly. "I'll fetch the crates."

"Yes, please."

She looked as excited as a kid. It made Kaiden want to smile despite the awfulness of Blaine. How she dealt with that guy every day he had no idea. He fetched the chickens, set the wooden box in the center of the enclosure, and bowed elaborately to Julia.

"My lady."

"Thank you." She crouched down, opened the latch, and half a dozen young hens came out and instantly started surveying their new territory. "They are awesome!"

"Indeed they are." Father Pascal was watching through the fencing as Kaiden released the cockerel. "Now, don't forget my eggs, Kaiden, lad, will you now?"

"You're right up there on my list," Julia reassured him. "Thank you for your help."

"I enjoyed it. Now, I'd best be off." The priest produced his car keys. "I've another parishioner to visit before I go home. Tell your father that I'll be back in a couple of weeks."

Julia went to rise, but he waved her back. "No need to stand on ceremony. I can see myself out."

"Bye, Father." Kaiden held up a hand. "Thanks for the help."

He smiled as the priest walked over to his modest car, backed it up, and went off down the driveway with a final wave.

"What a nice guy."

"Dad certainly liked him." Julia rose and came to stand beside him. "Jeez, what an afternoon."

He put a hand on her shoulder and gently rocked her back and forth. "How do you work with that dumbass Blaine every day?"

"Because at the moment I don't have any choice." She sighed. "Once my yearly review is done, I can contemplate changing jobs, but I'll need a good reference, and the only way I can get one is if stupid Blaine gives it to me."

"He sucks."

"I agree." She unconsciously leaned against him, and he put his arm around her. "I could really do with a drink right now."

"On a Sunday?" Kaiden pretended to be shocked.

"Scandalous, I know." She rubbed her cheek against the fleece he'd put on to protect himself against the wind. "But, as I said, it's been a bit of a day."

"I can't believe Blaine came all the way out here just to bug you." Kaiden shook his head.

"He's terrified of looking bad tomorrow at the meeting. He wants to be a senior partner before he's forty."

"He's not exactly a good example of cream rising to the top," Kaiden said. "Scum comes to mind. Now, do you want to feed the chickens, and see how your dad is doing? He said something about Dr. Tio's grandmother coming over to play cards with him this evening."

"Yes, Maria Rosa comes once a month. I'm not quite sure how they communicate because she speaks Portuguese, and my father's Spanish is pretty lousy, but somehow they manage."

Kaiden hesitated and decided to risk it. He was already in over his head. "If you really want that drink, do you want to come down to the Red Dragon with me? We can have dinner as well."

She looked up at him. "Like go out in public? Together?"

He shrugged. "You owe me, remember?"

She considered him for so long that he almost forgot how to breathe.

"If Dad's okay with it, I'd like that." She pointed at him. "But, it's on me, okay?"

He held up his hands. "I'm not going to argue with you. I'm just a poorly paid carpenter, Miss Hot Shot Lawyer."

She reached for his hand, which gratified him immensely. "Then, let's get these chickens fed and go and check in with Dad."

Julia glanced over at Kaiden as he opened the door into the bar for her.

"Ma'am."

"I think I preferred 'my lady,'" she joked as they made their way through to the bar where Nancy and Jay were working. It wasn't that busy seeing as it was a Sunday, and a lot of the older folk wouldn't dream of drinking on the Sabbath. Kaiden pulled out two stools.

"Hop up here, and I'll go check in with Bella about dinner."

Kaiden disappeared and Julia climbed onto the barstool.

"Hey." Nancy grinned at her. "Was that Kaiden Miller? The man you shouted at the other day? I told you he'd like it."

"He's been doing some construction work up at the ranch for Dad, so I thought I owed him dinner," Julia explained, not yet willing to consider why else she'd accepted his invitation, and what it might imply. "He's been great."

"He's certainly talented." Nancy put two beers in front of Julia and winked. "In *many* ways. Are you wanting a menu?"

"I think Kaiden's going to get us a table," Julia said.

"Wise choice. He probably doesn't want the whole of Morgantown listening in while he charms the pants off you."

"Hardly." Julia took a swig of beer and immediately coughed.

"Careful now, slugger." Kaiden patted her on the back and then perched on the edge of his stool. "Bella says we can go through right now if we like."

"Okay." Julia wheezed as he offered her a hand to get down. "Thanks."

"You're welcome." Kaiden turned to Nancy. "Hey, what's up?"

"Nothing much." Nancy cleaned the bar where Julia had spilled the beer. "Just watching the fools of Morgan Valley make complete asses of themselves."

"That's a bit hard on Julia," Kaiden protested. "She just choked on her beer."

"Ha ha." Nancy waved him off with her hand. "You're not as funny as you think you are, Kaiden Miller."

"I'm funnier." He winked at her and took Julia's hand. "So nice to come into my local bar and be insulted by a professional."

"You're welcome!" Nancy called out as they went through to the dining area.

"Do you ever leave without trying to get the last word?" Julia asked him.

"I just did," Kaiden pointed out. "I gave up trying to outdo Nancy years ago." He slid into the booth and she took the seat opposite. "The food here is really good.

Bella's got Sonali Patel working with her now. She just graduated from culinary college."

"I know." Julia unwrapped her silverware from her napkin. "I came to see Nancy the other night. I had the fish. It was really good."

"You drink by yourself a lot?"

"Yup, I'm a complete lush."

He shook his head, his gray eyes glinting. "I would never have guessed that in a million years. You've always struck me as someone with their head screwed on just right."

"I didn't really have much choice," Julia confessed. "After Mom left, Dad basically handed me the keys to the house and expected me to take on all her jobs."

Kaiden frowned. "But you were just a teenager."

"Yeah, but who else was there? Dad and Miguel needed to manage the ranch, they didn't have time for the house." She sipped her water. "It wasn't all bad. By the time I entered high school I knew how to manage a budget, take care of a house, *and* keep a four point two GPA."

"All by yourself."

She raised her eyebrows. "Don't feel sorry for me. You didn't have it much better when your mom left, did you?"

"There were more of us, and Adam took the brunt of it. And, we had Auntie Rae who turned up and took over everything."

"She was awesome." Julia took another sip of her water. "I often wished . . ." She stopped talking.

"You'd had someone like her," Kaiden finished her sentence. She wasn't sure if she liked it.

"Anyway, it taught me how to be self-reliant, how to manage stuff, and made me the independent person I am now." She smiled at him and picked up the menu. "What are you going to eat?

"The fish tacos. Don't ever tell my dad, but I sometimes get sick of beef."

She smiled, her shoulders relaxing, as he took the hint and changed the conversation to something far less personal.

"Me too and the same, although it can be hard to get good beef in the city without having to take a mortgage out on it."

"That's because you guys insist on building housing estates over the ranchland out there," Kaiden said.

"Didn't you say that had nearly happened here?"

"Yeah, unbelievable, I know, but luckily Rio Martinez stepped in and bought the place from Adam's old in-laws."

"Why would anyone want to build out here?" Julia wondered.

"When the housing prices in the rest of the state are so high, dormitory towns with a two-hour commute each way are apparently the next big thing."

Kaiden paused to give their order to Bella and then resumed talking.

"And we really do need housing here because of the success of Morgan Ranch and the growth of the businesses in town. Yvonne really struggles to get trainees for her bakery, I can't get apprentices, and finding ranch hands is almost impossible. We can pay them a living wage, but they either can't find somewhere to live locally, or the rent is too high, or the commute too long. We're currently trying to remedy that by refitting infill projects into affordable housing, but at some point, we'll run out of space, and the obvious thing to do is extend the town into one of the ranches."

Julia nodded as Kaiden spoke, aware that her initial snobbish thought that he hadn't left town, and therefore hadn't educated himself, had been way off base. She was familiar with both his arguments and the solutions, both from living in the valley and from her job.

He paused for breath and offered her a sheepish grin. "Sorry, it's a bit of a passion of mine."

"And a good one," she reassured him. "Can't the Morgans build more property to house their workers on their land?"

"They are trying to, but they also have to build guest accommodations, and keep it all sympathetic to the environment." He drank some beer. "And, it's a community problem. It's not just on them."

"I'm sure Chase Morgan can afford it," Julia said tartly.

"I'm sure he can, but as I said, that's not the point, is it?" Kaiden met her gaze. "We're all in this together. We've got to find a way to provide for the folks who want to live here, and yet try and keep the town how we like it."

"I think you're trying to do the impossible," Julia said. "Things always change and not always for the better."

Kaiden sat back. "Doesn't mean you don't *try* to make them better."

"You're such an optimist." Julia smiled at him.

"What's wrong with that?"

"Nothing, it's just that I've never seen it as one of your dad's strengths, and he basically brought you up, and you look just like him."

He shrugged. "Maybe that's why I'm like that. I don't

want to be Jeff Miller Two. I leave all that self-doubt to my brother Ben."

"Ben seems to have done pretty well for himself despite that."

Kaiden grinned. "He really hit the jackpot with Silver, didn't he?" He shook his head. "If I'd known who he was taking out on that trail ride I would've volunteered to go myself."

"That's how he met her?"

"Yeah. They got cut off by a storm at the top end of Morgan Valley. Ben fell off his horse, and Silver basically kept him alive until the medics turned up. It's almost as good as a romantic movie."

"Lucky Ben."

"And lucky Silver. My brother might be a slob, but he's really good person, and he'll always adore her."

He looked up as Bella returned with their food. "Thanks! This looks great."

Julia went quiet while they ate, and Kaiden didn't blame her because the food was that good. The fish was perfectly spiced, the coleslaw mellow, and the fries crisp and hot. She hadn't liked him implying that she'd had it tough, which didn't surprise him in the least. She was not the kind of person to ever feel sorry for herself. She just took life on the chin and got on with it.

She'd also just endured half a day with the obnoxious Blaine so her defenses were probably sky high. He got it, but for some reason he wanted her to feel able to relax with him, to let go, to *share* stuff. But she'd never had that luxury in her life so why should she want to begin now?

Especially with someone like him, who thought the best way to communicate was to poke fun at people.

He wiped his mouth on his napkin and pushed his empty plate away. His cell had remained uncharacteristically silent, which was slightly unnerving because he'd been away from home for hours, and his dad normally had a thing about that.

Julia sat back and sighed. "That was really good."

"Room for dessert?" Kaiden asked.

"Could we share?" She looked at him inquiringly. She'd left her hair down, and wore a crisp striped shirt and well-ironed jeans. If there was such a thing as an executive look for a cowgirl then she'd nailed it.

"It depends, how much are you likely to eat?" Kaiden pretended to be suspicious. "Half? More than half?"

He was back to gently teasing her again since it somehow seemed safer when she was smiling at him like that. She wanted to keep things light, so did he—apart from that nagging feeling that he wanted to lean across the table and kiss her stupid.

"Are you okay, Kaiden?"

He blinked at her. "Yeah, I'm good." He busied himself consulting the menu again. "What do you want to share?"

"The brownie and ice cream looks good."

"Then let's go for that. Do you want coffee?"

"Yes, please."

He caught Bella's eye, and she came over, and he gave her the order, which left them with way too much time to make conversation. Julia was leaving soon, and despite what everyone said, she was still way out of his league, and she wasn't interested in him anyway.

Apart from the fact that she'd kissed him . . . more than once.

She reached across the table and took his hand. "I really do want to thank you for sticking by me today. I can't imagine how I would've coped if I'd had to deal with Dad, Blaine, and the priest all at the same time by myself."

"You would've managed." Kaiden curled his fingers around hers. "You're a smart cookie."

"Maybe, but I'm not sure I would've kept my temper with Blaine, and being fired on the spot would not have helped matters at all." She met his gaze. "You were really great."

He shrugged. "Just helping out a neighbor."

"You'd do that for anyone?"

"Only the pretty ones." He held up a finger. "That was just a joke."

"I know." She sighed. "I feel like I should apologize to you."

"Again? What for?" Kaiden frowned.

"Not believing you were sincere."

"Why would you? I'm not exactly known for it," Kaiden said. "I make a joke out of everything, which winds most people up the wrong way."

She angled her head and considered him. "Why do you do that?"

He shrugged. "I've never really thought about it. I suppose it just came naturally to me."

"I suspect it's got something to do with your birth order." Julia nodded. "It usually does."

"Well, Adam's a grump, Ben overanalyzes everything, Danny internalizes everything, Evan's a wildcard, and Daisy's a nerd, so I suppose I had to be something different," Kaiden mused. "Comedy seemed to be my natural talent."

"And you're very good at it, but . . ." She hesitated.

"What?"

"I shouldn't say anything, it wouldn't be fair."

"You might as well spit it out. We're all friends here, right?" Kaiden said.

She fidgeted in her seat. "Okay, I always wondered even when we were kids whether you were using humor to hide something—like you were trying too hard to make everyone like you. It felt fake somehow."

"Wow, that's deep." Kaiden eased his hand away from hers and sat back. "Maybe I just found it a good way to get what I wanted."

"No, I don't think it was that, because you've got enough natural charm for ten people." She studied him intently. "Was it more as a means of protecting yourself? I can only imagine what it was like having to deal with your dad when you were a kid. Being the court jester might've deflected a lot of rage away from your siblings."

"So, you're saying I'm the rodeo clown of the family?" He crossed his arms over his chest.

"Why does that make you angry?"

"Why do you think it does?"

She sighed. "Kaiden . . . for one, you're glaring at me, and secondly, you're not brushing it off by making a joke."

He stood up. "Your lawyer is showing. For someone who hates anyone getting in their private business, you sure seem okay about diving into mine. Excuse me a minute, will you?" He dug out his cell. "I need to check in with my dad."

Julia stared in stunned silence at Kaiden's empty seat. What had possessed her to say something so unhelpful?

She'd seen the hurt in his eyes before he'd gotten as far away from her as possible.

"Here's your brownie."

Julia looked up at Bella. "Thanks so much." She bit her lip. "I hate to be a pain, but could you put it in a to-go box? I think Kaiden has to get back home, and I wouldn't want him to miss this."

"Sure! It's no problem, but you'll probably not want the ice cream, it'll melt too fast. I'll replace it with some cream. I'll do the same with the coffees, and bring you the check right away."

Julia made sure the coffee lids were tightly sealed as she placed them on top of the box containing the brownie, which was inside a sturdy paper bag. She walked out through the bar, but there was no sign of Kaiden.

Nancy called out to her, "If you're looking for your man, he went out to his truck. Said his phone was out of charge or something, and that he'd be back in a minute"

"Thanks!" Julia said. "I think I'll follow him out. Have a good evening."

"Will do, and don't be a stranger!" Nancy winked.

Julia waved and went out into the street. Despite it being officially spring, there was a cold wind whistling down Main Street, and she was glad she'd put on a warm jacket. Carefully holding the bag, she walked around to the parking lot at the side of the bar and headed toward Kaiden's truck. He was standing with his back against the door, arms crossed, head down as if contemplating the mud on his cowboy boots.

Julia continued her approach and he slowly looked up, his face still hidden in the shadow of his Stetson. She held up the bag like a peace offering.

"Nancy said your phone died. I thought we could eat this in the truck while it's recharging."

For a moment, she thought he was going to tell her to start walking, but he found a smile and straightened up as if there was nothing wrong between them at all.

"Yeah, sorry about that. I realized I hadn't heard from Dad for hours, which isn't like him, so I checked my phone, and it was out of charge." He gestured at the truck. "I just plugged it in."

"Then shall we get in and eat this before the whipped cream melts? I got the coffee, too."

"Sure." He went around and opened the passenger door for her. "Hop in."

She settled in the seat, inhaling the now familiar scent of wood shavings, leather, and whatever Kaiden's shower gel was. While he was busy turning the engine on she took out the coffee and set the box between the seats with two spoons at the ready.

"Here you go."

She wasn't sure she had much appetite for food anymore, but she had to make the effort.

"Thanks." He picked up the spoon. "Bella makes a really good brownie."

Julia forced down a couple of spoonfuls and then stopped eating. She couldn't just let this go. "Sometimes it's hard for me to forget that I trained as a lawyer, and I ask incredibly intrusive questions."

He shrugged. "Can't say I've noticed." He dug into the brownie and chewed slowly. "Maybe I'm just not used to people pointing out my flaws."

"Why should you be?" Julia said quickly. "And, you're right. It's none of my business, and it was an insensitive thing to question you about."

"I didn't say any of that," Kaiden objected.

"You didn't need to. I'm not stupid. I knew I'd messed up the moment the words left my mouth." She sighed. "I don't know why I'm behaving like this. It's not like me."

"You're under a lot of pressure right now."

"I'm always under pressure. It's the essence of what I do." She licked some cream off her spoon. "It's you."

"It's me, what?" Kaiden's gaze was riveted on her mouth.

"You unsettle me."

He sat back. "There's an easy fix for that, Julia. We just agree to keep out of each other's way for the next couple of weeks while you're here. It's not difficult."

"But, I don't want to do that."

Her words filled a silence he seemed unable or unwilling to end. Eventually, he stirred.

"What do you want then, Julia?"

She was equally slow to respond, and for once glad of the darkness and intimacy of the truck cab. Everything else—her job, her life, and her common sense—receded as she faced something far more instinctive and natural.

"You," she said. "I want you."

Chapter Nine

Kaiden drew a careful breath. "I hate to be that person, but could you be more specific?"

He surprised a laugh out of her, which made him want to smile in return. Ever since he'd walked out of the bar he'd been kicking himself for overreacting to her comments. But at some level, she got him like nobody else, and he wasn't sure he liked it one bit. Somehow, he kept talking even though it was like pulling teeth.

"I guess I'm the fun one because somebody had to be," he said slowly. "Dealing with my dad when we were kids was . . . hard. We all tried in our different ways to appease him, and I suppose sometimes, if I made a joke, it protected someone else, or lightened the mood, or refocused his ire on me, which was better because I could take it. I guess it became a habit."

She was quiet for so long that he almost forgot to breathe, and then she set her hand over his.

"Thank you."

"For what?" He shrugged. "Having to listen to me whine?"

"You're not whining. You're explaining how difficult things were for you, and how you learned to cope."

He stiffened. "Now you sound like you feel sorry for me."

"I do."

"So this 'wanting me' is some kind of gracious pity party for poor little Kaiden?"

She snatched her hand back. "Just because you admitted something personal doesn't mean you have to immediately lash out at me for being the person to hear it. I'm not exactly going to run around telling everyone that Kaiden Miller has a soft side."

He snorted. "Like anyone would believe that."

She regarded him seriously. "You're wrong. Everyone likes you, and you know it."

"That wise-cracking fake-assed guy who wants so badly to be *liked*?"

"Kaiden . . ."

He looked out of the window and slowly inhaled. What the hell was wrong with him? He rarely lost his temper, and certainly not over something so stupid as his *feelings*. His dad would've destroyed him if he'd thought any of his sons were so weak. He took another two, long, slow breaths before turning back to Julia and offering her a smile.

"So what were you saying earlier about wanting me?"

She opened her eyes wide. "That's what you're going with? *Really*?"

"It's not often that I get propositioned by the most beautiful girl in high school."

He could almost hear her teeth grinding together as he continued to smile and she breathed through her nose.

"Forget I ever said it, okay?"

He picked up his cell, which had revived sufficiently to light up the screen. "Sure!"

He thought she muttered something about idiots, but his attention was caught by the numerous messages now flashing up on his screen and he hissed a curse.

"Kaiden? What's wrong?" Julia's voice finally penetrated his terror and he looked up.

"My dad."

"What about him?"

"No wonder he wasn't chasing me down." He swallowed hard. "He's been flown out to Mammoth with a suspected heart attack. Everyone's been trying to get hold of me for hours."

She grabbed his arm. "Then let's get you back home. Go straight there and we can sort out my transport afterward."

He didn't remember driving back to the ranch, which probably wasn't a good thing. Julia had offered to take his place, but he'd needed something solid to hold on to, and a reason to overcome the sensation of terror that kept stealing his breath and making his own heart stutter in his chest. His dad might be the most god-awful pain in the ass, but he was as invincible and immovable as the Sierra Nevadas under whose shadow his family had made their home.

He couldn't die.

Could he?

"You're almost there," Julia encouraged him as they turned up the drive. She'd taken over his phone and had been texting away, telling him what was going on as he drove through the darkness. "Almost everyone is home except Adam, who went with Jeff to the hospital."

"Okay." Kaiden concentrated on not driving too fast as the truck climbed uphill to the flat pad the ranch house and barn stood on. "Got it."

He turned the engine off, didn't bother to wait for Julia, and ran straight for the house. His family was gathered in the kitchen just where he'd expected them to be, and they all looked up as he burst into the room.

"God, I'm so sorry. My phone was out of juice, and I—"

"No, it's okay!" His sister, Daisy, rushed over to him. "There's nothing you could've done anyway. We were right here when it happened, and there was no sign that anything was wrong." She drew a shaky breath. "One minute he was standing by the table arguing with Adam, the next he clutched his chest and just fell over."

Her fiancé, Jackson, came up behind her and looped an arm over her shoulders. "She's right, dude. Nothing anyone could've done. Adam was right on the chest compressions while Lizzie called Dr. Tio, who sent for the medevac team."

Kaiden sat down so suddenly he saw black spots and grabbed hold of the table edge.

"I should've been here, I—"

"Stop beating yourself up." Danny patted his shoulder. "You wouldn't have been able to do anything we didn't do. Dad's in the best place right now. Adam's going to call us when they get a proper diagnosis, okay?"

He managed to nod, and someone shoved a mug of coffee in his hand while everyone continued to tell him their version of what had happened. All he could think was that he was glad his father hadn't been alone, because what would have happened then? He shuddered and half the coffee slopped over the rim of his mug, scalding his fingers.

"Give that to me." Julia took the mug from him and set it on the table. He'd forgotten she was there. "You said they took him to Mammoth, Danny?"

"Yup." Danny, who had perched on the edge of the table on the other side of Kaiden, spoke up. "If he needs major surgery, they might transfer him to a bigger hospital, but we won't know that until Adam calls."

Kaiden struggled to find his voice. "I should take you home, Julia. You don't need to deal with this."

She took his hand. "I'd rather hang with you at least until we know how things stand. I already texted Dad and he knows where I am. He sent his best wishes by the way."

"Thanks," Kaiden replied automatically. "That's good of him."

Julia squeezed his fingers and looked over at Danny. "How long is it since Mr. Miller was helicoptered out?"

"About two hours. We should hear something soon." Danny sounded his usual quiet, reassuring self. "If it makes you feel any better, Kaiden, he was already complaining when they wheeled him out of here on the gurney."

Kaiden managed a smile. "Typical."

"So don't count him out just yet." Danny nodded at Julia. "If you're staying, can I get you some coffee?"

"That would be awesome," Julia said as she brought her chair as close to Kaiden's as she could manage.

"Did anyone let Mom know?" Kaiden asked just before Danny turned away.

"Yeah, Adam did. She's fully in the loop."

"What about Ben?"

"He and Silver were on a plane back to LA when it happened so I called Ben when he arrived. He's standing by to get Dad to an LA hospital if necessary."

"Good," Kaiden said as his brain finally decided to function more normally again. "Let's hope Adam gets back to us soon."

"Hey." Adam waved from the screen of Daisy's phone. He looked worn out and he wasn't wearing his cowboy hat, which made him look like a stranger. He appeared to be standing in a large parking lot, which Kaiden guessed belonged to the hospital.

Everyone waved back but kept the noise level to the minimum, not wanting to burst Adam's eardrums, or miss what he had to say.

"Dad had a minor heart attack. They did a whole load of tests and decided to do stent surgery to alleviate the blockages they found. He's got to stay here for twenty-four hours and then they will assess him again. If it's all looking good, he'll be discharged and he'll be able to come home."

Kaiden felt like a deflated balloon as his breath hissed out.

"So, he'll be okay?" Daisy got to ask the questions because it was her phone.

"Apparently so, although he'll need to take medication and change his diet and lifestyle." Adam managed a tired smile. "He was cursing up a storm when I stepped out to make this call, so I'd say he was on the mend. His color looked good too."

"Are you going to stay the night in his room?"

"You're kidding, right? I offered, and he told me he

wasn't five years old and to stop trying to mother him. He said he'd get enough of that when Mom turned up—which she is planning on doing, by the way."

Adam rubbed a weary hand over his unshaven jaw. "I'm going to get a hotel room and then I'll have to figure out how to get the two of us home if he's discharged tomorrow. I don't think the helicopter does return flights."

"I can bring your big truck and come get you," Kaiden offered.

"That's certainly an option. Can you hang tight on that until tomorrow, Kaiden?" Adam asked. "I'll get back to you as soon as I can."

"Sure." Kaiden nodded. "Just give Dad our love, okay?"

"Will do," Adam said. "I think I'll go back and check on him before I turn in. He won't appreciate it, but I sure will. I'll call if anything comes up overnight, but otherwise expect to hear from me in the morning."

"Okay." Daisy blew her big brother a kiss. "Thanks so much, Adam. We appreciate you."

Julia glanced over at Kaiden's uncharacteristically stern profile as he drove her home in his truck. She'd offered to drive herself back, but he'd seemed determined to take her, and she hadn't wanted to argue with him right now. His obvious shock at what had happened to his father still showed in his face, and she wished she could comfort him. So far he'd resisted all her helpful comments and attempts to get him to share his feelings. She relapsed into silence and instead watched the moonlight through the glass as it guided their way home.

He pulled up at the house and cut the engine before turning to her.

"Thanks for putting up with me this evening."

"As you said, we're friends and we support each other," Julia said. "Thanks so much for bringing me home. You don't need to get out. I'm sure you'd rather get back to your family."

She opened the door and stepped down onto the ground. There was a light on in her father's bedroom, but everything else was dark. Apparently, when Dr. Tio had arrived to pick up his grandmother, knowing what was going on at the Millers', he'd offered to help her father to bed.

Despite Julia's words, Kaiden was already out of the truck by the time she rounded the hood. He reached for her hand and she went still.

"Thank you." He reeled her expertly into his arms against the hard wall of his chest. "I really mean it. You kept me sane."

She couldn't resist cupping his chin and looking up into his eyes. "I'm glad I was there to help."

"Dammit," he muttered as his mouth crashed into hers and she kissed him back. "Julia . . ."

She pressed against him as he practically devoured her whole, his arm wrapped around her hips almost pulling her off her feet.

Words weren't working, so this was obviously the best way to comfort him, Julia thought dazedly. She couldn't say she minded his single-minded intensity one bit. She slid her hand into his hair, knocking his hat to the ground, and raked her nails over his scalp making him groan.

"Truck," he muttered, gathering her in his arms and flinging open the passenger door. "You and me, right now."

He somehow managed to get himself in the seat first

and then hauled her into his lap, which meant she ended up squashed against the hardness in his jeans. She slowly undulated in time with the thrust of her tongue in his mouth and his grip on her butt tightened.

"Let me touch you," he murmured between kisses. "I need to feel . . ."

She stripped off her jacket and placed one of his hands over her breast, gasping as he immediately thumbed her already tight nipple.

He expertly unbuttoned her shirt and slid his hand inside making her shiver with pleasure. He cupped her breast and pressed his mouth to the vee of uncovered skin at the base of her throat. She arched her back, offering him more as he kissed his way down to her now uncovered flesh and sucked her nipple into his mouth.

His other hand cupped her between the legs rubbing on the raised seam of her jeans. Even as she gasped his name, she was frantically unzipping her jeans. He took the offer and slid his fingers inside. Her panties were already damp, and he had no problem sliding his thumb over her already swollen bud.

She came so hard and so fast that it took her by surprise, and she bit his throat. Not that he seemed to care as he continued to play with her until she came again, now with his fingers thrusting inside her. She collapsed forward; her face cradled against his shoulder and she tried to gather her breath.

Kaiden didn't speak as he quickly set Julia to rights, buttoning her up, and smoothing down her hair until she eventually sat back and faced him. The sight of her reddened lips and the hint of sensual satisfaction in her eyes made his dick throb even more. He'd done that to her. He'd put that look on Julia Garcia's face, and for a moment he was the proudest man in the world.

She stroked his jaw. "Would you like me to . . . ?" She pointed down at his groin.

"No, I'm good."

If he let her touch him he'd start begging, and maybe say things that shouldn't be said, and then where would he be?

"Are you sure?"

She looked disappointed, which wasn't helping his resolve.

"I do need to get back," Kaiden reminded her, and her smile died.

"Oh! Of course." She attempted to climb off his lap. "I'm sorry."

"Nothing to be sorry about." Aware that he had erred in some way he opened the door and helped her out. "I'm the one who shouldn't have started anything while I'm in a state of shock."

She stilled. "It's okay. I know you didn't mean anything by it."

"Julia . . . that's not what I meant at all." God, he was too tired to deal with another complicated conversation with her. "If I offended you—"

"You didn't." She offered him a bright smile. "I'm the one who should be thanking you, right?" She stood on tiptoe and gave him a quick peck on the cheek. "Good night, Kaiden. If you have time tomorrow, can you let me know how things are with your dad?"

"Yeah, sure, I'll do that, but—"

She was already walking away like she didn't have a

care in the world and he—the man who was supposed to have all the answers—had no idea how to stop her.

He waited until she went through the door and then slowly climbed back into the truck, which smelled of her, and sex, and longing. God, she'd come for him . . . twice. He slowly thumped his head three times against the steering wheel and started the engine.

"You're an idiot, Kaiden Miller."

No one contradicted him, and he drove home with nothing but the silence of his own complicated thoughts to entertain him.

Chapter Ten

"So, he did okay," Miley said with great reluctance. "Not great, because when they asked him questions, he kind of didn't know the answers, but luckily the rest of us were able to cut in and answer most of the queries."

"That's great," Julia said.

She'd held off calling Miley to find out how the meeting had gone for as long as possible, but had eventually succumbed in the early afternoon. She'd had a restless night full of sexy dreams about a naked Kaiden, and horrifying images of hospitals and coffins. Not a good mix. She'd woken up early, done all the barn chores, taken her horse out for a ride, and it still wasn't lunchtime.

After an hour talking to her dad about the plans for the remodel, they'd settled on a design and a price point, and she'd promised to talk to Kaiden when the situation with Jeff had resolved. She'd had one text from Kaiden saying his father was doing well and was being flown back directly in a private plane to Morgan Ranch, courtesy of Silver and Ben.

She'd sent him her best wishes and left it at that. She

knew from when her own father had been diagnosed with MS and had medical issues that the last thing you needed was people bugging you for updates all the time. Back then, it had just been her dealing with everything because Miguel had been out of the country, whereas Kaiden had a big family willing to support each other.

When she was a kid, her parents had hosted regular family gatherings at the ranch after Sunday mass, where the women did the cooking, the men ate first, and the kids got to hang out with their cousins. When her grandparents hadn't wanted them to know what they were talking about, they'd switched to Spanish, which Julia's father hadn't taught her, although her mother had tried. After her parents split, her father hadn't continued the family Sundays, and Julia hadn't seen most of her cousins for years.

"I'm glad that Blaine didn't mess everything up for you," Julia said.

"He tried his best, but we were all on it," Miley said. "Is it true that he came out to your father's ranch?"

"Yes. He turned up yesterday."

"What an ass!" Miley shook her head. "That's why his presentation was so good. You wrote it for him, didn't you?"

"I did," Julia agreed. "He threatened to give me a crappy yearly review if I didn't."

Miley snorted. "I can just hear him saying that. I'm sorry he put you in that position."

"I'm sorry he's put us all in that position," Julia said, and then paused. "Now that the major crisis has passed, will you have time to look into something else for me?"

"Always, boss."

"I don't want you to make a big deal out of it, but I'm

looking to connect with a small boutique house builder that specializes in limited-sized sites, and is highly sensitive to the historical and environmental aspect of their work."

"In San Francisco?" Miley was writing notes in her book. "Like there is any space left to be sentimental."

"There must be some builders like that. Maybe out in Marin County, or the East Bay?"

"I'll definitely look into it for you. Anything in particular you want me to say, or don't want me to say?"

"I'm particularly interested in builders who have dealt with ranch owners. I'd rather you kept the name of our law firm out of it as much if possible, and focus on this being a personal inquiry rather than on behalf of a client."

"Got it. Unlike Blaine, I can do discreet." She hesitated. "By the way, I heard him mouthing off in the break room about you coming from a really 'poor and rural' environment."

Julia swallowed hard as she thought of the almost century of work her family had put into maintaining their land, and how much it meant to them.

"Hopefully, no one will listen to him," Julia said.

"If he says anything to my face, I'll be sure to set him straight. In fact, it would be my pleasure."

"Please don't worry about him. He's really not worth you losing your job over," Julia reminded her.

"Sometimes I doubt that because the satisfaction I'd get from dragging his ass would be such a high," Miley rallied. "Will we be seeing you back at the office any time soon?"

"In another week or so. The electrician and the plumber are coming today to discuss the remodel. If things go to plan my father will at least have a user-friendlier environment, and will be able to cope by himself. That's all he tells me he wants."

"He sounds like a tough old bird."

"He is." Julia smiled. "All ranchers are."

She ended the call and went back in to check on her father, who was happily finishing his lunch and watching TV.

"Mike Betts the plumber will be here in about ten minutes," Julia told him. "He just sent me a text."

"Good, you can deal with him, can't you, Julia? Or do I need to call Kaiden?" He rubbed his forehead. "I'm exhausted right now and my brain gets fuzzy. I definitely need all the help I can get."

Julia sat opposite him. It was so weird to hear her father admitting he needed help. "Kaiden's probably busy right now—what with his father coming back from the hospital sometime today."

"Well, we know what that's like." Her father sighed. "No fun at all. Have you heard from Miguel yet?"

"No." Julia picked up the various fishing magazines and tidied them into a neat stack.

"Did you tell him what's going on?"

"You know Miguel, Dad. If he doesn't want to be found, he'll just stay quiet until we stop bothering him."

"But this is different. I really need to talk to him about the ranch."

"I know." Julia patted his hand. Her dad's fixation on Miguel riding in to save the day was beginning to worry her. "I can't do anything unless he contacts me. I don't even know if he's in the US right now." She paused. "Have you ever considered that he doesn't want to come back and run the ranch?"

A familiar stubborn look passed over her father's face. "It is his duty to come home. He will be the fifth generation of Garcias to manage this land."

"If things go on the way they are, there won't be a working ranch for him to come back to, Dad." She gentled her voice. "Have you thought about what you want to do if Miguel doesn't come back? What you want to happen to the land?"

He went silent for so long that she was afraid he wasn't going to answer her. When he finally lifted his head, his mouth was set in a firm line that reminded her of herself.

"As long as I'm alive and functioning, the Garcia Ranch will be here. I'll continue to run it, and pray that Miguel will see sense and come home. After that?" He met her anxious gaze and winked. "I'll be dead and no longer have to worry about anything."

"You do have a will?"

"Goodness, you are full of doom and gloom today, Daughter. Yes, I do. It's lodged with Henry in town."

"That's good to know." She smiled at him. "I just don't want there to be any misunderstandings."

"Seeing as I'm not planning on dying right now, I think we'll have time to sort everything out. With you here helping, I can do so much more."

Julia met his gaze. "Dad, I've already told you. I can't stay here full-time, you know that."

"Why not?"

"Because I have a job in San Francisco."

He waved her livelihood away as if it was not important. "But family comes first, yes? When Miguel comes home, you can go back to doing whatever you want."

Julia slowly stood up. "It doesn't work like that, Dad.

And I can't wait until Miguel sees the light and comes home. It could be years."

He shook his head. "Maybe you are more like your mother than I realized, Julia. She, too, prioritized her career over her family."

"Dad . . ." Julia choked back all the things she'd like to have said before settling on "That's not fair."

He shrugged, averted his gaze to the TV, and turned up the volume.

She picked up his empty mug and walked out to the kitchen. After rinsing the cup, she stared out of the kitchen window, her gaze fixed on the mountain range where she could still see patches of snow. A familiar truck pulled into the parking spaces in front of the house, and she frowned.

After drying her hands and grabbing her fleece against the cold breeze, she walked outside to see Kaiden getting out of his truck. He had a thick sheepskin-lined jacket on, his usual black Stetson, jeans, and boots, but somehow the sight of him made her go still. He'd touched her intimately the night before and, even though she knew he'd been shaken, and off his game, she still wanted more.

He looked up as if suddenly aware of her presence and offered her a sunny smile.

"Afternoon, beautiful."

"What exactly are you doing here?" Julia asked.

His eyebrows flew up. "Are we back to that again? I thought we'd made some progress."

Her cheeks heated and she crossed her arms over her chest. "Your father is coming back today. I thought you'd be busy with him."

"He's not due home until five." He opened the tailgate and took out his toolbox. "I decided I'd rather get out and do something than sit around biting my nails and driving everyone else mad."

"Did Daisy make you leave?"

His natural grin flashed out and some of the tension left her body.

"Busted. She told the whole lot of us to find something to do, or she was going to kill us. I decided I'd come out here to meet with Mike and Bernie and talk through the plans."

He strolled over to her, his keen gaze roving her body. "Everything okay? You look a bit tense."

She debated what to tell him, worrying her lip until he reached out, and flicked her nose.

"Spit it out, honey. You know you want to."

She scowled at him. "Dad came right out and said I should stay here and look after him until Miguel comes back for good."

He raised an eyebrow. "That's a tall order seeing as you're paying for the remodel with your salary."

"Exactly. Except I couldn't bring myself to actually say that to him because I didn't want to hurt his feelings." She paused. "The thing is, he *does* need someone to help him keep the place clean and to cook his meals."

"Have you looked into finding someone around here who would be willing to do that?" Kaiden asked.

"Not yet. I can pay someone, but it would have to be the right person," Julia said cautiously.

"Does your Dad know Beth Baker?" Kaiden asked.

"Wes's mom?"

"Wes's stepmom, actually." He shrugged. "It's complicated. She's a really great person. She used to work as a physical therapist, so she'd be ideal to help your father. She probably knows him from church. Wes said she's looking for a job between school hours, so that might work out well for both of them."

Julia couldn't recall seeing Beth since she'd returned to Morgan Valley, but she would remedy that as soon as possible.

"Thank you." She smiled up at Kaiden. "I'll definitely contact her."

He angled his head lower. "Don't I get a kiss for being so helpful?"

"I thought we weren't doing that anymore," Julia said tartly.

"Whatever gave you that idea?" he murmured as he kissed his way up her throat.

"You did."

He grazed his teeth against her jaw, making her shiver. "I don't remember saying that."

Julia sighed, gave up the fight, and kissed him back. "You are so annoying."

"True." He carefully set her away from him. "Mike's just about to arrive, so unless you want to give him a show, let's save this for later, okay?"

"How do you know—?" She turned as a huge truck turned in through the gate. "Oh."

"I can't believe you didn't hear him coming," Kaiden said. "But, I guess you were so excited to be kissing me that everything else faded into the background."

She kicked him in the shin. He might be right, but she certainly wasn't going to admit it.

Mike was a big, redheaded guy with a long beard. He listened intently to all of them talking at once and some-how managed to understand everything they wanted in one go. Julia had no doubts he would be able to complete the job, and, as Juan knew his father, she was fairly certain he'd get it done as soon as possible.

While they were walking Mike through the house, Bernie, the electrician, arrived and joined the tour. He was also a good guy whom Kaiden said he'd worked with on several projects for the Morgantown Historical Society. When they reached the kitchen, Mike put his hand on one of the cabinets.

"I assume you're going to change these out too?"

"Yeah," Kaiden spoke up. "That part is on me."

Juan clapped his hands. "That's wonderful news. I can't wait to see what you do, Kaiden."

Julia met Kaiden's gaze over her father's head. "Are you sure you have time?"

He shrugged. "I'll make time. This project is important."

Thank you, she mouthed, and he winked at her.

Mike turned to Juan. "I can make a start this afternoon if you like, Mr. Garcia? You won't be able to use your bathroom tonight, but I promise I won't start on the other one until the master is fully functioning."

Kaiden was still smiling as he drove home. He'd stayed and had coffee with the Garcias, made sure Mike and Bernie were happy with the plans, and kissed Julia goodbye for at least five minutes before he'd finally let her go. While he'd talked to Bernie, he'd started thinking about how he wanted the kitchen to look, and what kind of wood he would use for the best finish.

It wasn't as huge a space as the kitchen at home, but he wanted to make it right for Julia and her dad. Hand building cabinets and countertops was his favorite part of the job, and what he'd trained for. The rest of the everyday stuff was useful and definitely paid the bills, but it wasn't the same.

He parked up near the barn because everyone was home, and there were trucks everywhere. He spotted a rental and guessed his mom had driven herself from the airport. Going in through the mudroom, he took off his boots, jacket, and hat, and put everything away before padding into the kitchen in his socks.

"Kaiden!"

He blinked as his auntie Rae and his mother zeroed in on him from either side of the room. They were both on the short side, but their coloring was different as were their personalities. Rae sparkled more whereas Leanne was a quiet presence. If he hadn't known them, Kaiden would never have guessed the lively Rae was actually Jeff's sister. They were as different as chalk and cheese.

"Wow!" He wrapped an arm around each of them and hugged them tight. "Double trouble. I didn't know you were coming as well, Rae."

"Leanne met me at the airport, and we drove over here together."

Kaiden was glad about that because his aunt's bad driving was notorious in Morgan Valley.

"Dad's going to hate this," Kaiden said in reverential tones.

"We know." Leanne and Rae fist-bumped each other. "But we figure that if we double-team him for a while he might finally get the message and do what Dr. Tio's been telling him for months."

"Good luck with that," Danny chimed in from where he was sitting at the table. "By the way. I just had a text from

Adam. They've landed at the Morgan Ranch airstrip so they should be with us in half an hour or so."

Kaiden went over to get himself some coffee while Rae and Leanne disappeared down the hallway toward his father's bedroom, arguing amicably about heated blankets and commodes.

"Did Ben and Silver come back too?" Kaiden asked Danny.

"They wanted to, but I guess Dad didn't want the fuss. Ben says they'll be back in a week and to keep him in the loop until then."

"Is Evan here?"

"Yeah, he's just taking a shower. He was out last night with a calving."

"Evan was?" Kaiden looked at Danny.

"Yeah, I know. He actually offered." Danny smiled. "For some reason he decided to stick to home and be helpful while Adam and Dad were away. To be honest, I've been glad of the help."

"I should be able to step up my game this week," Kaiden said. "Just let me know what you need doing, and I'll be there."

"It's okay, Bro. I'm more than happy to keep making Evan feel guilty enough to pull his weight for a change." Danny grinned at him. "It's kind of fun."

"Fun doing what?"

Evan spoke from the doorway. His spiky brown hair was still wet from the shower. He'd changed into PJ pants with a banana pattern and a bright yellow T-shirt, and his feet were bare.

"Nothing you need to know about." Kaiden winked at him. "How did the calving go?"

* * *

When Adam carried Jeff into the house, Kaiden stood back and let the women take over. The glimpse he got of Jeff's face wasn't reassuring. His father looked ghastly, and he was too tired to even shout at anyone, which was a first. Kaiden waited for a good hour before he ventured into his dad's bedroom. Only a lamp beside the bed shone light onto his father's gaunt features. Kaiden stayed by the door, one hand digging into the wooden frame like it was a lifeline.

"Well, don't just stand there gawping, Son. Either come in, or get out."

His father's voice was thin as a reed but somehow reassuring. Kaiden came in and sat on the chair beside the bed.

"I'm glad you're home, Dad."

"Me too, although I'm not sure what all the fuss was about."

Kaiden met his father's gray gaze, which was so like his own. "You damn well do know."

"Maybe I do." He sighed. "And even if I didn't, your mother and Rae will make sure I get it if I ever want them to leave."

Kaiden fought a smile. "You're lucky to have them, you know."

"Hmmph." His dad relapsed into silence.

"I just wanted to see how you were doing. I'd better go and let you sleep." Kaiden reluctantly rose to his feet.

"Good thinking. It's not as if I've been waiting for you to show up so I could do that very thing."

"Night, Dad." Kaiden bent to kiss his father's forehead.

"Now, don't be getting all sentimental around me,

Kaiden Miller. I'll have enough of that from the triple threat."

Kaiden paused at the door. "The triple threat?"

"Leanne, Rae, and Daisy."

Kaiden was still grinning when he went down the hallway and into the kitchen to catch up on all the news from Adam. His dad might look like a dog's dinner, but he certainly hadn't lost his crankiness. Kaiden wasn't the greatest believer in God, but he maintained a healthy respect for the Lord, and sent up a quick prayer of thanks to the heavens.

He suspected there was a long road of recovery ahead, which would not suit his dad's personality at all. From what Adam had already told them, he was going to have to change everything, and that was hard for anyone. After checking the kitchen, which was empty apart from two members of the triple threat who were deep in conversation, Kaiden decided he might as well turn in early. It had been an eventful day.

He sighed as he walked down the hallway to his bedroom and almost wished Ben was back home so they could talk it through. But Ben had Silver to talk to now, Adam had Lizzie, Daisy had Jackson, and Danny and Evan were as close as twins. Which left him—the wisecracking ass with no friends who wanted everyone to like him—all on his lonesome. Even as he considered starting his own pity party, his cell buzzed and he took it out of his pocket.

How did it go with your dad?

He sat down on the side of the bed and replied to Julia.

He's home. He looks exhausted, but he's cranky as ever.

He waited impatiently as the little bubbles danced and bounced in the corner of the screen.

That's good, right?

I suppose so.

Kaiden leaned back against the wall and made himself comfortable as he typed.

How did the work at the house go?

Lots of banging and mess, but Mike says it's all looking good so far ☺

Awesome.

Kaiden's thumbs paused over the keys. He wanted to tell her how the sight of his father's face had scared him; how he'd got the sense that nothing would ever be the same again. But he didn't have that right. She'd be expecting him to keep everything light.

I'll be over soon to measure up the kitchen.

Cool.

There was a longer pause. He'd almost given up hope she was still there when another text appeared.

Are you really ok? I know when my dad started to struggle with his MS it hit me hard. He was always the strong one, you know? Like my rock? And suddenly, there he was in a hospital bed looking at me to make decisions for him. I was terrified.

Kaiden stared at the screen until the words blurred as he tried to make sense of how they made him feel. He pictured his dad's face again and swallowed hard.

I wish I were with you right now, Kaiden.

For a moment, he thought he was hallucinating and that he'd typed the words on the screen rather than Julia.

Thanks

He winced at his own lameness. If he tried to explain how her words had hit him right in the feels, he would end up blubbering, and his dad would never allow that.

Kaiden, it's okay if you want to share stuff with me. I won't tell anyone, and I do totally get what you are going through.

He smiled at the screen. She got him, she really did, but that wasn't an excuse for him to give in and spoil her evening as well as his own.

I appreciate that. He paused and then carried on typing. **I really do.**

Coward.

He frowned at the single word.
Where the hell did that come from?!!
You know.
Maybe I'm just trying to keep things in perspective here.
Sure you are.

Kaiden typed furiously. **Maybe I'm better at explaining myself in person.**

Dude, you're worse in person. You just charm me and confuse me until I don't remember up from down, and then you avoid discussing anything painful.

He liked the first half of her response, but wasn't keen on the second. He reread the thread and considered what to say next. Part of him wanted to get in his truck, drive over there, and convince her of how wrong she was about everything. But, if she was right about his foot in the mouth syndrome, then he might just make things worse.

He let out a long, slow breath and replied.

Ok, you win. I suck. I'm going to bed now. Have a great night.

Will do.

He waited for a few seconds but she'd definitely signed off. From the shortness of her reply, he was pretty sure that she was as mad at him as he was with her, and hadn't bought his passive-aggressive attempt to apologize at all.

He got off the bed and went into the bathroom with the unsettling feeling that he'd missed an opportunity. What was even worse was that he knew Julia would make damn sure she didn't offer him the same chance again.

Chapter Eleven

Julia made quite certain that she was out when Kaiden texted her the next day to let her know he was coming up to the ranch. Her father was busy chatting to Mike and Bernie about the structure of the house and didn't need her help, and she had errands to run in town.

The whole conversation the night before had left her torn between annoyance that Kaiden was still putting up barriers, and an instinctive understanding that if he *had* succumbed and shared his feelings she would have to admit how much she'd come to care for him. And she didn't want to care. She was going back to San Francisco, and he would be staying in Morgan Valley, and that was the end of it regardless of how they might feel about each other.

She pulled into a diagonal parking spot in front of the post office and got out into the deceptively cool sunshine. It took a long time for Morgan Valley to emerge from the cold clasp of the winter months. Spring was short, and often rushed into summer far too quickly for Julia's liking. She'd never been a fan of the scorching hot days when the creek almost ran dry and finding water for a ranch full of cattle became all-consuming.

Not that they had many cows right now as her father had sold off most of his breeding stock two years ago and not brought in any youngsters. If Julia had her way, she'd ask Roy, the foreman at Morgan Ranch, to help her round up what remained and get rid of them so her father had more money in the bank. But she didn't have the authority to do that, and, if her father had his way, she never would.

Julia stomped up the wooden steps to the raised walkway and went into the post office to check the ranch mailbox. Most of the mail was feed catalogues and Western wear, but there was the occasional letter from a friend or her mother's family back in Guatemala that would cheer Juan up. She took the pile back to the truck without sorting it through and set it on the floor on the passenger side where she wouldn't forget it.

After checking out the various shops on the way, she went into Yvonne's and saw Nancy already sitting at a table waving at her.

"Hey!"

She walked over and took the seat opposite. "Hey, to you too. What's up?"

"Nothing much." Nancy indicated the third chair. "Beth's just gone into the bathroom. She'll be back in a sec."

"Cool."

Julia had decided to approach Beth Baker about looking after her dad. After consulting with Nancy, who knew everyone in town, she'd decided that a casual meet and greet with Nancy and Beth in Yvonne's was the best way to go. If she liked Beth, she could always approach her more formally.

Beth was tall like her brother Ted, who ran the local gas station, and had the same friendly smile and quiet way about her. Julia already knew, courtesy of Nancy, that Beth's recent past hadn't been great resulting in her leaving her abusive husband and coming back to Morgantown. She had a teenage son and also gave Wes, her stepson who worked with Kaiden, a home.

Beth smiled as she spotted Julia. "Hey! How are you?"

"I'm good," Julia replied. "I hope you don't mind me butting in like this."

"Not at all." Beth reclaimed her seat. "It's nice to see you again. Are you back for good, or are you just visiting?"

"I'm just here to help my dad with some family stuff and improvements to the ranch house for a couple of weeks."

"Mr. Garcia has MS, doesn't he?" Beth asked.

"Yes, and he's had a major flare-up resulting in him needing to use his wheelchair more so we need to adapt the house."

"At least it's all on one level." Beth nodded. "I hear you've got Kaiden Miller on it, so you're gold."

Julia might have snorted because both Nancy and Beth looked inquiringly at her.

"You're still pissed with him?" Nancy asked.

"He is a giant pain in the ass." Julia crossed her arms over her chest and dared either of the women to contradict her.

"I've always thought he was lovely," Beth said. "He's been so good with Wes. We were beginning to think he'd never settle into any kind of routine or work, but Kaiden has been helping with that."

"Wes was great when I met him," Julia said.

"Which wouldn't have been the case pre-Kaiden." Beth grinned. "Wes ran through three jobs before the carpentry apprenticeship opened up. Kaiden was the only guy left in the community college program who was even willing to give him a chance."

"That's really awesome," Julia agreed. "I can't say I've ever seen Kaiden Miller as a role model."

The other two laughed.

"Nope," Nancy said. "He was always the class clown, wasn't he? Maybe karma does exist."

Lizzie Taylor came over to the table, her tablet at the ready.

"Hey, guys, are you eating, or is it just a beverage kind of day?"

Julia's avid gaze slid to the array of pastries behind the glass counter. "I think I might just have room for something sweet. How about you two?"

She came away from the coffee shop full of delicious cake and fairly certain that if Beth was interested, and her dad okay about it, she had found the perfect person to help him. She'd heard nothing from work all day, which indicated that both Melanie and Blaine were happy with how things had gone. In fact, it had been fun talking to Nancy and Beth, who had no idea what her kind of lawyer actually did, or any interest in exploiting her contacts.

As the sun was still shining, she checked in with her dad to make sure either he or the guys didn't need anything, and then went in the general store with her list of groceries. Maureen, Nancy's mom, who ran the store, was sitting at the checkout playing some kind of game on her phone.

"Hi, Julia, how's your dad doing?"

"He's doing great, Maureen," Julia called out, as she

picked up a basket and headed into the store at some speed. If she stopped to chat on the way in as well as the way out she would be there all day.

She'd done the food shopping and had gone into the back where the Western wear and ranch supplies were located, when her cell buzzed. Thinking it might be her father remembering something he'd forgotten, she pulled it out.

"Hey, Sis."

She gripped the phone tightly. "Miguel?"

"Yeah, what's up?"

For a moment her brain filled with so many words that the idea of sorting them into coherent sentences seemed impossible. She already knew that if she started off by complaining about how hard he was to get hold of, he'd simply end the call. She settled on the most important thing.

"Dad's not been well."

"Yeah?"

His indifferent tone implied that was old news and nothing to do with him.

"His MS has gotten worse, and he's having to use his wheelchair to get around most of the time. He isn't able to get out on the ranch."

There was a long silence as Miguel obviously digested that.

"Are you with him?"

"Yes, I am at the moment. I'm sorting out the remodel of the house and trying to set up some everyday care for him."

"I don't have any more money to send him."

Julia suppressed a sigh. "I didn't ask you for any. I can handle the bill for the renovations."

She waited, but he made no effort to ask what else he

could do to help, leaving the burden of the conversation entirely on her. Not for the first time, Julia wondered what had happened to her brother to make him so uninterested in her and his family. He'd changed when their mother had left, and nothing had ever been the same since.

"Dad would really like to see you, Miguel."

The silence was so long this time that she thought he'd cut the connection so she talked into it.

"He's worried about the future of the ranch. You know he wants you to be the fifth generation of the family to run it."

"I can't come back."

Julia's patience grew ragged at the edges.

"Can't or won't, Miguel?"

"Does it matter?" He sighed. "Look, Julia, tell the old man that I don't want the place, okay?"

Even though there was no one in the store, Julia straightened her back. "No, you need to come back and tell him yourself."

"Why? What difference does it make?"

"Miguel, you owe him that at least. You know it will break his heart."

"I already told him years ago."

"And he didn't believe you."

"So, why would he believe me now? Better to leave it as it is and wait for the inevitable. Listen, Sis—"

"No, you listen to me." Julia struggled to contain the shake in her voice. "Are you saying you'd rather wait until he's dead, Miguel? That you'll only come back when he's gone, and you can take what's yours? If that's your plan, then you should know that there might not be anything worth having if you even bother to turn up for his funeral."

He abruptly terminated the connection leaving her

staring at the poster on the back wall of the shop of a grinning PBR world champion who looked about twelve years old. She shouldn't have lost her temper, but his callous disregard for their father had enraged her.

Yet again, Miguel expected her to pick up the pieces, to make everything right. For the first time in her life she wasn't sure if she was willing to do it. She knew he'd been through a lot—that his military career in covert ops had hardened him into an even tougher version of the boy who had left home. But hadn't it instilled a sense of responsibility in him too?

She put her phone away and walked over to the veritable wall of denim that covered the back wall of the shop. She'd buy herself and her dad some new jeans and shirts. Shopping always calmed her down. Working her way through the sizes would keep her occupied until she regained control of her emotions and could face Maureen, who was almost as good at ferreting out gossip as her daughter Nancy.

"That man." Rae stormed into the kitchen, her hands on her hips, and her cheeks flushed. "Is impossible."

Kaiden, who had been about to leave for the Garcia Ranch, looked inquiringly at her. "What did he do now?"

Twelve hours into his convalescence and Jeff had already set everyone's backs up. Daisy had almost been in tears before she'd gone to work, and even Leanne, who had a calm disposition like Danny's, had almost shouted at him.

"What's the current issue?" Kaiden asked.

"He threatened to throw the bowl of oatmeal at me,"

Rae said ominously. "And demanded eggs, bacon, and fried bread."

Kaiden frowned. "He doesn't even eat that stuff anymore."

"He *says* that if he's going to die from all the mollycoddling, he's going to go out on a high."

"Stay there." Kaiden set his toolbox on the countertop. "I'll be back in a minute."

He walked down the hallway to his dad's bedroom. The door was open. His father was sitting up in bed, his arms crossed over his chest, and his scowl prominent. Kaiden went in and shut the door.

"You are behaving like a giant ass." He pointed at his father. "Knock it off."

He braced himself for his father's fury, but Jeff looked away from him out the window and said nothing. After a stunned moment, Kaiden went and sat by the bed.

"What's going on, Dad?"

"This is the first day in fifty years that I've been stuck in bed and not out working the ranch."

"You just had surgery. You need a few days to get over it," Kaiden pointed out. "If you do what Dr. Tio says, and take your meds, you'll be back out there in no time."

Jeff slowly turned back to look at him. "Will I?"

"That's what the doctor said. Didn't you hear him this morning?" Kaiden searched his father's face. "And what does this have to do with you wanting to stuff your face with eggs and bacon rather than oatmeal, and being rude to Rae?"

"It's all part of the same thing, isn't it?" Jeff looked down at his work-scarred hands. "I've never been good with change."

"Can't disagree with you about that," Kaiden said. "But, this time I think you're going to have to do what you're told."

"I hate—"

"—doing what you're told," Kaiden finished the sentence with him. "Do you think you could give yourself a break for a few days? Just let us look after you for a change?"

"Nope." Jeff shook his head.

Kaiden fake sighed. "Then, we'll have to go with option two, tie you to the bed and stick all your food in a blender so you can suck it out of a straw."

Jeff's scowl returned. "You wouldn't dare."

Kaiden held his gaze. "I will if you continue to disrespect the people who love you and are just trying to do their best for you."

For the first time ever, Jeff blinked first. "All right. I'll apologize. I'll even eat the damned oatmeal."

Kaiden stood up. "Good." He half turned to the door. "We all know how hard this is for you, Dad. Give us a chance, okay?"

His father's brief nod was the best he was going to get, so he went back to the kitchen where his aunt and mother were comparing notes on Jeff's insufferable behavior. They both looked up when he entered.

"Did he get mad at you?" Rae asked.

"He tried, but I told him to stop disrespecting the people who were trying to help him."

"And how did that go?" Leanne pointed at his head. "I'm surprised you're not wearing the oatmeal."

"He said he'd apologize. Let me know if he doesn't." Kaiden picked up his toolbox and hesitated. "I think he's scared, and he doesn't know how to deal with it."

His mother nodded, her thoughtful gaze fixed on his

face. "You might be onto something. He's never reacted well to being challenged."

"That still isn't any excuse for being mean to everyone. I told him that as well. In fact, I threatened to tie him to the bed and feed him through a straw if he didn't get his act together."

His aunt and mother stared at him in silence for so long that he frowned.

"What?"

"You're a genius," Rae said in hushed tones. "There we are, all trying to be nice to him, and what does he respond to? Threats."

Kaiden held up his hand. "I wouldn't recommend you guys—"

Leanne and Rae exchanged a speaking glance.

"Oh, we won't be shouting at him, Kaiden, don't you worry about that." Rae winked at him. "We'll just tell him that if he won't behave we'll send you in to deal with him."

Kaiden was still thinking about his conversation with his dad when he left the Garcia Ranch. He'd checked in with Mike and Bernie, taken some more precise measurements for the kitchen cabinets, and pointedly not asked where Julia had gone. He shouldn't have sent her that text announcing he was coming over. He should've known she would do anything to avoid seeing him right now.

Satisfied that everything was going well, he continued down into town where he had a few things to pick up at the lumberyard and feed store before he returned to work on the old movie theater. He'd offered to stay home and help out, but Evan had decided to step up, and Danny and Adam said they could manage without him.

He parked in the lot beside the feed store and pictured his dad's face. Whatever Jeff was saying, he wasn't coping well with being stuck in bed. He never sat down and he was always working. Kaiden considered that relentless drive anew as he got out of the truck. Could his dad ease off? Was it even possible? But what was the alternative? He pushed himself too hard and had another more serious heart attack?

"Hey."

He spun around to see Julia standing behind him. She wore a baseball cap, her usual fleece, jeans, and boots and looked like she belonged in Morgantown. His gaze narrowed on her face.

"What's wrong?"

"Why would you think anything's wrong?"

"Because you look like you're about to burst into tears."

"How do you know?"

Mentally, Kaiden sighed. Lawyers sure loved asking questions. He pointed at her forehead. "Because when you're worried, you get this weird crinkle effect right over your nose."

Her fingers flew to her face and her eyes widened. "Do I?"

"It's a definite tell." He held up his hand. "If this is about what I said last night, I'll save you the trouble of getting your mad on and apologize without the snark, okay?"

"Last night?" She frowned. "Oh, I'd forgotten about that, thanks for reminding me." She considered him for a long moment. "How's your dad doing?"

He grimaced. "It's complicated."

"Tell me about it."

He forced a laugh. "I know."

"I meant *really* tell me."

It was his turn to stare. "I have to do some stuff first."

"Okay, then do you want to meet somewhere when you're done?" she asked. "Or, I could just follow you around, and keep you company?"

He gestured at the feed store like an idiot. "I'm going in there and then in the lumberyard."

"Sounds good to me. I've already done my shopping."

Kaiden began to feel that his day was just destined to be weird all around. His father hadn't shouted at him, Julia was seeking his company . . . maybe he should go to Maureen's and get a lottery ticket.

Chapter Twelve

Even as Julia followed Kaiden into the store, she kept surreptitiously pressing on the indentation above her nose. If she wasn't careful, she was going to have a permanent frown. She couldn't wait to get home and check it out in a mirror. It was also easier to fret over her frown lines than to wonder why seeing Kaiden standing there right when she needed him had been such a relief. Her conversation with Miguel had left her feeling so frustrated and angry.

By the time Kaiden finished with his purchases and she practiced keeping her face as line free as possible, she was definitely calmer. He turned to her as he finished loading the back of his truck.

"Do you want to come get coffee with me before I go to work at the theater?"

"I've already had coffee with Nancy and Beth, thanks, but if you want to get some I'll wait with you."

He angled his head to one side. "Why are you smiling like that?"

"I'm just keeping my face in a positive alignment."

"Jeez, it's just a little frown line." He flicked her nose. "Don't get all bent out of shape over it."

"I'm not. It's just that in my business any 'tell' is not helpful so I need to stop doing it."

"Okay." He started walking again. "I don't get it, but I'm not going to argue with you."

"That must be a first," Julia muttered.

He grinned as he opened the door into Yvonne's and stood back to let her go past him. "After you, honey."

She was already scowling before she remembered she wasn't doing that anymore. As he got his coffee, black with no fancy additions, he was ready to go in less than five minutes. They walked together along the boardwalk and then descended the steps to diagonally cross the corner to the old movie theater.

Julia waited as he unlocked the doors and made sure the space was safe enough for her to venture inside.

"Where's Wes?" she asked as she inhaled the smell of freshly shaved wood.

"It's one of his college days." Kaiden set his coffee down on his workbench. "He won't be in until tomorrow."

"So what's going on with your dad?" Julia asked, obviously surprising him. He'd probably expected her to tell him all her problems and forget about his.

"He hates being stuck in bed, he makes the worst invalid ever, and if someone doesn't murder him in the next few days, I'll be very surprised."

"So, pretty much as expected, right?"

"Yeah." He rubbed his hand over his jaw. "I had to have a few words with him this morning about his attitude."

"How did that go?"

He paused. "He didn't react as badly as I thought he

would. I think underneath all the bluster he's scared, and he doesn't want anyone to know it."

"My dad was the same." She nodded. "They just don't know how to stop working and take care of themselves."

"So what did you do to help him get out of that mind-set?" Kaiden asked. "I feel like I'm letting Dad down here."

"I just kept asking questions, I gave him space to talk, and I tried really hard not to jump in and tell him how he *should* be feeling." She shrugged. "It took quite a while to get him to admit that things would never be the same again, but eventually, he worked it out, and adapted. I'm sure your dad will do the same."

"Eventually." Kaiden grimaced. "It's hard seeing him like this."

"I know. Just remember how much harder it is for him right now."

He nodded. "Thanks, that was helpful." He took a tentative sip of his coffee. "So what put that frown on your face this morning?"

She leaned back against one of the sturdy supporting poles. "Miguel finally called me."

"And?"

One of the things she really liked about him was that he always gave her one hundred percent of his attention.

"He doesn't want to come back, he doesn't want the ranch, he doesn't care that Dad is ill, and he expects me to somehow convey all that to Dad without him having to lift a finger."

"That's totally unreasonable," Kaiden said. "I hope you told him so."

"I told him he was a coward, and that he needed to come back, face Dad, and tell him straight out."

"Knowing Miguel, I bet that didn't go down well. He

always had a problem facing up to the consequences of his actions."

Despite the fact that Kaiden was criticizing her brother, Julia didn't have the heart to contradict him. She'd spent years making excuses for Miguel's behavior and she wasn't prepared to do it any longer.

"It's not fair for my dad. He deserves better." Julia met Kaiden's concerned gaze, and she had to swallow hard. "Miguel suggested he'd wait until Dad was dead, and then he would turn up and sort it all out. I kind of lost my temper with him at that point, and he hung up on me."

"*Shit.*" Kaiden moved so fast that Julia was in his arms before she realized it. "It's a good job your stupid brother isn't around because if he was I'd be kicking his ass again."

"You kicked his ass?" Julia looked up at him. "From what I remember, you were the one on the bottom of that particular pile."

"I was just letting him wear himself out."

"Or praying my father and I would pull him off you," Julia said. "And, seeing as he's special ops now, he'd probably kill you. What was that last fight all about, anyway?"

His face hardened. "You'd have to ask Miguel."

"Why can't you tell me? It happened a long time ago."

With her faith in her brother so shaken, she was actually interested in hearing Kaiden's side of the story.

"Because it's not my tale to tell." He kissed her very deliberately on the forehead. "You're frowning again."

"I can't believe Miguel won't come back." Realizing she'd lost that particular battle and more than willing to get back on topic, Julia carried on speaking. "What am I supposed to say to Dad? He'll be heartbroken."

Kaiden hesitated. "Can I tell you what I really think, or will you get mad at me?"

"Go ahead." She sighed. "It doesn't matter if I do get mad at you anyway, it never seems to bother you."

"What I *think* you mean to say, Julia, is that you can't resist my charms, but you do you." He continued to hold her in his arms, his gray eyes now searching her face. "Number one, I don't think it's your job to be Miguel's messenger. Number two, why doesn't your dad see you as an alternate who would keep the place together?"

"He doesn't trust me." Unable to look at him, Julia stared at the open top button of his work shirt. "He thinks I'm like my mother, that I'll up and leave whenever I feel like it."

"That's . . ." Kaiden let out a breath. "Stupid."

"Not that my mother did that," Julia said fairly. "She tried everything to convince Dad to let her go back home to work at the clinic when the ranch wasn't busy, but he got really stubborn and tried to stop her going entirely."

Julia fidgeted with the collar of Kaiden's shirt. "She got so depressed, Miguel and I were really worried about her. The tighter my father tried to hold on to her, the worse he made things. As soon as Miguel and I were old enough to look after ourselves, she gave Dad an ultimatum. Let her go back to Guatemala during our vacation times to practice medicine at her clinic, or she would leave him. He didn't take her seriously until she refused to come back at the end of the summer."

"But, what's that got to do with you?" Kaiden asked. "You're not her, and from what I've seen you've basically been holding that ranch together financially for the last few years."

"Tell that to my dad." She smoothed a hand over his chest. "He loves me dearly, but he can't get over his fears, just like he couldn't with my mother. He's probably going to leave the ranch entirely to Miguel. He doesn't think a woman can run it."

"You could manage that place with one hand tied behind your back," Kaiden scoffed.

She raised her eyes to his face. "But, I don't want to run it, Kaiden. I don't ever see myself being a full-time ranch manager."

He went still. "Which is your nice way of reminding me that you're never coming back home, and there's no chance of us ever having a relationship, right?"

"It wasn't, but let's be honest, maybe it needed to be said." She cupped the hard line of his jaw. "I'm obviously attracted to you, but I can't offer you anything right now."

Kaiden raised an eyebrow. "Have I asked you for anything?"

"No, but—"

"You just assumed I would." Any spark of humor evident in his eyes vanished. "I'm not stupid, Julia."

"I never said you were."

She had a horrible sense of the conversation slipping away from her.

"But, here you are, graciously telling me that although you might have the hots for me I shouldn't get my hopes up because I don't stand a chance? Like I didn't *know* that?" He stepped back with a fake smile on his face. "You set the limits here, okay? Tell me what you want from me, and I promise to abide by your rules. No strings attached."

"I don't *have* any rules," Julia objected. "I was just trying to be honest with you."

He retreated behind his workbench, picked up his coffee, and took a sip before looking at her again, but he didn't speak.

"I'm the one who is confused here, Kaiden," she said

unsteadily. "Not you. I don't do this kind of thing. I don't know how to deal with these feelings I have for you. I'm scared that you'll get the wrong idea, and I don't want to hurt you."

"The wrong idea." He half smiled. "What's that? Like you'll settle down here, have half a dozen little Millers while we run the ranch together until Miguel turns up and kicks us out?"

There was a long silence while they measured each other.

"Are you trying to make me smile?" Julia asked incredulously. "After everything we just said to each other?"

He shrugged. "Right now, I think you just need a friend, okay? So why don't we just stick to that?"

Long after Julia had gone, Kaiden was still running through their last conversation and rethinking every single one of his answers. He'd allowed her to get him riled up again, but this time he'd just about managed to downplay the effect her words had on him. And, she was right. There was no future for them. But she'd admitted to having feelings for him, and that made him want to cheer. The trouble was—he had feelings for her, too.

"Pathetic," Kaiden muttered to himself as he tightened up the last bolt in the beam. "She was just trying to be honest with you, as a friend would."

He needed to keep his hands to himself and try not to remember how she'd felt when he'd had his fingers inside her, his mouth on her skin . . .

"Keep it down." Kaiden glared at his groin. "We're at work."

"Talking to yourself again, Bro? Maybe you miss me more than you realize."

He looked up to see his brother Ben grinning at him from the doorway.

"I miss you like a fly swarm." Kaiden came around the bench to give his brother a bear hug and an attempt at a noogie, which was difficult when Ben was built like a linebacker. "Where's your better half?"

"She's at the store getting some supplies."

"And you're not helping her?"

"I wanted to see how you were." Ben looked down at his scuffed boots. He wasn't much better at communicating than Adam. "Like, check in with you, and stuff."

Kaiden sighed. "You've been in LA too long, buddy. All this checking in with my feelings crap has got to stop."

Ben gave him the finger, which somehow made Kaiden feel so much better.

"Did you come back to see Dad?" Kaiden asked.

"Yeah, and we've got some scheduled vaccinations to do at the ranch, which would be too much for Mr. Gomez to handle alone."

"I can lend you a hand if you need me." Kaiden looked up at the repaired ceiling. "I'm just about done on stage one of this place. Gotta let the architect back in to decide on the new wiring, floor plans and partitions."

"It's going to look great," Ben said. "And, sure, any help is welcome at the ranch." He paused. "How are things going with Dad?"

"About as well as you might expect. I had to read him the riot act this morning about disrespecting everyone."

Ben winced. "How did he take that?"

"He didn't like being told, but he was surprisingly subdued." Kaiden hesitated. "I think this is hitting him harder than he expected. He just doesn't know how to react, or how to deal with it."

"At least he listens to you."

"Sometimes." Kaiden shrugged. "I'm just more direct than the rest of you are."

Ben nodded. "Because you're the most like him."

"I'm nothing like him," Kaiden protested. "I'm the charming one, remember?"

"Okay, maybe I phrased that wrong," Ben said. "You're as straightforward as him, but you don't choose to express yourself in anger, but use humor to get your point across."

"Too long in LA, Bro. You've finally lost it." Kaiden sighed even as he noted that Julia and Ben were basically singing the same song. "You should go back and live there permanently."

"Not happening." Ben hesitated. "If you think Dad needs to talk to anyone, let me know, will you? I'll see if we can find him a therapist. He might appreciate the opportunity to share his concerns with a professional." Ben frowned as Kaiden started laughing. "What did I say?"

When Kaiden finally got ahold of himself again at the thought of his dad meeting a therapist, Ben was still talking.

"Silver was thinking of having a few friends around for dinner tomorrow night. We wondered if you'd like to come, and bring Julia with you."

"Julia who?"

"Don't be cute. You know who I'm talking about." Ben met Kaiden's gaze head-on. "You've always had a thing for her, and Silver thinks she likes you."

"Does she now?" Kaiden smiled. "Well, maybe you could tell Silver that while Julia might 'like' me she has no intention of sticking around in Morgantown for the duration."

To his annoyance, Ben just smiled.

"What?"

"You're just pissed because she's the first woman in a long time who hasn't immediately fallen into line and worshipped you."

"As I said, it really doesn't matter whether I like her or not." Kaiden was sick of playing games. "She's not hanging around for the likes of me, and why should she?"

"That's what I said about Silver." Ben was positively smirking now.

"So what?"

"And we made it work."

"Look, I love you, Ben, but you made it work because Silver has the kind of career and money that can transcend normal problems," Kaiden said.

"Nah."

Kaiden resisted the urge to punch his smug big brother. "Wow, that's profound. What am I supposed to learn from that?"

"We made it work because we learned to trust each other, and our love was strong enough to deal with whatever happened."

"Man." Kaiden stared at his brother. "You sound like a cheesy greeting card. If that's what love does to you, I want nothing to do with it."

Ben chuckled. "Look, what I'm trying to say is that Silver and I made a pact that we would try our best to make our relationship work however awkward it felt. And, that if we were truly meant to be together, love would find a way."

Kaiden pretended to gag until Ben thumped him hard on the back.

"It worked, Bro. Look at how happy we are."

"So you think I should just waltz up to Julia Garcia, look worshipfully into her eyes, and suggest we give our love a chance to 'find a way'?" Kaiden asked, sarcasm dripping off every word. "Not that we even love each other or anything."

"Yeah. Why not? What do you have to lose?" Ben who was oblivious to sarcasm at the best of times thumped him again. "Look, I've got to go and find Silver and help with the shopping bags. We'll see you tomorrow at six at our place, if not before at Dad's."

Chapter Thirteen

"Yes, I'm still planning on coming back next week, Melanie," Julia said as she opened her closet and considered what on earth she should wear to have dinner at a famous movie star's house.

"That's good because Blaine got the impression that you were settled back home with some kind of hick cowboy boyfriend." Melanie laughed.

"Did he now?" Julia set her jaw. "Mind you, as Blaine is doing so well, maybe he doesn't need me back at all, and I'd just be in the way. Is it time for me to ask for a transfer into a new team for a fresh start?"

Leaving the team she'd created to Blaine would kill her but she wasn't prepared to go down without a fight.

"I still think he needs you there as a stabilizing presence for a while yet, Julia. I know he did a great job at the last presentation but he's still relatively new." Melanie rushed to get the words out. "I certainly wouldn't be comfortable moving you *just* yet."

Surprise, surprise, Julia thought. "Is there anything you'd like me to be working on while I'm here?"

"Well, there is a land negotiation we're keeping an eye on in Bridgeport, which is quite near you, right?"

"Yes, it is. What do I need to know?"

"Our client is considering acquiring some land adjacent to the existing town. I gather the land runs alongside a great fishing river."

"I can definitely help with that," Julia said. "Do you want me to go out there and take a look?"

"That would be great. You're really good at assessing the potential of land acquisitions. I'll send over the details as soon as I get off the phone." Melanie paused. "I am looking forward to seeing you back at work, Julia. I do hope such . . . interruptions won't become a feature of your continued employment at MZB."

"I'll see you next week, Melanie," Julia said evenly. "Have a great day."

She ended the call and stared into her open closet. Did Melanie really believe that caring for one's family was an interruption? What was she supposed to have done? Ignored her father like Miguel did? The only reason her brother could get away with behaving like that was because he knew she would step up. After her mother had failed to return home, Julia had felt like it was up to her to take on everything so that her father and brother wouldn't notice the loss.

She shook off the call and grabbed the flowered shirt she'd bought at Maureen's, paired it with her new tapered jeans and her favorite fleece, and called it a win. There was no way she could compete with Silver Meadows, and she wasn't even going to try. Not that Silver would turn up in a custom designer gown or anything, she wasn't like that, but she just had that glowing star thing going for her.

Mike's Dad, Brian, was coming to spend the evening with her father, so she knew he would be fine. Kaiden had offered to pick her up on his way back from town, but she'd declined. Getting into his truck seemed to banish her inhibitions, and she couldn't go down that path again.

She held the shirt up against her and looked in the mirror. But she wanted to touch him very badly. It didn't seem to matter that her logical brain was telling her it was a bad idea, her hormones were screaming at her to jump his bones and get real close while the opportunity presented itself. He was just so . . . in tune with her sometimes it scared her.

She grabbed her clothes and went into the Jack and Jill bathroom between what had been her and Miguel's bedrooms. Her hormones needed to take a back seat and let her leave Morgantown without ruining Kaiden Miller's life as well as her own. She snorted. Like she'd ruin his life. He'd be onto the next woman the second she left.

She paused in the doorway. But Kaiden had told her he'd play by her rules. So did that give her more opportunities than she thought? Her hormones perked up. Sometimes, her refusal to give up on finding a solution to every problem was a curse. Julia gave herself a firm stare in the mirror.

"Stop it, ladies, or I'll have the coldest shower possible."

By the time Kaiden pulled his truck up outside the fancy house his brother and sister-in-law had built on the Gomez Ranch everyone else had already arrived. He'd stayed late talking to May, the architect working with the Morgantown Historical Society on the movie theater.

She'd shared her new plans for the space and he'd been so intrigued that time had escaped him. When he'd gotten back home, he'd popped in to see his dad, spoken to his mom and aunt, and taken a much-needed shower before he could get back out the door. Adam, who had also been invited, had gone into town to pick up Lizzie earlier bringing Roman back to stay with the Millers for the evening.

Ben's house was all lit up, probably because he and Silver never had to worry about how to pay the electricity bill. Kaiden grinned as he climbed the steps up to the covered porch. Even though he knew Silver had insisted on every energy saving available in the construction, he still liked to tease her. The house suited the land it occupied, blending seamlessly in with the lush pastureland surrounding it.

He knocked on the door, which had a huge floral wreath Daisy had made on it. If he ever built himself a house, he'd probably go with something similar. Not that he'd ever actually do that. He was probably destined to live at home for the rest of his life.

"Hey!"

He composed his features into a smile as his hostess opened the door, and he offered her a large wrapped box.

"Hey! Happy late wedding day present."

Silver eyed the box and held up her hands. "I'll let you carry that in. I'd hate to drop whatever it is."

"Yeah, you wouldn't want to drop a little baby puppy, would you?"

She rolled her eyes as she set off back toward the kitchen. She wore leggings, a really long knitted sweater that reached her knees and looked suspiciously like one of Ben's, and yet she still managed to look striking.

"Like you think I'd mind that? Ben's dogs are working dogs so I'd quite like my own."

"Then you'd better make sure I don't drop this box."

He paused on the threshold of the family room to check out who was there, his gaze immediately sticking on Julia, who was sitting on the couch with Lizzie and Adam.

"Hey." Ben came over and punched him gently on the shoulder. "What's up?"

"Ouch." Kaiden set the box on the large pine kitchen table he'd made for the kitchen and pretended to rub his arm as Silver rushed to get a pair of scissors to cut the twine. The main kitchen cabinets were stained pine so he'd constructed the table to match.

"It's your wedding present," Kaiden said. "If I'd known you were eloping I would've had it ready sooner."

Ben grimaced. "Don't you start. I'm still getting heat from Mom and Dad about that."

"Mom, too?" Kaiden watched as Silver peeled off the brown paper. "I thought her favorite son could do no wrong?"

"Obviously not." Ben leaned in as Silver removed the last piece of paper and gasped. "Wow, that's so cool!"

Aware that everyone had gotten up to take a look, Kaiden shrugged. "It's just something I knocked together to keep your stuff in, okay? Nothing fancy."

"It's beautiful," Silver whispered as she used the small key to open up the marquetry doors he'd labored over to reveal interior drawers of various sizes. "It must have taken you ages."

She turned to Ben. "Look, he's even carved our initials into this heart at the top."

Ben nodded as he reached out to run his finger over the

tiny turned wooden knobs on the drawers. He pulled one drawer out and examined the corner joints. "It's absolutely beautiful, Bro."

"Thanks." Despite his father's "nothing is ever good enough to praise" ethic, Kaiden had taught himself to accept compliments on his carpentry work without any qualifiers. "I really enjoyed making it."

In fact, he loved making things for people he knew and always tried to put some of their personality into the work. Carved into the sides of the chest were intertwined images from both Ben's and Silver's lives that he hoped they'd eventually notice.

"It's beautiful, Kaiden."

Julia spoke in his ear making him jump. She was so close that he could smell her perfume and feel the press of her body against his side.

"It came out good." He took a step back so that he could see her properly, leaving everyone else still crowded around the table. "I'm just glad they seem to like it."

"How couldn't they like it? It's so personal, and unique, and . . ." She waved her hands in the air. "I'm running out of words here."

"That's not very lawyerly of you," Kaiden said. "By the way, you look beautiful tonight."

She blushed and looked right into his eyes. "Thanks."

"Not going to tell me to knock it off, or anything?"

"No." She smiled. "It's a long time since anyone has said anything so nice to me so I'm taking it."

"What? Are they all blind in San Francisco?" Kaiden asked. "You have always been the most beautiful woman I have ever known."

She pointed over her shoulder at Silver, who was still examining the cabinet. "Yeah, right."

"Are you suggesting I covet my brother's wife?"

"You know what I mean. How can any mortal woman compete with that? And she's so nice as well."

"She is, but I'd still much rather look at you," Kaiden said.

Her gaze softened, and she just stared back at him. "Kaiden . . ."

He couldn't do it. Despite what Ben said, he couldn't ask her whether she'd try and have a relationship with him anyway, because with her logical lawyer's brain she'd pick apart any proposal he made and leave him for dead on the ground.

He turned back to the table. "Any chance I could get a drink around here?"

Julia could put her finger on the exact moment Kaiden Miller had shut her out, but she still wasn't sure why. He was a great dinner companion, considerate of her needs, and willingly listened to her going on about the current state of the bathroom remodel, but something had changed. He even rested his hand along the back of the couch as they sat together after dinner, but he didn't actually touch her.

She reminded herself that he was doing what she'd asked—keeping his distance, allowing her the space to just be his friend. But she didn't like it at all. Which just showed what a selfish, inconsiderate person she really was.

At some point, Kaiden went off with Ben and Adam to look at a horse in the barn at the back of the house leaving Silver to entertain Julia and Lizzie. The three of them curled up together on the couches in the family room drinking hot chocolate and eating brownies.

"Is everything okay, Lizzie?' Silver set her mug down on the coffee table. "You looked a bit tense when you came in."

"Adam and I had another argument in the truck on the way here." Lizzie sighed. "Well, not exactly an 'argument' because arguing with Adam is about as productive as getting annoyed with a rock, but we definitely had a disagreement. He just keeps on making these not-so-subtle comments about how if I lived up at the ranch he wouldn't have to keep coming and fetching me."

"Did you tell him you were quite capable of driving yourself wherever you want to go?" Silver asked.

"I did mention that, and then he started worrying about the state of my car, and how long it would last doing all these journeys, and what would happen if me and Roman got stuck." Lizzie rolled her eyes. "I know he's doing it out of love, but he just won't stop."

Julia sat forward. "I hope this doesn't sound rude, and obviously I don't know the full story. But is there a reason why you are reluctant to move up to the ranch?"

Lizzie smiled. "I don't mind you asking at all. Sometimes, it's good to get a fresh opinion on something you've been going round and round on for ages." She paused as if to gather her words. "I guess it's because I'm afraid that once I give up all those things I fought so hard to get, like my apartment, and my job, that I'll be powerless again."

"Does Adam really expect you to give up your job?" Silver asked.

"No, of course not, but I guess if I moved up to the ranch there would be plenty for me to do there." Lizzie smiled. "I'd probably want to go all in and help him and then what happens to my job at the café? What about all the commuting to work and to take Roman to school?" She hesitated, and then blurted out, "And what happens if Adam and I break up, and I've got nothing to go back to?"

"I can't see you and Adam breaking up," Silver said thoughtfully. "He absolutely adores you."

Julia nodded in agreement even as her mind played out various scenarios. "Have you thought about a trial period with strict conditions about what both your roles are?"

"Like a contract?" Lizzie looked interested.

"Exactly. For example, even if you move up here you agree to keep the lease on your apartment for six months. You keep your work hours exactly the same at Yvonne's, and just see how it goes."

"But what about Roman?" Lizzie asked. "If things don't work out, I'll have moved him up here, made him think he's got a family, and then ruined it for him."

Silver glanced at Julia before she replied. "I understand why you're being so careful, Lizzie, but if you do as Julia suggests and work out an agreement with Adam and things don't work out then you'll have a backup plan and a life to return to. You can explain it to Roman like that too. He's a smart boy. He'll get it, but I really don't think it will come to that." She sat forward, her arms clasped around her knees. "Sometimes, when you love someone, you've got to take that leap of faith, you know?"

"Like you did with Ben?" Lizzie asked.

"Exactly." Silver laughed. "Although, man, did he make it hard because he worried so much about *everything*."

"He sounds like me." Julia didn't mean to speak, but the words just fell out of her mouth. "I have a lawyer's brain. I always think of at least two thousand possible things that can go wrong before I commit to anything."

"Does Kaiden know that?" Silver grinned.

Julia sat up straight. "I wasn't actually talking about my personal life."

"Oh God, I'm so sorry!" Silver held up her hands. "That was really rude and intrusive of me. Please forget I opened my mouth." She turned back to Lizzie. "I *meant* to say that I think Julia's idea is a really good one. Why don't you write some thoughts out when you get home, and take it from there?"

After the brothers returned, Adam and Lizzie went almost immediately because they wanted to get back to Roman. Before they left, Lizzie took a quiet moment to thank Julia for her idea and to ask if she could get back to her if she managed to get something concrete down on paper. Julia was quick to agree, and glad that Lizzie at least was still okay with her.

She had a sense she'd hurt Silver's feelings by clamming up on her when things had gotten too personal, and she didn't know quite how to fix it. When her hostess suggested she come with her to check out her new Korean skin care routine, Julia jumped at the chance. As soon as the door closed behind them she turned to Silver.

"I'm sorry if I came across as rude earlier."

Silver shrugged. "The only person who was rude was me. Sometimes I forget that I haven't lived here very long, and that I should keep my nose out of other people's business. I come from a very involved family where everyone is in each other's faces, sometimes way too much, so I should've known better."

"I'm . . . just not used to having the kind of friends I can confide personal stuff to," Julia said awkwardly. "Most of the women I know in San Francisco are either my competitors who I would never share a weakness with, or they simply don't have time to listen because their lives are already crammed full with stuff."

"I know the feeling," Silver said wryly. "The only people I trust are my immediate family. I guess that seeing as Ben's been keeping me up-to-date about how he thinks Kaiden feels about you, I got a bit ahead of myself. It really is none of my business, and I'm sorry I said anything."

"Kaiden knows I'm going back to San Francisco," Julia said. "He agrees that we should just stay friends."

"Then that's great." Silver nodded. "As long as you are both on the same page, then you have nothing to worry about. I'll tell Ben he's totally on the wrong track about everything." She switched on the lights of the huge en suite bathroom. "Now, come and take a look at this skin care stuff. It's absolutely amazing."

She went to move past and Julia reached out her hand. "I really do appreciate you treating me like family. Even if I don't deserve it."

"Everyone deserves a family," Silver said warmly. "And, whether you like it or not, I already consider you part of mine. Now, before I forget and we get stuck into skin care, what were you saying earlier about a grant from the Morgan Valley Heritage Foundation?"

Kaiden followed Julia out the front door of Ben and Silver's house and immediately did up his jacket. There was a cold wind blowing off the top of the snow-covered Sierra Nevadas that chilled his bones. Julia had her head down as she approached her dad's truck. He wasn't sure if it was because of the cold, or because she hadn't enjoyed her evening.

Despite trying to keep his distance and keep things light, he hadn't quite succeeded in not checking up on her every thirty seconds. When he'd come back from the barn with his brothers she'd been tense, which made him wonder what Silver had been saying to her. It wasn't like his brother's sunny-natured wife to upset anyone, so he had no idea what had happened, or even how to ask.

He called out to Julia as he approached the truck.

"Do you remember the way home?"

She fished out her keys to open the door, but didn't turn around. "I'm good, thanks."

"Hey." He reached her side and put a tentative hand on her shoulder. "Are you okay?"

"I'm fine." She offered him a brief, dismissive smile. "Silver's really nice, and their home is lovely."

"I like it a lot myself." He hesitated, aware of the tension in her frame. "Are you sure that everything's okay?"

"Why wouldn't it be?" She opened the door, which meant he had to step aside, as she got into the truck. "Thanks for asking me for dinner."

"I didn't." Kaiden gave her the truth before he thought it through. "Ben just told me he'd invited you on my behalf. Is that why you're mad? Did Ben or Silver say anything about me?"

She wouldn't meet his eyes, and he slowly exhaled.

"They stuck their big noses in, didn't they?" He briefly tilted his head back and looked up at the heavens. "I didn't ask them to do that, I swear. I'll go right back in there and maybe kick some famous movie star ass if they upset you."

"Please don't do that," Julia finally spoke. "It was nothing, really, and definitely not what you think. Silver was just trying to be nice, and I . . . well, I wasn't ready to confide in her, that's all."

"Confide what?" Kaiden asked cautiously.

"Nothing—that's the point."

Kaiden was fairly certain he was being deliberately led away from the point. "What did she say?"

"*Nothing.*" She finally turned to look at him. "I told her we were on the same page, and that was that."

"On the same page about what?"

She fussed around with the keys. "Just being friends."

Even as he instinctively wanted to protest that point, he still managed to nod and take the necessary step back.

"Cool, then I'll wish you good night."

"Okay. Good night, Kaiden."

He waited until she'd pulled away in the truck, the red lights flaring in the darkness before he turned to face the house again. Should he go back and ask what the hell had happened? Would it do him any good? Knowing his just married and horny brother, he might get an eyeful if he walked back in there, and, in his present celibate state, he really didn't need to be any more jealous of his brother.

He got into his truck and drove home in the darkness almost by instinct. He parked and went in through the mudroom where he took off his boots and coat. There was a light on in the kitchen but most of the house was dark. He contemplated making some coffee, but he was already too hyped up to sleep. As he walked down the hallway, he sighed. The thing between him and Julia couldn't go on like this so he knew he was doing the right thing, but man it was hard. . . .

"That you, Kaiden?"

He looked up and saw his dad's door was ajar and went toward the light.

"You still up?" he asked as he entered the dimly lit bedroom.

"No, I'm talking to you in my sleep." His dad frowned at him. "How am I supposed to sleep when I've done nothing but sit around all day?"

"You're allowed to walk around the house, now, and annoy everyone," Kaiden pointed out. "You seem to enjoy that."

"It's not enough and you know it." Jeff huffed. "I hate being cooped up."

"I get it." Kaiden tried to remember the advice Julia had given him. "It must be difficult for you when you're used to being so active."

"Got it in one." Jeff sniffed. "Dr. Tio says I can walk outside tomorrow as long as someone comes with me— like I'm a child."

"I'll walk with you. That new foal looks like it'll be coming early."

"That fool of a doctor won't let me help with the birth. I can tell you that now."

"Dr. Tio is not a fool, Dad. I'm sure you can still be there, and tell us we're doing it wrong, and how to fix it. You'll like that."

"Maybe." Jeff took something off his nightstand and handed it to Kaiden. "Leanne gave me this. She said I can watch movies, read books, and e-mail people on it."

Kaiden opened the tablet. "Yeah, they are great devices. Did she set it up for you?" He flicked through the settings and icons on the screens.

"Apparently."

"Did she give you any headphones?"

"Yes, you know your mother. She's always prepared." Jeff hesitated. "Which is why I don't want to ask her how to make all this stuff work."

Kaiden fought a smile. "I can do that. Here, take a look, it's really easy."

Fifteen minutes later, his dad was compiling a wish list of movies and had worked out how to plug in his headphones, which gave Kaiden a weird sense of pride.

"Should I do that twittering thing?" Jeff asked.

"God, no. You'd be banned in a heartbeat," Kaiden said. "You might want to avoid Facebook for a while, too."

"Okay." Jeff looked up from the tablet. "What's going on with you, then?"

Startled by this unexpected parental interest, Kaiden blinked.

"Nothing much. Ben and Silver liked the memory cabinet I made them."

"Good. How are things with Julia Garcia?"

Kaiden's smile died. "Nothing is going on with Julia. Why would you think otherwise?"

"Because I lie here all day with the door open, and listen to everyone gossiping, and your name comes up a lot." Jeff set his tablet aside. "Do you still like her?"

"Do we have to do this now?" Kaiden complained. "I'm not a kid, Dad."

"Then don't take that whiny tone with me."

"Julia is an amazing woman who is going back to San Francisco next week," Kaiden said evenly. "That's all you need to know."

"So, she's not interested in you." Jeff nodded. "That's what I told your mother."

"You've been gossiping about me? Really, Dad?" Kaiden let out a breath. "For the record, she likes me a lot, but we're both being responsible adults who understand that sometimes things just aren't meant to be."

His father snorted. "You sound like Ben when he messed everything up with Silver. I thought I'd taught you all to fight for what you wanted."

"You can't force someone to love you, Dad."

"You're telling me that? Look what a mess I made of things with your mother." Jeff pointed at his chest. "I let my anger and stubbornness take over, and lost the best thing I ever had."

"But both you and Ben eventually worked things out, didn't you?" Kaiden reminded him, aware that his father didn't need to get too excited about anything right now, and it was usually his job to be the peacemaker. It was probably way past time for him to leave.

"So why can't you?" Jeff asked. "Do you think you're too special to even make the effort?"

Kaiden stood and looked down at his father. "I don't think that at all. I'm not even sure how I feel about Julia, so maybe I shouldn't jump in and make things worse?"

"Is that how it's always going to be with you then, Son?" His father looked him square in the eye. "Losing someone you might come to love because you're too damned scared to reach out to them?"

"After what you did to this family, you are the last person in the world to give me advice on my love life, Dad." Kaiden just managed to keep his voice even as he walked toward the door. "How about you just stop talking crap and go to sleep?"

"But I worked it out! I learned from my mistakes! I'm the perfect person to give you advice."

"Bullshit." Kaiden swung around. "Mom came to find

you. You did nothing but keep her away from us and blame her for it." Kaiden knew at some level that he was the one who should be shutting up, but somehow his mouth just kept moving. "If she hadn't contacted Rae you'd still be sitting here making everyone's lives as miserable as your own!"

"Kaiden."

He started when his mother spoke from behind him and touched his shoulder.

"Honey, this isn't helpful, okay?" She ran her fingers down his arm and gripped his elbow hard. "How about you come into the kitchen, and I'll make you some hot chocolate?"

"Sure." Kaiden cast one last look at his father's furious face. He couldn't find it in himself to apologize so he said nothing and walked away.

By the time his mom came into the kitchen, he'd taken a seat at the table and had his head in his hands. She set a pan of milk to boil on the range and walked over to sit opposite him.

"I'm sorry." Kaiden stared down at the table. "I don't know what came over me."

"It's okay, Kaiden." She patted the top of his head like he was five again. "You had cause."

"But I'm not *like* that. I don't get mad, I—"

"Then maybe you should."

He finally looked up at her. "And give my old man another heart attack?"

She smiled. "He's way too tough for that little skirmish to upset him. And, maybe this will teach him to keep his nose out of your business." She glanced back at the stove. "Hold on while I check the milk. I don't want it boiling over."

He stayed where he was because the spat with his father had somehow exhausted him. He listened to his mother stirring in the chocolate powder, the spoon clinking against the side of the mugs. She brought the cocoa over to the table and placed one in front of him.

"Here you go, sweetheart."

"Thanks." Kaiden took a dutiful sip and found she'd made it just how he liked it. "It's great."

She let him drink in silence as the house creaked and settled around them. Kaiden had a weird sense that the calmness flowing into him was coming directly from her.

"I heard what you said to your father about me."

Kaiden grimaced. "Yeah, I'm sorry about that. I have no idea where it all came from."

"From your heart." She set her mug down on the table. "It can't have been easy for any of you growing up without a mother."

"I don't blame you, Mom." He looked her in the eye. "Dad caused all of this."

She sighed. "I wish I had your confidence that was true. I still beat myself up regularly, like, how hard did I try to get back? What kind of mother walks out on her own kids? Maybe I should've just knuckled down and let him win?"

"But you did try," Kaiden pointed out. "I remember Dad and Rae having a terrible fight once because you were in Bridgeport, and she was trying to sneak us all out to see you. Dad took her car keys and kept us in the house for the whole day, and no one else knew why."

"You remember that?" his mother asked. "I had no idea."

"I never told anyone what I overheard. I wasn't that

stupid." Kaiden wrapped both hands around his mug. "I cried myself to sleep that night."

"I still could've tried harder," Leanne said. "At one point, Declan asked if I'd like him to set his lawyers onto Jeff to insist I had visitation rights. That he'd be happy to pay to fly you all out to New York if it put a smile back on my face. I thought about it, but I was terrified that it would make things even worse, and that taking you away from the ranch you all loved would just confuse you more, and cause resentment."

"I don't think Dad would've cared if the courts had ordered him to do something. He would've just ignored them anyway," Kaiden reminded her.

"That's probably true." She bit her lip. "Also, by the time I saw Ben again, he was so angry with me that I was afraid I'd left it too long, and that you all hated me."

"We never did that," Kaiden said. "Most of us thought you were dead because Dad just wouldn't even say your name."

Leanne groaned. "Neither of us would win parent of the year, that's for sure."

"I guess you both did your best."

Leanne reached for his hand. "There you go again, trying to make me feel better about myself. At some level I know I did the best I could, but my heart tells me differently."

"I'll apologize to Dad tomorrow, okay?" Kaiden finally stirred.

"You don't need to do that."

"I'll feel better if I do." Kaiden shrugged. "I don't like falling out with people."

"It's hard to deal with other people's anger, isn't it?" Leanne said.

"That's not the thing I have a problem with. I'm used to . . ." Kaiden said slowly. "I'm way more worried that I'll be the angry one, and I'll sound just like Dad."

Chapter Fourteen

"We're going to store most of this lumber in the barn, Wes, so you can help carry everything in."

Kaiden let down the tailgate of his truck as Wes got out and ambled toward him, yawning so hard Kaiden could see his tonsils. He hadn't particularly wanted to go to the Garcia Ranch this morning, but he didn't have much choice. Mike's truck was already parked outside the house, which meant that at least Kaiden wouldn't have to face Julia alone.

"Isn't that stuff, like, heavy?" Wes frowned.

"Just think of the muscles you'll have to flex when we're done." Kaiden grabbed hold of the first long plank. "Get the other end, will you?"

With a long-suffering sigh, Wes pocketed his phone and did as Kaiden asked.

"Ouch." After they'd set the plank down, Wes sucked his thumb into his mouth. "I think I got a splinter."

"I've told you a million times to wear your gloves, Wes."

"I left them in the truck."

"I suppose that's progress. Last week you didn't even

manage to bring them," Kaiden muttered as he stalked back to the truck.

"You're super salty today, boss. What's up?" Wes called out to him.

Kaiden yanked hard at the next piece of wood, which, typically, refused to budge. "I'm good, thanks."

"No, you're not."

For a second, Kaiden debated the merits of getting into a stupid argument with a teenager, and reluctantly decided it wasn't worth it. Just because he *was* salty, wasn't a reason to take out his frustrations on Wes.

"Is it because of your dad?"

Kaiden looked up at his apprentice.

"Beth said I should be nice to you, because, like, your dad is sick, and that you must be feeling worried about him," Wes said. "So, if you are worried, you can, like, talk to me about it, you know? Because I, like, know how it feels when you've got a sick parent." He frowned. "Although, my mom died, and I don't think that's going to happen to your dad, okay?"

"That's . . . really thoughtful of you, Wes," Kaiden said, then blew out a breath. "I appreciate it."

Wes grinned at him. "Awesome!" He pointed at the bed of the truck. "If I climb in there I should be able to move that piece."

"Thanks."

Jeez, his emotions really were rattled if the awkward offer of help from a teenager was making him feel like welling up. Behind him, the ranch door opened and shut and his shoulders tensed.

"Hey," Julia said brightly. "Dad and I decided to take a walk while the weather was holding up."

"Good morning, Kaiden and Wes," Juan called out.

He turned to see Juan smiling from his wheelchair with Julia behind him pushing. He'd laid the new wider and graded path for the wheelchair a couple of days before, and he was glad to see Juan taking advantage of it.

"Hey, Miss G and Mr. G!" Wes said. "How's it hanging?"

"Er, great! Thanks!" Juan replied.

Kaiden finally got a good hold on the end of the wood as Wes eased it clear of the congestion and managed to wrestle it out of the truck.

"What's all that for?" Juan asked after Kaiden and Wes returned from the barn.

"Most of it is for the kitchen cabinets." Kaiden stripped off his jacket as he started to warm up from the exercise. "I won't be starting yet, but I wanted to bring the wood over so I could measure up." He nodded at the barn. "I can set up my workshop out here so I'm not in Mike and Bernie's way."

"I can't wait to see what you do with it," Juan said.

"I've got some ideas." Kaiden smiled at him. "But, don't worry, I'll consult with you as I get going."

"I trust you," Juan said. "I'd rather wait and get a surprise."

"You sure?" Kaiden joked, aware that Julia was keeping really quiet. "I could totally get it wrong, and you'd hate it."

"I doubt that." Juan looked up at his silent daughter. "Julia was telling me about the memory cabinet you made for Ben and Silver and how beautiful it was."

"Thanks." Kaiden couldn't help but look at Julia, and wished he hadn't. The last thing she needed was his puppy dog eyes begging for scraps of affection. "I love making things like that."

"I can tell," Julia spoke finally and Kaiden breathed more easily.

"Wes and I are going to be in and out of the house most of the day, measuring up the new bathroom shower wall and re-siting the closet into its new spot, so don't mind us."

"We're getting used to all the comings and goings these days," Juan said. "It makes life interesting."

"That's a good way to look at it." Kaiden nodded. "Now, we'd better get on with unloading the truck, or we won't be building anything today."

Julia gave her father his mug of coffee and avoided looking out of the window where Kaiden had now shed his shirt, and was working in a tight, black T-shirt that showcased his biceps and flat stomach way too well.

"Is there anything I can do that is away from the house today?" Julia asked.

Juan looked at her. "I would've thought you'd appreciate Kaiden hanging out here all day."

She found a smile. "I doubt he'd appreciate me stopping him every five seconds to chat. Didn't you say that you needed to check up on those cabins way up on the northern fence line? The ones we used to rent out to hunters?"

"Jose and Andy can do that."

"No, they can't, Dad," Julia said patiently. "They are busy trying to round up the cattle, and that's taking a while."

From what she'd observed, the two old-timers were doing it cow by cow because that was all they could handle. Not that she was complaining. It was better than nothing.

"So, would you be okay with me going up there this

afternoon?" Julia asked. "I can make sure the cabins are secure, and report back to you this evening."

"If you really wish to go, then be my guest." Juan sipped his coffee. "I've got plenty of company today."

"As to that." Julia took the seat opposite him. "Do you remember Beth Baker?"

"Ted's sister? Yes, of course." Juan frowned. "She moved back recently, didn't she? Some trouble with her marriage."

"Well, she's looking for a job as a home helper during school hours. I wondered whether you'd like to talk to her about coming up here and taking care of the cooking and the cleaning for you when I'm gone?"

Julia held her breath as her father studied her.

"You're really not staying, then?"

"I can't, Dad." She held his gaze. "I will come back more often though, I promise. At least once a month."

He looked away from her. "What does Miguel think of this plan of yours?"

"Miguel will like anything that doesn't involve him having to lift a finger to help."

"That's not fair. He's a good boy."

Julia pressed her lips together hard and counted to thirty before speaking again.

"So, would you like me to ask Beth to come up here so you can have a chat with her?"

"I'll think about it."

"Great!" Julia said way too enthusiastically. "Or speak to her after the church service on Sunday." She rose to her feet. "I'll just make sure there's something ready for lunch for everyone, and then I'll leave for the cabins."

* * *

Kaiden had just dropped Wes home after a long day up at the Garcia Ranch and gone back to the theater to pick up the rest of his tools when his phone buzzed. He took it out and studied the unfamiliar number and text message.

Julia not home yet and it's getting late.

Kaiden frowned and hit the call button. "Mr. Garcia? What's up?"

"Hey, Kaiden, thanks for calling. Julia went out to check up on the cabins in the northern section of the ranch, and she hasn't returned yet. I'm getting worried about her."

"Has she called or texted you?" Kaiden asked.

"No, I haven't heard anything, although the reception up that way is pretty rough. I know I'm probably worrying over nothing, but you never know if there are bad people up there who have taken over the cabins."

Kaiden mentally drew a map in his head of where Julia had gone and silently agreed with Juan. There was a problem with small pot farms springing up in isolated spots in the valley and there was a lot of illegal hunting and poaching.

"Do you want me to check up on her?" Kaiden offered.

There was a long pause and then Juan finally spoke. "That would be very kind of you. I wish I could go myself, Kaiden, but I can't, and I don't want to worry the emergency services if this is just because we can't connect with each other."

"I'm in town right now, so I'll let Nate Turner know what's going on before I head up there. If you don't hear from me, then assume all is good. If there is an emergency, I'll talk to Nate, and you'll hear from him, okay?"

"Thank you, Kaiden. I really appreciate it."

"No worries, Mr. Garcia. I'm glad to help."

Kaiden packed his toolbox in the back of his truck, stopped for gas at Ted Baker's, and called in at the sheriff's office beside the post office.

Nate was already shutting up shop ready to go out on patrol when Kaiden came in the front door. He stopped long enough to approve of Kaiden's plan, and gave him a radio pack to take with him, which would work anywhere in the valley.

Kaiden took the bulky radio. "Thanks, Nate."

"You're welcome. There's a late storm coming in tonight over the mountains so watch out for that."

"Will do." Kaiden walked out into the parking lot behind the sheriff's office with Nate. "I'll keep you in the loop."

He checked to see that he still had his winter gear stowed in the truck along with a few basic supplies and decided to head out. He'd already texted his mom so she could tell everyone at home where he was. He still wasn't ready to talk to his dad, and the urgency of his mission gave him the perfect excuse not to go home.

"Coward," Kaiden chided himself as he turned onto Main Street. "Conflict avoider."

He checked his phone again, put the map coordinates Juan had given him into the truck navigation system, and hoped to hell the signal would last long enough to get him close enough to Julia in the dark.

"Damn!"

Julia shivered as her attempt to light the fire in the stone hearth of the cabin failed once again. She got a firmer grip on the lighter and this time managed to create a flame, which immediately flickered out as she tried to set fire to the crunched-up newspaper in the grate.

She sat back on her heels and took a deep breath.

"You can do this, Julia. You were a Girl Scout, remember?"

She finally connected the flame to the kindling and, sheltering it with her hands, managed to coax the small, curling strands of wood she'd stripped to take fire. Five minutes later the smaller twigs started to burn vigorously and she sat back on her butt to monitor further progress. She glanced out of the window noticing how quickly it was getting dark. With a groan, she got to her feet and went back outside, carefully closing the door behind her. She knew her dad usually kept some supplies in the truck. She just hoped he'd replenished them recently.

The sound of an approaching vehicle had her backing out of the interior and turning to face the rutted track. She eased the hunting knife she'd found in the glove box out of the back pocket of her jeans and held it behind her back. With the glare of the headlights directly in her eyes she couldn't see a thing.

"Hey!"

She blinked away the spots of vivid color behind her eyelids and stepped cautiously to one side.

"Anyone need help around here?"

Her breath tumbled out as she pocketed the knife and practically ran toward Kaiden, who was smiling. His expression changed as he took a good look at her, and he drew her in for a hug.

"It's okay, hon. We've got this. What happened?"

"The rear tire on the truck got a puncture." Despite her best efforts, Julia's voice shook.

"I'll help you change it, then."

"I might have lived in the city for years, Kaiden Miller, but I still know how to change a tire." She pushed her hair out of her eyes. "I got the truck jacked up, found the spare, and put it on. Ten minutes later, it was also flat, and I had to come back here."

She didn't tell him that it had taken her well over an hour to get the job done and that watching the sun disappearing behind the Sierras had made her as anxious as hell.

"That at least explains why you smell like a mechanic," Kaiden said.

She gave in to temptation and leaned into him, rubbing her cheek against his jacket.

His hand settled gently over her hair. "It's okay," he said again. "We've got the same truck, and I definitely have a working spare tire. We can put it on your truck so we both can leave."

"It's too dark to do that now," Julia said against the solid warmth of his chest. "And, it's just about to start raining."

"Then we'll stay the night here and get it done in the morning."

She nodded as he steered her toward the cabin and opened the door.

"Looks like you've already got this place all warmed up."

"There are a couple of lanterns and I brought some wood in," Julia said as she surveyed the one-room log cabin. "There wasn't much there."

"I can fix that." Kaiden turned around the compact space, his presence making it feel way smaller. "Any food here?"

"Three tins of canned chili and beans," Julia reported. "Still in date."

"Cool." Kaiden walked her over to the small couch.

"How about you keep an eye on the fire while I go and get some stuff from the truck?"

"Don't tell me you've got a blow-up bed in there."

Kaiden grinned and glanced back at the bare mattress and bed frame. "Nope, but I do have a sleeping bag." He pointed at the couch. "Sit. I promise I'll be back as soon as I can."

She grabbed his hand. "Wait, what about my dad? He'll be worried sick."

"How do you think I knew where you were?" He gently rubbed her palm with his thumb before releasing her hand. "He called me, I talked to Nate, and when I'm outside, I'll call Nate and let him know the situation."

"There's no reception out here."

"Which is why Nate gave me a radio." He pointed at the couch. "You look worn out. Stay put and tend the fire."

Julia only realized how exhausted she was when she didn't mind Kaiden giving her orders. The thought of her father knowing she was safe was a huge relief.

Eventually, Kaiden came back through the door with a pile of stuff that he dumped on the small table. "I think there's still some coffee left in my flask, if you want it."

Julia was already on the move before he left again searching through the pile to discover the promised coffee. Not that she considered herself an addict or anything, but six hours without caffeine had been horrible. After finishing the dregs of the coffee she took an inventory of what he'd brought inside.

He took quite a while to come back the second time, but as the wind was rising, and the fire needed help to survive the gusts coming down the chimney, she was too busy to be worried. When he finally returned, his jacket was dark from the rain, and he carried a huge stack of wood.

"This should see us through the night."

"You didn't have to do that," Julia said. "You're soaked through!"

"And now I'll have a fire to warm me up and dry my clothes with." He set the wood down and straightened with a groan. "I haven't chopped wood that fast for a while. I'm going to be stiff tomorrow."

"How come you have so much stuff in your truck?" Julia asked.

"Because you never know when you'll need it out here." Kaiden dusted off his hands and came toward her. "Is the water on?"

"Yes." She showed him how to work the pump. "Just cold. We'll have to boil it on the stove."

"Sounds just like home." He stripped off his jacket and shirt, washed his hands and face, and dried them on the sleeve of his flannel shirt. "My dad didn't believe in wasting hot water when we were kids."

Julia shivered at the thought.

"He said it toughened us up." Kaiden studied her. "You might want to wash up yourself. You've got a streak of oil on your forehead."

"Really?" Julia groaned. "I got so busy starting the fire that I forgot about how I looked."

"Well, you weren't exactly expecting visitors, were you? You'd look even better minus the oil. I left some soap on the side of the sink." Kaiden walked toward what passed as the kitchen. "Are you hungry? Where's the chili?"

The can opener was rusted and useless, so he used his knife to open two of the cans of chili, dumped them in a pan, and heated them on the stovetop, which still had gas.

He'd packed some sandwiches and chips he'd picked up from Maureen's in town for the journey and set them out, too. Julia washed up some bowls and silverware and they were ready to eat.

Despite its obvious age, the cabin had been well put together, and apart from the wind whistling down the chimney, the fire managed to keep the small space warm. To his relief, Julia appeared unharmed by her experiences. He tended to forget she'd spent the majority of her life in Morgan Valley and had the necessary resources to survive among the elements.

He'd spoken briefly to Nate, who had seconded his decision to stay put. Hearing the rain now beating down on the cabin roof and the thunder and lightning made him glad Julia wasn't stuck out in a thunderstorm in a metal truck. He'd fetched all three of his spare jackets from the truck and persuaded her to add his fleece to her thin sweater. He kind of liked seeing her wearing his stuff.

"I wish we had more coffee." Julia sat on the couch and drew her knees up to her chest. "Why didn't you think of that when you packed your emergency supplies?"

"I promise I won't forget next time."

He sat next to her because there was nowhere else to sit and laid his arm along the back of the couch. The fire had taken hold and was crackling away nicely, filling the room with the scent of pine. The drapes shut out the rain and he'd folded up the mat and pushed it against the crack under the door to keep the wind out. All things considered, he was happy where he was right now.

"This happens to you a lot?" She arched an eyebrow in his direction. "This rescuing thing?"

"All the time." He shrugged. "Damsels in distress gonna damsel."

"I was managing quite well without you, you know."

"You were." He wasn't going to argue with her, but he couldn't resist a quick tease. "What was your plan for getting home tomorrow? Were you going to walk?"

She pinched his chest. "I hadn't decided whether to walk down the valley until I could pick up a signal and call for help, or drive the truck anyway and see how far I could get on a flat tire."

"Both good plans." He nodded and made as if to rise. "I might as well just head back out and leave you to it."

She came up on her knees and wrapped an arm around his neck. "Not so fast. I don't want you getting struck by lightning or anything."

He smiled down at her, bringing his hand to her waist. "I'm not stupid. I'm not going anywhere."

She smoothed her thumb over his jaw. "Thank you."

"For what?"

"Coming all the way out here to make sure I was all right."

"That's what neighbors are for." Kaiden reminded himself to keep things light. "I didn't want your dad worrying unnecessarily."

She sat back down again and he followed her.

"Do you think we'll be okay?" Julia asked.

"I don't see why not." Kaiden looked around the cabin. "We've got food, shelter, and warmth, transport for tomorrow, and each other."

"I am glad you are here."

"You would've managed without me," Kaiden said.

"But I'm glad I came." He hastily covered his mouth as he yawned. "Sorry about that. It's been a long day."

"What time is it?" Julia gestured at her phone. "My cell ran out of battery."

Kaiden slowly rolled up his sleeve. "Then it's a good job I wear one of these old-fashioned watches on my wrist. As long as I keep moving, it keeps ticking."

He checked the time. "It just turned nine, which explains why I'm so tired. That's usually when I turn in."

"That early?" Julia asked.

"Remember, I have to squeeze in two or three hours of ranch work before I leave for my day job or Dad gets on my back."

"That's tough."

"That's the life of a rancher. Long days, low pay, and no one to blame but yourself and the current government if things go south."

"Dad can't do it anymore," Julia said flatly. "Miguel won't, so what am I supposed to do?"

"Hire a competent manager until your dad either makes his mind up to sell the place, or Miguel comes home?" Kaiden suggested.

"Yes, that's what needs to happen, but the place isn't profitable enough to pay anyone a decent salary right now. I'll have to subsidize it."

"Which means you have to keep working with pond slime like Blaine." Kaiden's hand dropped onto her shoulder and he automatically started working the kinks of tension out of her muscles. "I don't know what the answers are, Julia. I just admire the hell out of you for trying to keep everything afloat."

"Thank you." She leaned her head against his shoulder and sighed. "This is kind of nice."

"It is until you need the bathroom, which we both do before we turn in." Kaiden deliberately didn't take advantage of the moment to kiss the top of her head. "You'll need to put on your rain slicker and head off out back to the lean-to."

"You're right." She sat up. "Oh God, do you think there are spiders in there?"

"Probably." Kaiden hid a grin.

"Will you go first, and get rid of them for me?"

The mixture of horror and hope on her beautiful face undid all his resolve.

"I might if you are willing to pay a forfeit."

"Anything." She clasped her hands together like she was praying.

He pretended to consider all the more outrageous things he could ask for, and settled on the simplest.

"A kiss."

"Just the one?" She knew him well enough to be wary, and she was also a lawyer.

"That's up to you. I've noticed in the past that you don't seem to want to stop at one. But for the record, just one kiss on whichever part of my anatomy I ask for."

Her gaze immediately dropped to his dick and then shot back up to his face.

"That's way too much territory."

"Then you go first to the bathroom." He rose to his feet. "I'll find you a flashlight."

He was already smiling when she tapped him on the back and he swung around.

"All right. One kiss wherever you want it." She stuck out her hand. "Deal?"

"Deal." He shook her hand. "Let's get our jackets."

He went in first, armed not only with a stick, but also

with a ton of disinfectant, and made sure the place was okay for his ladylove before she went inside. He even stayed and shone the flashlight over the door so that she could pee and continue to monitor the spider situation while he got soaked in the rain again.

After escorting Julia back to the cabin, Kaiden took a moment to check that both of the trucks were locked and to remove his gun and ammo from behind the back seat. Like most ranchers he always carried a weapon in his truck just in case. He also spied his medical kit and brought that in too.

Julia was drying her hair on the towel he kept in the truck for the dogs, not that he would mention that. She looked up as he came in and discarded his wet jacket.

"Why do you have your gun? Are you expecting trouble?"

"Not necessarily, but I don't want to *invite* trouble and leave it in the truck in case someone decides to break in overnight." He set it in a safe place away from the fire. "Better to be safe than sorry."

"Dad said there were pot growers and rustlers up here last year."

"There's a lot of it about." Kaiden took off his fleece-lined shirt. "I wouldn't normally have come up here by myself, to be honest."

She sighed. "Dad didn't want me to either. I just didn't want to spend the whole day looking at you outside my window so I made the suggestion. It wasn't my finest moment. I can see that now."

Kaiden paused as he took the towel from her. "If you don't want me at your place—"

"That's not it. The problem is me wanting what I can't have, and trying to stop myself mooning over you all day."

Kaiden slowly dried his hair, using the time to work out what he wanted to say to her frank admission. He liked the idea of her watching him work way too much. But, what was the point of going around the same old rodeo again? Nothing had changed. Neither of them could make a relationship work right now. . . .

Right now.

Kaiden set the towel over the back of the chair.

"You owe me."

She straightened up, pushing her hair behind her ear. "I know."

"Twice, actually."

Her nose wrinkled. "I don't remember that."

"I saved you from Blaine."

"No, you didn't." He was about to correct her when she carried on speaking. "You helped me by keeping an eye on my dad, and managing Father Pascal."

"And by not killing Blaine for being so damned insensitive he turned up at your father's ranch just to harass you about work."

"Okay." She folded her arms over her chest. "I'll give you that."

"So, given that you owe me twice, can you agree that right now, we're kind of out of our own time and away from all our problems?"

"Kind of." She eyed him curiously. "What are you getting at?"

"That being said, maybe we could do what we both want?"

"Which is?"

He reached forward, cupped her chin, and kissed her mouth. "This."

"I thought I was the one who owed you a kiss."

"Oh, you do." He kissed her again, running the tip of his tongue along the seam of her lips. "I'll make you pay up very soon, honey, don't you ever doubt it."

She pushed gently on his chest and he immediately let her go.

"You're suggesting we give in to our . . . needs?"

"Oh, yeah." He kissed her ear and down her throat. "All of them."

"And, then when we go back we forget it ever happened?"

He met her gaze. "I'm not sure I'll ever be able to forget you, but I certainly won't hold it over you, or have any expectations of more."

He held his breath as she considered him, her expression serious.

"I'm not sure," she whispered. "It sounds impossible."

Even as his faint hopes died, he offered her a smile, moved away, and gestured at the bed. "If we put the two fleece blankets down on top of the mattress, and spread the unzipped sleeping bag over us, we should be warm enough." He paused. "That is, if you're okay with us sharing the space. I can go sleep in my truck if you want."

"Don't be silly, you'd freeze out there." Julia stood and brought their mugs over to the sink. "I'll just finish this washing up, and then I'll be ready for bed."

Julia took off her jeans and wiggled out of her bra without removing her shirt and sweater, and walked over to the bed where Kaiden was unzipping the sleeping bag.

"It's a good one." He nodded for her to get in. "Should keep us nice and warm."

"Great." Julia crawled across the space and waited as Kaiden did his final check around the cabin. He tested the locked door, built up the fire so that it hopefully would stay alight all night, and extinguished all the lamps except one, which he brought to sit beside the bed.

"Anything you need before we turn in?" he asked, his expression inscrutable in the shadows cast by the lantern.

"I think I'm good." She smiled up at him, but he didn't respond, as he was busy shucking his jeans and thick fleece jacket.

He climbed in next to her and the suddenly roomy bed took on the dimensions of a dollhouse. She often forgot how broad his shoulders and biceps were. She tried to squeeze farther into the corner, but there was no way she wasn't going to be touching at least some part of him while they slept.

"You okay?" he asked as he drew the sleeping bag over them both.

"Great," she whispered. "Just peachy."

"If you don't mind me saying so, you don't sound peachy."

She resolutely closed her eyes. "Shut up and go to sleep, Kaiden Miller."

"Okay, good night, honey."

"And, don't call me that."

Time slowed along with Kaiden's breathing until Julia ended up wide awake and counting every second in her head. The storm ebbed and flowed above her making the cabin rock and shift. She could only hope that whoever had built it had done a good job and reminded herself that it had stood for at least fifty years without a problem.

Her treacherous mind kept circling back to Kaiden's

offer of time-out-of-mind sex. He'd been totally respectful of her decision not to go along with him, which she appreciated more than she could say. But the longer she lay there, in such an unfamiliar and unexpected environment, the easier it became to believe that anything they did together here would be such an anomaly that they could return to their regular lives afterward without any remorse or guilt.

She turned on her side and studied him. He lay on his back, one hand cradling his head, the other trailing over the side of the bed. Even in his sleep, his face was mobile and alive. He exuded a kind of restless energy that kept her off guard, which was an unfamiliar sensation for the girl voted "most prepared for any emergency" in high school. Was she making excuses for herself because she already knew she wanted to go ahead? Touching him, breathing in his smell just made her want him so badly.

"If you think any louder you'll wake the spiders," he murmured without opening his eyes.

She came up on one elbow and stared down at him. "I thought you were asleep."

"I was until I felt you staring at me." He opened an eye. "It's like being stalked by a predator. Damn terrifying."

She leaned over and poked his chest. "Good."

"Ouch." He collected her fingers in his and entwined their hands together over his heart. "Go back to sleep, I promise I'll keep you safe."

"I'm quite capable of taking care of myself, thank you," Julia retorted. "And I'm not worried about the surviving part."

"Then what are you worrying about?" He sounded like he was about to drift back to sleep.

"The usual."

"I told you my take on it earlier." He paused. "You changing your mind?"

"I might be."

"Yeah?" He finally opened both his eyes and gave her one hundred percent of his attention, which was both gratifying and slightly nerve-wracking.

"If we do this—and I said 'if'—we both have to agree that it's not the start of a relationship. That it's just for now," Julia said.

"What happens in the cabin stays in the cabin." He winked. "I'm good with that."

"And we don't tell anyone, ever," Julia added.

"Okay." His gaze never left her face. "Before you ask, I have protection in my medical kit, so we're good."

She was also on birth control, but he didn't need to know that. She took a deep breath and gathered her courage.

"Then, maybe we should do this." She waited hopefully, but he didn't sit up and immediately start kissing her. "If you're still all right about it."

"Sure I am." He stayed where he was, one hand behind his head, and beckoned to her. "You're the one who owes me a kiss or two, so I'll let you set the pace."

Even as she marveled at his absolute and complete audacity she briefly considered turning over and forgetting the whole thing. But, she'd always been competitive, and this was an outright dare of epic proportions.

"Okay, then." She wiggled out of her panties and climbed onto his stomach, her knees on either side of his hips. "Don't be scared."

She slowly leaned down, planted one hand beside his head on the blankets, and licked a line along the slightly parted curve of his lips. He obligingly opened his mouth as she delved deeper tasting a spiciness and a richness that was all him. He made an approving sound and brought one arm around her hips.

"That's nice, honey. Do it again."

She considered biting his tongue, but she was already too caught up in the sensual spell of discovery and redis-covery that he represented to her. She'd known him most of her life, but this part of him? The part that seemed made just for her was new, and exciting, and terrifying. This wasn't a man who didn't know her, or get her, in fact he knew her far too well, and sometimes that scared her.

He rocked his hips making her very aware that she was sitting across his stomach and that he was very happy about that indeed. She ended the kiss and smiled down at him.

"That was the first one I owed you. Where do you want the next one?"

He raised an eyebrow. "I'm a man. Where do you think?"

She pretended to consider the question, one finger pressed against her lower lip, which he couldn't seem to look away from. She deliberately licked the tip of her finger and he groaned.

"Yeah, just like that."

"You want me to kiss your fingers?" she inquired.

"How about you give me your hand, and I'll show you exactly what I want."

"Only if you take your T-shirt off first." Julia was totally ready to bargain for what *she* wanted.

"You want me to freeze to death or something?" Kaiden complained.

"No, I want to get a good look at those fine shoulders, pecs, and abs I suspect you're hiding under there." Now that she'd committed herself, she was enjoying ordering him about.

"If you insist." He sat up dislodging her from her perch and pulled his T-shirt off one-handed.

"Oh . . ." Julia sighed and leaned in to rest her palm on the heavy slab of muscle layered under his lightly haired chest. "That's damn fine." She traced her fingers down over his perfect abs to the elastic band of his boxers. "It's a shame you have to wear clothes at all, really."

He flexed his arms. "Thank you, ma'am, and unlike Blaine the pain, I've never been inside a gym in my life." He held out his hand and took hold of hers. "Now, it's your turn."

He brought her fingers to the hard length making his boxers bulge almost open at the top. "Kiss this."

She kept her fingers where he left them, lightly grazing his boxers, and lowered her head. His breath hitched as she looked right at him and used her teeth to delicately pull the soaked cotton of his boxers away and drag it clear of his stiff, heated flesh.

"Julia . . ."

She waited, but apparently, for a change, he'd said everything he wanted to say. He was gazing down at her with a mixture of lust and trepidation that made her feel very powerful indeed. She licked him like an ice cream, enjoying the way his hand fisted in the covers and his body arched toward her, seeking each lavish stroke.

"That's . . . good, that's damned good." He breathed. "Don't stop, okay?"

Seeing as she had no intention of stopping anytime soon, his bossiness was easy to ignore. Having Kaiden Miller at her command and in her power was not something any woman would relinquish easily. She wanted him to beg, she wanted him pleading to come, and, even though she knew at some point he'd get even, it didn't bother her in the slightest.

She peeled his boxers farther down, pausing to explore the firm curves of his ass, which made him curse under his breath, and then returned her attention to the main attraction. She kissed her way down his shaft with slow deliberation, aware that he was already wet for her, and that the sight of so much brazen maleness was having a very specific effect on her own sex.

If this was to be her only night with Kaiden, she was determined to examine him as minutely as possible, and to explore as many of her fantasies of what to do with a supremely fit and hot cowboy she could manage. With that thought firmly in mind, she took another leisurely tour of him, pausing to caress his balls and the firm root of his shaft. He smelled delicious, like leather and horse, like he was . . . *hers.*

Which was stupid, but there it was.

She reached his crown and lapped at the wetness, making him say her name again, his fingers coming down to her shoulder, not to direct, but simply to touch her. She slowly took him inside her mouth and sucked him hard enough to make him groan. His hand moved to her covered breast and squeezed, making her hum with pleasure.

"You need less clothes," he said hoarsely. "A lot less clothes."

She released him and sat up straight before peeling off her sweater and T-shirt. His eyes went so dark when she revealed her breasts that her breath caught in her throat.

"May I?" He reached out a hand.

"Not yet." She wrapped her fingers around his pulsing shaft. "I haven't finished."

He added his fingers to hers. "If you keep that up, I'll come, and I know where I'd rather be when that happens."

"Then perhaps you'd better come up with a solution that benefits us both?" she challenged him.

He stared at her for a second, and then nodded.

"Okay."

Before she could do anything except gasp, he grabbed her by the waist, turned her around, and set her over his torso. "This work for you?"

As her nose was now practically touching his shaft she couldn't even nod. She settled the matter by drawing his thick length into her mouth and almost screeched when his tongue licked her most sensitive parts.

Trying to concentrate on pleasuring him while he teased and played with her, while he rubbed his stubbled chin against her bud and thrust his tongue deep, was almost impossible. She climaxed in a heated rush and blatantly writhed against his face, not caring if he could breathe or not.

"Damn." He lifted her off him again with an easy strength that still shocked her. "I need to be inside you right now."

She helped him find the medical kit and the precious foil packages inside, and waited with barely concealed impatience for him to cover himself and lie back on the covers.

"Come on, cowgirl." Kaiden breathed. "Take me for a ride."

She made a face. "So corny."

"Replace the 'c' with an 'h' and you're closer to the mark."

She straddled him and slowly lowered herself down over his cock, watching his face as she took him deep.

"That's so good, honey." He briefly closed his eyes as she settled over him. "Can I touch you now?"

"Yes, of course." She deliberately squeezed her internal muscles and his eyes nearly crossed. "But don't put me off my stride."

"I wouldn't dare."

She rose slowly up and then sank down again, finding a rhythm that pleased her and also seemed to drive him wild. He used his formidable core strength to roll upward to meet each of her downward thrusts, causing enough friction to make her freeze over him and come again.

She planted one hand on his chest and felt the slam of his heart against his ribs as he set his jaw and fought not to come with her. Holding him under her, *keeping* him there at least for a while, suddenly seemed vital. If she allowed him to surge over her and take control would she ever find herself again?

Kaiden counted backward from a hundred and tried to think of the kind of winter day in the great outdoors that would freeze his nuts off. But Julia gasped his name and bent forward, her breasts swinging against his face in an invitation he couldn't resist. Holding her steady over his thrusting hips, he scooted backward until he was in a sitting position, his thighs spread wide, her knees clinging to his sides.

She kissed him again, and he slid his fingers between them to finger her bud, urging her on, knowing at some desperate level he never wanted to stop feeling her pulsing around him. She moaned into his mouth as she climaxed again, and he couldn't hold back any longer. With a harsh cry he joined her, his whole body shuddering with the effort to satisfy her as he climaxed.

She fell forward over him, her hair all in his face and mouth as she sobbed in completion and held him like he meant something to her. He stared up at the rafters of the cabin, automatically checking the joinery as he slowly regained his breath. He waited to see what she would do next. Would she say thank you, turn her back on him, and go to sleep? Or would she want more?

She sighed and stroked his hair. "That was wonderful. . . ."

He allowed himself to relax a little.

"Good to know."

"Do you want me to get off you?"

He shrugged. "It's up to you. I'm okay being used as your own personal mattress." In fact, he loved the way she was cuddled up against him, and didn't really want to move again in this lifetime, but he wasn't going to be that guy.

"I suppose you'll want to clean up."

"Yeah! Of course, right." He lifted her off him and immediately swung his legs over the side of the bed to take care of condom disposal. "Would you like a drink or something? I can boil some water—"

She touched his hip. "I'm fine."

"That's great." He paused. "Do you want—"

She knelt up behind him, wrapped her arms around his torso, and bit him gently on the neck. "I want you to stop fussing, come back to bed, and sleep with me before we get to do this again."

He tried to keep his voice light even though he knew he was smiling like a fool. "Wow, you really are bossy in bed, aren't you?"

She bit him again, this time harder, which made his dick twitch ready for round two, and attempted to pull him backward into the bed. The resulting skirmish left her on her back with him looming over her, one thigh planted between hers. Her gaze lowered to his groin.

"You can't possibly be ready for more?"

"It sure looks like it. Sleeping is for sissies." He slicked a hand over his most prized possession. "You make me so hard."

Her smile was beautiful enough to make him speechless.

"That's so sweet of you."

"I don't feel sweet." He cupped her mound, his voice rough. "I want you again right now."

She pretended to sigh and crooked her finger at him. "Then, come down here, cowboy, and show me what you've got."

Chapter Fifteen

She'd been right about one thing. He was a demanding lover who gave everything, and expected the same in return. He'd coaxed her, teased her, laughed at her, enraged her, and effortlessly offered her everything she'd ever wanted in a sexual partner. And she'd drowned in his demands, aware that he'd willingly gone along with all of her fantasies too.

A slight snore escaped him and Julia smiled. She was currently curled up against his side, one bent knee over his stomach with the hardness of his thigh pressed against the softness of her well-satisfied flesh. He lay on his back, his mouth slightly open, with one arm draped around her shoulders. Normally, she hated sleeping with her boyfriends after sex, but this just felt right.

The rainstorm had finally abated, and it was quiet outside—apart from all the night creatures that howled, chirped, and squeaked through the darkness. Julia had never felt so much at peace. Both her body and her mind were in harmony for the first time in years.

How could she possibly have thought he'd be forgettable? That one night with him would be enough to satisfy her desires for the rest of her life? She stroked her fingers through his chest hair and reminded herself of all the reasons why they couldn't be together. They argued all the time, he teased her too much, she got in his face . . . none of those things were good indicators of a stable and lasting relationship. She craned her neck to check the time on his watch and considered getting up, but that would mean the end of their idyll, and she wasn't quite ready for it to be over yet.

With a sigh, she pressed her cheek against his warm skin, pulled the sleeping bag back over her shoulders, and allowed herself to enjoy the uniqueness of Kaiden Miller for as long as he kept sleeping.

The next time she woke she was alone in the bed, and sunlight from the opened window slanted across the cabin. There was no sign of Kaiden, but he'd obviously been busy. The fire had been raked out and was stacked with wood again, there was a kettle of water steaming on the stove and a protein bar sitting on the table had her name written on it.

Julia got out of bed, wincing at her own stiffness, and walked over to the window. Outside, Kaiden was already busy changing the tire on her truck. She considered rushing out there just to remind him that she was perfectly capable of doing it for herself, but something stopped her. For the first time in about twenty years she didn't feel sure of herself. What the heck was she going to say to Kaiden? God, what did she even want to say?

She hurried back to the bed and discovered that he'd picked up her clothes and set them in a neat pile beside the fire. The kitchen had been scrubbed with something that smelled lemony and he'd also set out a bowl and washcloth for her beside the kettle. Despite his easygoing attitude, he was a surprisingly organized and tidy person.

She had a quick wash, shivering as she uncovered each portion of her skin, and climbed into her clothes, not caring they weren't fresh because she was so glad to be warm. She stuck the protein bar in her pocket and eyed the door. She needed the bathroom, which meant she'd have to walk past Kaiden and at least acknowledge his presence.

"This isn't high school prom, Julia," she muttered to herself. "Grow up, get out there, and just be your normal self."

Except she didn't feel like her normal self. She felt super aware of everything, the rasp of the washcloth against her skin, the slight swelling on her lip where he'd accidentally bitten her as he climaxed, the languorous ease of her limbs . . .

"Stop it," she said firmly. "You really need to pee."

Just before she went out the door, she grabbed the dish mop and brought it out with her to deal with any spiders.

"Hey," Kaiden called out to her as she came down the steps.

"Hey, sorry I slept in." She raised her hand to shield her eyes against the sun to try and see him. "I've just got to use the bathroom. I'll be right back."

She scurried off, scolding herself for the totally fake cheerfulness of her voice, knowing that he wouldn't miss it. She was horribly aware that unless she wanted to spend the rest of the day with the spiders she'd have to come back out at some point and talk to him.

When she did return, he had his back to her and was

busy jacking up her father's truck. He'd already removed the spare tire that had failed and had the new one standing by.

"Anything I can do to help?" Julia went toward him.

"Yeah, can you find my other glove? I must have dropped it when I moved the tire."

Julia glanced around and discovered it beside his open toolbox.

"Here you go."

"Thanks." His attention was all on the positioning of the jack, which she quite understood. "Can you put it down beside me? I'll have this done in no time and then we can be on our way."

He sounded his usual easy self, like nothing had changed between them at all and why shouldn't he? They'd had very specific rules, and he'd obviously taken them to heart and was abiding by them, which was exactly what she'd wanted.

"Great!" Julia replied. "How about I pack up all the stuff in the cabin while you do that so we won't waste any more time."

"If it's not too much trouble." He stood up and checked the height of the truck with a critical eye. "I already spoke to Nate. He said to tell you that your dad is fine and that Mike's father, Brian, stayed over with him so not to worry about rushing back."

"That's great." Aware that she was repeating herself, Julia went back toward the cabin. "I'll get started."

Two hours later they were on their way in their separate trucks, which meant that Julia didn't have anything else to do but follow Kaiden and keep an eye out for rough spots on the trail. He had dropped a kiss on her forehead as she'd gotten in her truck, but other than that, he'd kept his hands to himself, and so had she, which made things a lot easier.

To her surprise, he drove straight up to the front door of her home, parked, and waited for her to join him. He grimaced as she approached.

"Lots of work going on here today. It's going to get loud."

"And I'm probably going to be in the way." She paused, her gaze on his face. God, she wanted to touch him so badly. "If Dad is okay about it, I might skip out for the day. I have to go to Bridgeport for a work-related matter. Would you like to come with me?"

He blew out a breath and looked over at the collection of trucks parked by the barn.

"You're not making this easy, Julia."

"Maybe I'm just not ready to let you go just yet."

He gazed down at her, his usual smile absent, and didn't reply.

"Maybe we can spend the day together and find our friendship again?" Julia asked. "Or am I just being stupid here?"

"Like decelerating the threat level?" Kaiden offered.

She shrugged. "Something like that. Unless you have to work—which I quite understand."

Kaiden stared into her brown eyes and mentally berated himself about a thousand times for what he knew he was about to do.

"I'll need to talk to the guys and make sure they don't need me for anything first."

Her face lit up. "That's . . . awesome! I'll have to ask Dad, too, but he loves having everyone here. He's been happier than he's been for ages so I think he'll be fine with it."

She started for the door. "I'll be back out in an hour. I'll come and find you."

"Great, you do that." Kaiden waited until she'd gone inside before he found a rock to kick against the side of the barn. "You're a fool, Kaiden Miller. You just don't know when to let things go."

Yet, Julia was right, wasn't she? They had to find a way to go on together that didn't involve them both being naked. He pictured the way she looked when she came, her head thrown back, her whole face contorted in ecstasy, and groaned again.

Yeah, he was a fool just like his father said. Too scared to ask for what he really wanted and content to live off the scraps everyone else threw his way.

Despite his best efforts, none of the contractors needed either his help or advice. For once, the job was progressing smoothly, everyone was getting along, and so far there had been no major problems. He got the sense that the guys were working extra fast to get the work done for Juan, who was well known and liked in the local community.

By the time Julia came back out, he'd also spoken to his mom, who now knew where he was but was still wondering out loud why he was avoiding his father. He hadn't had an answer for her, but the thought lay heavy in his mind. Maybe he was becoming some kind of expert at avoiding anything unpleasant in his life.

"Wow." He did a double take as Julia sashayed down the path toward him. "You look . . . different."

She smoothed down her pencil skirt with her fingers and offered him a slightly anxious smile. "It feels weird wearing a skirt and heels again."

"You look great," Kaiden hastened to reassure her although she didn't look like "his" Julia anymore.

In some weird way, seeing her dressed up in her business attire reminded him of the gulf between them, so maybe it was for the best. She seemed to have taken their parting of ways and return to the real world in her stride, and he wasn't going to spoil it for her.

"Thank you." She'd tied her hair up at the back of her head and carried a navy jacket over her arm. "Are you still okay to come with me?" She paused. "I know it was kind of presumptuous of me to ask, and probably came out of left field, but—"

He held up his hand. "It's okay, I get it. The sooner we get back to normal the better, right?"

"Yes." She nodded so hard her ponytail bobbed along. "That's what I was hoping." She took a quick breath. "I still want us to be friends."

He had nothing constructive to say to that so he changed the subject.

"We should go in my truck."

"Why?"

"Because yours is almost out of gas and you need to get that tire changed out again. When you get a moment, take it down to Ted Baker's place, and he'll set you right. I can pick up my spare from him when he's finished."

"Oh, yes, Dad wanted to know how much he owes you," Julia said as he opened the passenger door for her.

"Nothing. Like I said, I'll get the tire back." He waited

for her to get in and frowned as she hopped around like a demented frog. "What's wrong?"

"I can't reach the running board in this skirt," Julia admitted.

As he reached for her, he pretended to sigh. "Women and their stupid fashions."

"So, you'd rather we dressed in jeans and boots all the time instead?"

"I wouldn't go that far." He picked her up and deposited her easily in her seat. The scent of her, up close and personal, made him never want to let her go. "Do you want me to do your seat belt up for you too, honey?"

She raised her eyebrows. "Do you want me to kick you in the nuts?"

"Wow, harsh." Kaiden shook his head. "I'll leave you to it, then."

Julia plugged the coordinates Melanie had given her into the navigation system and sat back to review the case notes while Kaiden drove. There wasn't much to go on, yet. Melanie wanted a visual of the potential land to assess its proximity to the town, the major services, and the highway system. Sometimes potential sellers weren't quite accurate in their descriptions.

MZB always tried to make sure that at least one of their associates actually went and viewed each potential site. It meant that future negotiations between clients and sellers were less likely to fall apart over something basic. Normally, it was the kind of job Julia would give to a new hire, but as Melanie had asked her personally, and she needed a few allies at the firm right now, Julia was more than willing to help out.

"So what are you doing today in Bridgeport?" Kaiden asked as he turned off the county road.

"Assessing a land parcel for a potential client."

"For a new home?"

"I'm not sure yet." Julia wasn't about to spill any office secrets. "This is only a preliminary assessment of one of several possible sites."

"Do you do this a lot?"

"Go out and see places? Not much anymore. I need more billable hours." She half smiled. "Got to pay for that remodel."

"I wish I'd never suggested it now." He glanced over at her and then back at the road, which was getting bumpier. "Thanks to me, you're stuck in that place."

"I think you're taking on way too much responsibility for something that is definitely not your fault," Julia said evenly. "I'm 'stuck' at that place because I love the work. The money isn't really the issue. I have enough saved to cover all your bills, so please don't worry."

"I wasn't actually thinking about myself," he said abruptly. "I was thinking about you."

"Oh." Julia stared out the window. "That's . . . very sweet of you." She checked the navigation, which seemed to have disappeared. "Are we close now?"

He pointed toward a roofline at the end of the road. "I'm going to take a guess and say we're supposed to end up there. I can't see anything else that looks like a structure, can you?"

"No."

She collected her paperwork in a tidy pile and replaced

it in the folder. There was a jeep parked outside the small dwelling and a man was watching their approach. He was dressed quite smartly so she assumed he had to be the seller's representative.

"I think that's our guy, there." Julia pointed out of the window.

"Ya think?" Kaiden brought the truck to a stop. "Do you want me to stay here, or would you prefer me to get out with you?"

Aware that they were in the middle of nowhere with very patchy cell coverage, Julia opened her door. "You're welcome to join me. It shouldn't take long."

She walked up to the guy and extended her hand.

"Hi! I'm Julia Garcia from MZB and associates. You must be Cameron."

"That's me." Cameron's gaze drifted over her shoulder toward where she assumed Kaiden was standing. "Hey."

Kaiden spoke up. He'd left his Stetson in the truck and donned his dark glasses. "Don't mind me. I'm just here to protect Ms. Garcia."

Julia fought a smile as Cameron looked way more impressed than he should've.

"I've got some additional information from the ranch owner since I last spoke to your colleague at MZB." He handed over another file. "There is a map of the boundary fences, the access to the river, and the best places to fish. He also said that there is an old roadway within the property that used to connect right through to the outskirts of the town, which maybe could be revived?"

Julia opened the folder and looked at the maps. "This is all really helpful. Thank you. Is it possible to take a tour of the boundaries noted here?"

"Yes, of course. I've got permission from the family to access the property and all the relevant keys and codes for the gates." He patted his pocket and gestured at his jeep. "Would you like to come with me, or follow along behind?"

Julia turned to Kaiden and raised her eyebrows.

"What do you think?"

He regarded her impassively and took a long, slow look at the jeep as if assessing its defensive capabilities. "I'll sit in the back."

It wasn't a big ranch. From the style of the fencing and the general layout, Kaiden guessed it had been started about the same time as his own family's place around a hundred and fifty years ago. The Millers had arrived from the East Coast after a long and perilous journey in a wagon train where they'd lost several family members and eventually settled in Morgan Valley alongside the Morgans, the Lymonds, and the Gómezes.

It was also evident that the place was run-down, something that became even more apparent when they pulled into the yard of the ranch house. There were a few chickens about, but no other signs of life. Kaiden made sure to get out of the jeep first so that he could come around and get the door for Julia. Her decision to go along with his bodyguard fantasy was giving him life.

"All clear, Ms. Garcia," he said as he scanned the area.

"Thank you, Miller." She stepped out of the jeep like the queen she was and turned to Cameron. "Does anyone live here right now?"

As if in answer to her question, the front door of the

house creaked open. An extremely old dog came out, cast them an inquiring glance, and lay down on the covered porch like it was far too much effort to bark.

"Can I help you, folks?"

Kaiden looked at the elderly man who had followed the dog out of the house and frowned. The guy looked vaguely familiar.

"Oh, hey, Mr. Evans! How are you doing today?" Cameron advanced toward the old man. "Do you remember me? I came out here with your granddaughter Jackie last week."

"I remember you." Mr. Evans didn't look as if the memory gave him any joy.

"Is it okay if I walk Miss Garcia around the barn and the other structures here?"

"If you like." He turned back toward the door. "Come into the house for a glass of lemonade when you're done."

"Thank you, sir," Julia called out to him, her smile fading as he shut the door. "I feel bad disturbing him."

"Just FYI, I don't think he's very happy about the decision to sell the place." Cameron lowered his voice. "He can't keep it going. His three daughters decided to step in to make sure he has enough money to live on for the rest of his life."

Julia nodded, her expression thoughtful. "That's a tough choice." She pointed at the barn. "Shall we take a look in there?"

Kaiden touched her shoulder as she moved past him.

"Are you okay if I go into the house ahead of you?"

"Sure. I don't think I'm going to be assassinated just yet."

"Tell Cameron I'm checking for bugs or something,"

Kaiden added before heading up the steps to the porch where he paused to pat the dog.

He knocked politely on the door and wasn't surprised when it swung open. Ranch hospitality was usually informal and, as long as he wiped his boots on the mat, he was probably good to proceed.

He found Mr. Evans in the kitchen sitting at the table reading the local newspaper. He glanced up briefly at Kaiden and gestured at the refrigerator. "Lemonade's in there if you'd like some."

"Thank you." Kaiden helped himself. "Excuse me for bothering you, sir, but are you related to a Jennifer Evans Hollister?"

"I have a granddaughter named Jennifer." Mr. Evans looked him up and down. "She's probably around your age."

"I think I know her," Kaiden said slowly. "In fact, I think we dated about ten years ago when we were both taking evening classes at Bridgeport College."

"She did go there to get her associate degree. She's a nurse now. Works in the hospital in Mammoth." Mr. Evans set down his paper. "And what's your name, son?"

"Kaiden Miller."

A brief look of horror passed over Mr. Evans's face. "Not one of Jeff Miller's boys?"

"Yeah, sorry about that." Kaiden had to smile. "I think Jennifer decided to stop dating me the first time she met my dad. I didn't blame her. He's something else."

"I'm glad you said that first, son." Mr. Evans nodded. "He's a hard man to get along with. We had a few spats in the Cattlemen's Association over the years."

Seeing as his dad had been politely asked to leave that organization, Kaiden wasn't surprised to hear that.

Mr. Evans jerked his head in the direction of the door. "What are you doing hanging around with those ghouls?"

"Ghouls?" Kaiden took the chair his host indicated at the table.

"Well, to be fair, I don't know about the lady, but Cameron Stravinsky is working for my daughters, not me."

"You don't want to sell the place?" Kaiden asked.

"Hell no." Mr. Evans sat back. "I don't care how much they think it's worth. It's my home, and I don't want to see it go to strangers."

"I know how you feel. We've had a couple of similar issues in Morgan Valley recently with legacy families either dying out or not having anyone interested in taking the place on. I guess your daughters aren't interested?"

"My middle daughter would take the place on, but her husband and family aren't willing to make the move out here." Mr. Evans grimaced. "It's a damned shame."

"Maybe if you have to sell, you could ask the new owners if you could stay here and run it for them?" Kaiden asked.

"Like I'd want to stay here under those circumstances. I don't want to be a hired hand on the land my father bequeathed to me." Mr. Evans sighed. "It's the first time in my life I ever envied your father anything—having all those boys."

"That brings its own problems," Kaiden said. "Dad decided to leave it all to Adam, which means the rest of us are out of luck."

"Sounds just like Jeff. Is your brother going to make you all leave?"

"No, he's already promised we can either stay and build

our own places on the ranch or he'll buy us out. He's a good guy."

"It's not the same though, is it? You're no longer part of the land."

Kaiden took a long drink of his lemonade as he considered that painful truth and tried to make the best of it. "Yeah, I suppose I've never thought of the place as mine anyway—what with being the third son, and my dad looking like he would go on forever. But, he recently had a mild heart attack, and the world feels like a very different place right now."

"I'm sorry to hear that, Kaiden. Give him my best, won't you?"

"I will." Kaiden finished his lemonade. "Can your daughters sell the place if you don't want them to?"

"Pretty much." Mr. Evans scowled. "A couple of years ago I had prostate cancer, and I made the decision to set up a trust with my girls having power of attorney so they could make medical choices for me. Since the damn disease has come back, they keep telling me it's for my own good, that I'll have less to worry about while I recover, but what's the point of recovering if my ranch is gone?"

Kaiden grimaced. "I hear you. I'm still not sure they can sell the place from under you. Maybe you should talk to another lawyer?"

"I suppose I should. Is Henry still working in Morgantown?"

"Yeah, he is."

"Then maybe I'll give him a call. I trust him." Mr. Evans gave a decisive nod. "They keep telling me this place is worth millions, but I don't see it myself. Maybe if they try and sell it and can't, they'll get off my back and leave me alone."

Kaiden raised his empty glass. "Here's to that." The kitchen door opened and Cameron came through with Julia. "Hey, would you guys like some lemonade? It's really good."

Julia glanced over at Kaiden as they pulled away from the ranch. He hadn't said much as they'd toured the house, but she'd noticed his hand lingering on the carved finials of the staircase, and his appreciation for the wide, plank flooring saved from the original house, which had been built over a century before.

"Mr. Evans doesn't want to sell the ranch," Kaiden finally spoke.

"So I gathered." Julia kept her tone neutral. "But I understand he has recurrent cancer. His family wants him closer to town so he can get his treatments done, and his eldest daughter can keep an eye on him."

"So he has to move out to keep everyone else happy?"

"If it makes sense for the family, then yes."

"You'd make your dad move out of the home he loves if he was sick?" Kaiden asked.

"That's totally not a fair thing to say. The situations are totally different." She glared at him, but he kept his profile averted. "Why are you taking this so personally?"

"Why wouldn't I? Mr. Evans is dealing with exactly the same kind of shit as half the ranchers in this part of the world. And who's going to buy his ranch? Some billionaire from the Bay Area who wants a second home in the countryside?" Kaiden snorted. "What's a person like that going to contribute to the community? Nothing."

Julia had never felt less like walking the corporate line than she did right now. With her father in a similar, precarious position, her sympathies were all with the ranchers.

"Progress and change can hurt people."

This time he did look at her, and she wished he hadn't. "That's it? That's all you've got?"

She raised her chin. "Kaiden, I'm not sure why you're yelling at me. I'm just the representative of one of several companies that are looking at this real estate opportunity. I'm not single-handedly bringing down the whole of the ranching community."

He went silent on her and kept it up as they drove back to Morgan Valley.

Great, after asking him to come with her to reestablish their friendship, she'd simply widened the gap and reminded them both of all the reasons why they would never get along. She stared out the window and tried to enjoy the scenery, aware that in a few precious days she would be in her apartment in the city and back at work.

The thought of leaving him tore at her heart.

When they reached her home, he parked and offered her a brief smile.

"Give your dad my best, okay?"

"You're not coming in with me?" Julia asked.

He raised an eyebrow. "Why would I?"

"To see how the work is progressing, to say hi to my dad?" Julia intentionally didn't mention herself.

"I'll check in tomorrow if I have time."

She reached for the door handle. "Okay, I'm sure you must be tired after having come all that way to help me."

"As I said, that's just what we do for our neighbors around here."

Seconds ticked by as Kaiden drummed his fingers on the steering wheel and Julia studied her hands. For someone who was so keen to leave, he seemed damned reluctant to go. Julia gathered her courage.

"For some reason you seem to have decided that I'm the bad guy in all of this, and you're obviously still mad at me."

"Why would I ever be mad at you? I just had the best sex of my life!"

"We agreed—"

He cut her off. "Yeah, we did, so why don't you just say good-bye and get out of my truck?"

"Because I'm trying to make things right, here. I don't want—" She struggled to find the right words through an increasing sense of hurt.

"You don't want what?"

"I don't want to leave things between us on a bad note," Julia said. "I . . . wanted today to be about setting things right, not making them worse, and I'm sorry."

He stared out at the barn for a long moment, his face uncharacteristically somber. "You're right. I'm being an ass. It isn't your fault." He let out a breath. "We're good, okay? No hard feelings, we had a great time together, and we're still friends."

"Are you sure?" Julia asked hesitantly.

"Absolutely." He offered her another smile that didn't reach his eyes. "If I don't see you before you leave, Julia, take care. I'll keep in touch about how the work is going."

There didn't seem to be anything left to say. She opened the door of the truck and stepped down. Kaiden didn't even wait for her to close the door, but reached across and did it himself. He turned the truck in a circle and headed back down the drive with a final wave, which felt very final.

Julia stood where she was way longer than necessary, with some stupid hope that he'd turn around, come back, and agree with her that what they had together was way too important to let go. But he wouldn't do that, would he? They'd both made it abundantly clear they had no chance of a relationship, and the awful thing—the really awful thing—was that they were both still one hundred percent right.

Chapter Sixteen

By the time Kaiden had done his chores, apologized to Danny, and taken a much-needed shower he was late for dinner. He arrived at the table to find the rest of his family including his father eating chicken casserole. Jeff looked like some kind of survivor grimly clinging to a piece of driftwood, but at least he was upright and apparently mobile.

"Hey." Kaiden nodded to him. "Glad to see you up and about."

"Did you find the Garcia girl?"

"Yeah, the tire and the spare on her dad's truck went flat, and she had to take shelter in one of the hunting cabins up there." Kaiden went to get the extra iced tea out of the refrigerator. "I ended up using my spare on her truck so we could get back."

His dad waited until he took his seat and helped himself to a plate of food. "Took you that long to change a tire?"

"Nope, it was too dark to see when I got up there and starting to rain so I did it this morning. I followed the truck back to the Garcia place to make sure she made it home."

Kaiden kept his gaze on the glass as he poured himself some iced tea.

"So where have you been all day?"

"I took Julia into Bridgeport. She had an appointment. I didn't think her dad's truck was going to make it."

"There's no need to interrogate him, Jeff. I told you where he was." Leanne leaned over and took her ex-husband's hand. "He's not a child."

"He still works for me. I have a right to know where he is, when he's leaving his chores for his brothers to do."

"It's not a problem, Dad," Danny spoke up. "Kaiden did all my stuff when I was at college the other week. It all comes out even."

Kaiden set his fork down and slowly looked up at his father, unaccustomed anger churning in his gut. "If you really think I'm not pulling my weight around here, why don't you just fire me?"

Danny put his hand on Kaiden's arm. "Kaiden . . ."

"Maybe I should." Jeff met his stare head-on. "I sure don't like your attitude right now, Son."

"Then let's consider it a done deal, shall we?" Kaiden looked around at the stunned faces at the table. "We all good with that?"

Adam frowned. "Hell no, we aren't." He turned to their father. "What's wrong with you? You're out of commission, I need all the help I can get to keep this place running, and you're firing your own son?"

Jeff shrugged. "He's the one who suggested it. I'm just following along."

"Then maybe you could tell him you'd like him to stay?" Adam suggested. "Make him feel like he's a valued and appreciated member of our family?"

"If he doesn't know that by now, there's nothing I can

say to convince him otherwise." Jeff shrugged. "He's had a bee in his bonnet ever since that Garcia girl turned up, and because he's too much of a wuss to do anything about it, he takes it out on me."

"Bullshit," Kaiden snapped. "My problems with you go back way longer than that. And, by the way, she's not a girl, she's a woman, and she has a goddam name."

"Look," Adam said in a calm voice. "I don't know what's going on between you two right now, but this isn't the place to have it out." He glared at both of them. "This is why Lizzie won't come and live with me. She doesn't want Roman having to deal with all this crap every day."

"Also bullshit." Kaiden stood and tossed his napkin on the table. "Lizzie won't come live up here because she's scared of losing her independence, any fool can see that."

Adam opened his mouth and then closed it again as Kaiden grabbed his plate and left the table. He knew that at some point he'd have to make his peace with his big brother, but right now, after the day he'd just had, he wasn't in the mood to deal with anyone.

He went into his bedroom and locked the door, glad for once that Ben wasn't there to barge in on him, but also kind of wishing that he was. They were very different, but Ben had always had a way of cutting through the crap and bringing Kaiden back down to earth.

He managed to force down his food and set the empty plate beside his bed. There were no messages on his phone or texts so it looked like no one needed him. He checked his thread of texts from Julia one more time, but there was nothing new. He glanced over at his pillow. God, he wished she were there right now, smiling back at him, begging him to make love to her. . . .

The door to the bathroom banged open and Kaiden glared at his dad.

"What do you want?"

"I've thought things over, and with Evan stepping up, I don't need you to work for me on the ranch, okay?"

For a weird second, Kaiden felt like someone had just pushed him off a cliff.

"Fine, then."

"Good."

His father turned around and made his way back out into the hallway shouting at Leanne for more coffee. Kaiden sank down onto the side of the bed and stared at the open door. He hadn't thought his day could get much worse, but somehow he'd managed it. He'd said good-bye to Julia, pissed off his father, and lost his job at the ranch.

For the first time in ages he felt like all the tethers that bound him to Morgan Valley had been broken. He could leave now, he could move to the Bay Area, set up as a carpenter, and see Julia whenever the hell he wanted. So, why did he feel like his whole world had crashed around him and he was suffocating?

Julia's father smiled at her as she came into the family room. She'd been so busy answering his questions about what had happened up at the cabins and catching up on housework that she'd managed not to think that much about Kaiden for hours.

"There you are, Julia. I asked Beth Baker to come and see me this evening to talk about the job. You'll probably have some good questions for her, and you can talk about her salary and hours. She seemed really keen on the idea."

Julia shoved all her muddled thoughts to the back of

her mind. Sometimes it was better to suggest something to her father, let him raise his objections, and then leave him to make up his own mind.

"That's great! I think you're going to like her a lot."

Juan nodded. "I can't see why I wouldn't. The Bakers are good people."

"What time is she coming?" Julia asked.

"Around seven. Ted's bringing her. Veronica is minding all the kids."

"Cool, I'll text him and ask if he can bring a new tire for the truck so I can return Kaiden Miller's to him." She turned to the door. "I'd better make a start on dinner if Beth's coming over."

"No need. Bernie left us a casserole from his wife," Juan said. "It's in the oven right now."

"That's so kind of him." Julia grimaced. "I'm sorry I wasn't here all day."

"I told you to go to Bridgeport," Juan reminded her. "I'm more than happy to see you spending time with Kaiden. He's a good boy."

"He's . . ." Julia sighed. "Definitely that."

"You two an item now?" Juan asked hopefully.

"With me going back to San Francisco and him living here?" Julia forced a laugh. "So not happening."

"Maybe it's a sign that you should stay here, Daughter," her father suggested. "I've seen the way that boy looks at you. One word, and he'd be all yours."

"Maybe he'll still be around when I retire," Julia joked. She'd already decided there was no point trying to argue her side again. "And I can come back here, and live my best life."

"That won't give me grandchildren," her father

grumbled. "Between you and Miguel, I will never have the pleasure of holding the next generation of Garcias in my arms."

"You never know, Dad," Julia said. "Miguel is always full of surprises."

She left the room before she said something that would clue her dad into realizing how much she'd come to care for Kaiden. The thing was, it felt like Kaiden was *already* hers. That despite everything, all the disagreements, the teasing, the sheer Kaiden Millerness of him, he was her perfect match. And it wasn't as if they both didn't know that, which somehow made everything worse.

She checked the timer and took the casserole out before calling for her dad to come and eat. Bernie had even put some baked potatoes in the oven to go with their meal so she didn't have to do a thing. She'd been amazed to see how far the work had progressed on the master bathroom in the twenty-four hours she'd been away. Mike said it would be ready for use in two days, which was just before she had to go back to work.

He'd even managed to stick to her budget, which made her really thankful because the thought of going into debt always frightened her. The quicker she could make enough money to retire comfortably, the happier she would be.

Just before she set the table, she checked her phone. Kaiden hadn't texted or called, which told her everything she needed to know. What was there left to say that hadn't already been said? She glanced around the familiar room. Would he fulfill his promise to build her father a new kitchen, or would he designate it to someone else? She reminded herself that with her absence, he would be free to visit the ranch without worry. As long as she kept paying everyone's bills no one would miss her at all.

"Kaiden . . ."

Kaiden looked up to see Adam leaning against the doorway of the tack room and deliberately turned his back on him.

"It's okay, just don't expect me to be up doing this tomorrow night. I'm not trying to take anyone else's job."

His brother's sigh was loud enough to hear without him turning around.

"Look, we both know that Dad can be a real dick sometimes, but that doesn't mean you have to be one too."

Kaiden finished cleaning the halter and went to hang it back on its designated hook. He'd come out to the barn after trying to get to sleep for an hour intending to work off some of his frustrations. He wanted to punch something, or yell, feelings so unusual for him that he didn't know what to do with them. He should've known that someone from his way too invested family would track him down for a little chat.

Adam obviously didn't know when to shut up because he kept talking.

"I get why you're frustrated with Dad, but he's still sick, Kaiden. Can you just give him a break for once?"

"For once?" Kaiden finally faced his brother. "Come on, Adam, we've been making fricking excuses for that man our entire lives. He'd already made up his mind that he wanted me out of here, so don't try and lay this all on me."

Adam's brow creased. "I don't follow."

"He left the ranch to you. He's got Mom back even if it

is on her own terms, Evan's finally on board, Danny's got the qualifications to take us forward, so why the hell does he need me hanging around?"

Kaiden couldn't quite believe what he'd just said, and how easily it rolled off his tongue. Had he secretly been resenting everyone all along?

"Because you're his favorite son?" Adam wasn't backing down. "Because you've always been the one who's been able to get through to him?"

"I get it." Kaiden shrugged. "I'm useful to everyone else, but maybe that's not who I want to be anymore."

Adam straightened, his frown deepening. "I guess I didn't realize you felt like that about helping your own family."

"Maybe it suited you not to see it as long as I toed the line and took the hits for everyone."

"That's not fair," Adam retorted. "We all took our hits, Kaiden. They just never seemed to bother you as much."

"Yeah, because I'm so thick-skinned, right? Good old Kaiden will just laugh it off. . . ." He shook his head. "Can we stop this? I need to go to bed. I have a lot to do in the morning." He went to push past Adam, but his brother didn't budge an inch and he was built like a linebacker.

"What you said about Lizzie—" Adam paused.

"This is why you're really mad at me, isn't it?" Kaiden stared into his brother's eyes. "Because I said something about Lizzie that was staring you in the face and you refused to acknowledge it."

"I'd never stop her being independent, you know that."

"Look, any fool can see that she's worked hard to get herself to a place where she can support herself and her kid. She's proud of that."

"I'm proud of her too."

"Then why can't you see that if she gives it all up to come and live here for your benefit, that would make her feel vulnerable?"

"But, we love each other!"

"Sometimes love isn't enough," Kaiden said.

"You think we should continue to live separate lives? Me here, and her down there? How the hell is that supposed to work?" Adam demanded.

"Have you ever considered moving 'down there'?"

The flash of shock on his brother's face told Kaiden everything he needed to know.

"How could I run the ranch from Morgantown?" Adam asked.

"So you're saying that what you do is more important than what Lizzie does? But you expect her to run the café, get Roman to school, and take on whatever you want her to do at the ranch without complaint?"

"Don't be stupid."

It took a lot to rile up his big brother, but Kaiden was doing an excellent job of it.

"You're just talking out of your ass now."

"How would that make you feel, Adam?" Kaiden refused to shut up. "If you were stuck in town, with a whole new routine, no family around you, and the knowledge that sometimes relationships don't always work out, and you might have to move again? Wouldn't you feel a tad vulnerable?"

Adam's hands fisted, and for a second Kaiden wondered if he was about to get his just desserts. He almost wanted his brother to hit him, God knew why.

"When is Julia Garcia going back to San Francisco?"

It was Kaiden's turn to blink like a fool. "What the hell does that have to do with anything I just said?"

"Because Dad's right. I've seen how you look at her. We all have. You're pissed because you can't be with her, and you're taking it out on us." Adam took a step back so Kaiden could get past him and held up his hands. "Maybe you should take your own advice, Bro, and leave here, and go live with her."

Kaiden let that low punch sink in and then offered his brother a ferocious smile. "You first, okay?"

He walked away knowing that he'd hurt his brother's feelings. For the first time in his life, he was unwilling to laugh it off and apologize. Maybe because he was at odds with Julia he was seeing his own family more clearly than usual. As the old saying went, two wrongs didn't make a right. If he was upset about Julia, Adam was still definitely in the wrong about Lizzie.

Chapter Seventeen

"I've set up a couple of meetings for you with some small developers this week." Miley handed Julia a fresh cup of coffee and a couple of files. "The actual meetings are already in your calendar, but I know you like to have stuff to read in your hand as well."

"Too much screen time gives me migraines," Julia said. "This is for my personal information only, right?"

"Yep, I scheduled them during your lunch breaks so you won't really be on company time." Miley perched on the corner of Julia's desk. "You look tired. Is Blaine driving you up the wall?"

"He's been surprisingly quiet this week," Julia mused. "Like he's up to something."

She'd been back at work for three weeks having successfully avoided Kaiden while overseeing the completion of the master bath and installing Beth as her father's housekeeper. She'd promised her dad she'd be back once a month to check on everything, and she intended to keep her word.

The fact that she'd spent most nights missing Kaiden

and meticulously running their night together through her head was irrelevant. She hadn't done much more than have drinks and dinner with her two best girl pals where she'd tried not to share too much about her shattered love life. It was still too personal and too close to share with anyone yet.

"Blaine's a snake. And I don't like the way he's always in Melanie's office." Miley was still opinionating. "It's creepy as hell. She's old enough to be his mother."

Julia definitely didn't want to go there so she changed the subject. "Mr. Bashear is coming in from New York next week for his annual review of our branch of the company. If you can coordinate with his PA and get me some face time with him, I'd love you forever."

"Mr. B of MZB himself?" Miley fanned herself. "Do you know him?"

"He's the one who hired me. We've always gotten along."

"Maybe he'll promote you and take you back to New York," Miley speculated. "Where you'll definitely need a really cute almost up-and-coming young lawyer to keep you company."

Julia grinned. "I wonder who that might be? If you can avoid mentioning me trying to meet with Mr. Bashear to Melanie and Blaine I'd appreciate it."

"Like I'd tell them anything." Miley stood up. "Do you want to come out for lunch in about an hour with the good part of the team?"

Julia looked at the files stacked on her desk. "I think I'll be working through lunch. It's tough when I have to do all my work and my boss's as well."

"It sucks and I don't care who hears me say that," Miley said. "Maybe I'll mention it to Mr. B myself."

Julia was just about to start work when her cell phone buzzed. She picked it up and saw a text from Silver, which immediately raised her heart rate.

> Hope you'll be back for our party next weekend!
> We're expecting you!

Julia hesitated over her reply.

> Do you really want me there? What with the Kaiden thing?

To her surprise, Silver had turned out to be someone who refused to accept that Julia didn't need a friend. She regularly texted Julia with tidbits of gossip about Morgan Valley, updates on the formation of the heritage foundation, and even the occasional mention of Kaiden, who had apparently been setting the Miller family on fire.

> According to Ben, Kaiden's still being an ass.
> Apparently he's now insisting on paying rent to live at the ranch and is looking for his own place.

When Silver had told Julia about Kaiden being fired by his father, she'd wanted to contact him so desperately that she'd handed her phone over to Miley for an entire weekend. She didn't understand what was going on, but she had a feeling that if she had been there he would've talked to her.

Silver continued.

> We don't even know if he's going to come to the wedding party. ☹

> I'm sure he will. He's got no issues with Ben.

But you will come regardless, right? I really want you
to be there.

Sure, Julia typed. I can't wait.

Awesome!!! Avery Morgan will send you all the
information. It's being held at Morgan Ranch because
they have more space. My family is flying in from LA.
Gotta go, cow needs milking! x

The thought of Silver milking a cow was enough to
make Julia smile before her thoughts returned to Kaiden.
Whatever was going on with him was worrying her. She
yearned to contact him, but what good would it do? If she
went back to Morgan Valley and happened to see him
around, maybe she could get a sense of how he was feeling
and at least talk it through. He'd wanted them to remain
friends. She could at least do that for him.

She put her phone away in the drawer before she gave
in to temptation to text and ask him what the hell was
going on. He *loved* his family, he always had, and they
loved him right back, so why were they currently at war?

Kaiden smoothed his hand over the wood and stood
back to gauge whether the surface was level. It was a lot
quieter up at the Garcia Ranch than it had been a week ago
when Bernie, Mike, and their crews had been remodeling
the bathrooms. That had all been completed now leaving
Kaiden to deal with the kitchen.

Beth moved past him to get at the newly installed stove.
"Sorry, Kaiden. I'll be out of your way in a minute."

"No apologies necessary." He smiled at her. "I'm the

one who's getting in the way here. I've just got this bit to finish up, and I'll be done for the day."

"Are you going to the party next Saturday?"

"I've been invited," Kaiden said as he put his spirit level away.

"Well, of course you have. Ben's your brother." Beth smiled at him. "I think pretty much the whole town has been invited alongside you."

"Yeah, Ben and Silver like to go big or go home," Kaiden agreed. "It's going to be one hell of a party."

"Wes is looking forward to it."

"He's planning on going?" Kaiden looked up. "I wouldn't have thought it was his kind of thing."

"Oh, he loves dressing up." Beth grinned. "And I think he's got a bit of a crush on Julia, so he's hoping she's coming, too. Do you know if she is?"

"I've no idea." Kaiden shrugged like the thought of seeing her again wasn't giving him life. "You should ask your boss."

"Juan says she was definitely invited." Beth set the covered dish on the table. "I just wondered whether she'd said anything more definite to you, personally. Wes seems to think you are his main competition."

"Wes is—" Kaiden paused, remembering he was talking to his apprentice's adopted mother. "Welcome to try his luck."

"Like she'd pick him over you." Beth chuckled. "Poor Wes." She flicked the tea towel at him. "I think Julia's already made her choice."

"Yeah, well, she's in San Francisco, and I'm here, so I can't see that working out, can you?" Kaiden pocketed his tape measure and set about putting his stuff back into his toolbox.

"Some people make long distance relationships work," Beth said. "Look at Chase and January."

"Sure helps being a multimillionaire with a private jet," Kaiden muttered. "Not all of us can manage that."

"What's up, Kaiden?" She studied him intently. "You're usually one of the most positive people I've ever met. Now, you can barely manage a smile."

He shrugged and focused on what he was doing, hoping she'd take the hint and stop asking him stuff.

"Are you worried about your dad?" Unfortunately, Beth kept talking.

"He's doing much better. Dr. Tio says he can start doing some basic ranch work next week."

"Then if it isn't him, what is it?"

Kaiden stared at her. "Why does it matter?"

She put her hands on her hips. "Because I like you? Because you've sorted Wes out, and you got me this job, and I wish I could help you?"

"I'm just . . ." He shoved a hand through his hair. "Changing stuff up right now, and it's hard, okay?"

"I get that. I had to make some difficult decisions myself a couple of years ago." She hesitated. "Are you sure this doesn't have anything to do with Julia Garcia?"

He picked up his toolbox. "We've already talked about that, and there's nothing left to say. She's gone, I'm here, and that's the end of it."

Beth rolled her eyes. "So, basically, you've decided to be stubborn."

"Yup." He set his Stetson on his head. "I'll just put this away in my truck and come back for the rest of my stuff."

He walked out through the mudroom, put his boots on, and stalked over to his truck. The problem with living in the place where you were born was that everyone knew you too well and thought they should give you advice all the time. Beth wasn't the first well-meaning person who'd tried to help him, and she probably wouldn't be the last.

He glanced up as an unfamiliar car came bouncing up the rutted driveway and stopped behind his truck. It looked like a rental, and for a second Kaiden wondered if Julia had come back early. The thrill that thought gave him indicated that despite everything he kept telling himself, he still wasn't over her.

A guy got out, shut his door, and turned a slow circle before finally seeming to notice Kaiden was there.

"Hey. Long time no see."

Kaiden blinked hard. "Miguel?"

"Yeah." He came forward, his hand extended to shake Kaiden's, his eyes hidden behind dark glasses. He wore a leather jacket with military badges on it and khaki pants. "Good to see you, Kai. Is my old man around?"

"He's inside." Kaiden gestured vaguely at the house. "What brings you back here?"

"Family business." Miguel set off for the house and Kaiden followed him. "No need for you to announce me."

"I dunno, maybe I should," Kaiden said. "I don't want to stress your dad out. I don't think he's expecting you, or he would have said something."

Miguel paused in the doorway. "May I ask what you're doing here?"

"I'm remodeling the kitchen. I'm sure Julia told you about it," Kaiden said. "Since your dad's MS has gotten a lot worse he needed the place to be wheelchair accessible."

"Oh, that's right. Julia did mention it."

Miguel went to push past Kaiden, but he refused to budge.

"Seeing as we're asking questions right now, Mig, does Julia know you're here?"

"Definitely. I was just talking to her." Miguel shrugged and took off his sunglasses to reveal his cold brown eyes and a scar that ran diagonally across his forehead. "She's certainly been nagging me to visit Dad."

Kaiden stepped out of the way, aware that Miguel was army trained and perfectly capable of breaking his neck, and that he really had no right barring the man's way into his own home. But something felt wrong and all the hackles on his neck had risen.

Beth's screech had him chasing after Miguel into the kitchen.

"Is everything okay?"

"Oh, my goodness, he startled me!" Beth clutched the tea towel to her chest and stared over Miguel's shoulder at Kaiden. "I'm so sorry."

Miguel looked her up and down. "It's Beth Baker, right?"

"Yes," she said, nodding rapidly. "Sorry, I just turned around, and there you were. . . ."

"It's all good." Miguel's attention was already moving on. "I've come to see my father. Is he in the family room?"

"Yes, he was just about to take his afternoon nap." Beth edged toward the door. "I'll go and see if he's awake, and tell him he has a special visitor."

After Beth almost ran from the room, Miguel turned to Kaiden.

"Why's she so jumpy?"

Kaiden wasn't about to share Beth's personal history with Miguel.

"Have you seen yourself in the mirror recently, dude? You look like an assassin."

The corners of Miguel's mouth flicked up in what might have been a smile. "So I've been told." He unbuttoned his jacket. "Looks like you're doing a nice job on the new kitchen. What are you, a plumber now?"

"Carpenter." Kaiden wasn't going to let Miguel get a rise out of him. "Kitchens are my specialty but I do a lot of restoring old buildings as well."

"Plenty of those around here, although from what I hear, Morgan Valley is thriving."

"Who told you that?"

"Lots of people." Miguel shrugged. "I took a drive down Main Street before I came out to the ranch and I was impressed. Lots of new buildings and no boarded-up shop fronts, which is rare in this part of the world."

"We're doing okay," Kaiden said cautiously. "You thinking about finally moving back?"

"Me? Hell, no."

Beth came back in and Miguel nodded at Kaiden as he walked toward the family room.

"Nice talking to you, Kai. You take care now."

"I'll bring you some coffee," Beth called after Miguel.

"Thanks, I could use some."

Kaiden barely waited until Miguel was out of earshot before he locked gazes with Beth, who looked uncharacteristically worried. He lowered his voice.

"Look, I know this is none of our business, but if you could keep an eye on him, and let me know what's going on, I'd appreciate it."

"I've never liked Miguel. He's bad news." Beth wrapped her arms around herself. "If I find out anything I'll definitely let you know, okay?"

Kaiden was still thinking about Miguel as he pulled up his truck at home and got out. He was tempted to text Julia to let her know her brother had turned up, but Miguel had said she knew, and he didn't want to get in the middle of anything. He was having enough problems with his own family to want to dive in and disrupt hers and make things worse between them.

Even as he made the decision not to interfere, he still got out his phone and pulled up her number. His call was immediately put through to voice mail and he hesitated again. Was there any point in leaving a message? She'd probably ignore it anyway.

Unfortunately, he'd arrived home earlier than planned, which was awkward because he wasn't really on good terms with anyone right now and had started spending as much time as possible in his room. He entered the house, took off his boots in the mudroom, and walked through to the kitchen where of course his dad was sitting at the table.

Kaiden nodded at him and went to get himself some coffee. As far as he knew, Evan was now doing his ranch work, and that was just fine with him. He tried to keep out of all the discussions about the ranch, which meant he often ate his meals in silence.

Auntie Rae had gone home and Leanne was staying until Jeff had his final clearance from the hospital, which was expected a week after the party.

"How's the kitchen going at the Garcias?"

Kaiden turned to look at his father, who had his tablet out in front of him and was playing some brightly colored game. To his knowledge it was the first time his dad had asked him a direct question in three weeks.

"Great."

He added cream to his coffee and stirred it slowly.

"When do you think you'll be done?"

"I'm not sure."

"Leanne went into town to pick up my prescriptions and see Lizzie about something so she said she'll bring pizza and wings back from Gina's."

"Okay." Kaiden mopped up the countertop and then went toward his father. "Here's my rent." He dug in his pocket and pulled out a wad of bills.

"I don't want your stupid money," Jeff snapped.

"Too bad." Kaiden tossed it onto the table. "I don't work here anymore so I can't pay you back that way."

"Yeah, well, as to that." His father shut the lid of his tablet. "Maybe I was too hasty."

Kaiden shook his head. "I'm not playing this game, Dad. I'm taking a shower. When I come back I'll set the table for dinner."

He walked out, aware that he really wasn't in the mood to tangle with his father again, and walked straight into Adam.

"Hey, can I talk to you?"

Kaiden repressed a sigh. "I'm just about to take a shower."

"It'll only take a minute."

"Fine." Kaiden went down the hallway to his bedroom, opened the door, and walked over to the window. "Shoot."

Adam leaned back against the closed door. "I talked to Lizzie."

"Okay."

"She basically said everything that you did."

Kaiden didn't know how he was supposed to respond to that so he just nodded.

"She's scared that if she gives everything up for me, and things go south again, then she'll be left picking up the pieces." Adam cleared his throat. "I tried to tell her that will never happen, but I do understand where's she's coming from. I haven't exactly been reliable. I mean, you don't go into a marriage expecting your wife to die at twenty-one of inoperable brain cancer, but that happened, and just to make things worse, I lost Lizzie as well."

Kaiden winced.

"So, we've decided to try something different. She'll keep her apartment for six months and we'll try it both ways. Her living up here and commuting back into town for the first month, and then me doing the reverse for a month."

"Hold up—you're going to move down to *Morgantown*?" Kaiden asked.

"Isn't that what you told me I should do?" Adam raised his eyebrows. "Lizzie was originally suggesting that she was the only person who should be making the monthly move, and I said it should be both of us."

Kaiden stared at his big brother. "That's . . . pretty awesome of you both."

"Roman's okay with it too," Adam added. "We sat him down together and explained everything, and he totally got it."

"Have you told Dad yet?"

Adam looked down at his boots. "I thought we'd wait until after the big party and his final checkup at the hospital."

"Makes sense." Kaiden nodded. "You know he's going to hate it?"

"Good." Adam's elusive smile appeared. "Maybe it will take some of the heat off you."

"I made my own bed," Kaiden reminded him. "I don't need you to save me."

"Yeah, I forgot you made that very clear." His brother's smile disappeared and he straightened up. "You don't need or like any of us right now, period."

He grabbed the door handle. "I just wanted to let you know that even though I didn't like what you said at the time, it kind of stuck in my side like a saddle burr. When Lizzie approached me with her plan, it all suddenly made sense, so thanks."

"You should thank Lizzie, she's the smart one around here," Kaiden said.

Adam opened the door. "She got some help from Julia, of all people. She said that having someone talk everything through with her from a new perspective really helped."

"Julia's good at that."

"So it seems. Is she coming back for the party next Saturday?"

"I've no idea." Kaiden undid his shirt. "Mom's bringing pizza back, so I need to get a shower and go help set up the kitchen."

"Okay, thanks again." Adam finally left.

"Why does everyone keep asking me about Julia?" Kaiden muttered as he stripped off his T-shirt and turned on the shower. "Like I'd know?"

All he had to do was send her a text, and ask. . . .

Kaiden stripped off the rest of his clothes and stepped under the hot spray. And, if he did that, he'd be right back where he didn't want to be. Wanting something he couldn't have, and even more miserable than he was already.

Chapter Eighteen

"Good morning, this is Julia Garcia, how may I help you?"

Julia uncapped her pen and found a legal pad just in case she needed to make notes. She had to record every billable second.

"*Julia? Esta es tu madre, Lupita.*"

For a second she couldn't find any words in either of the languages she'd grown up speaking. "*Mama? Esta todo bien?*"

"*Si, querida. Todo esta bien.*"

"Did you forget my cell phone number?" Julia gave up on attempting that in Spanish.

"*No, mi hija.* I wanted to call you here—if that's all right." Her mother switched back to English.

"It's totally fine, what can I do for you?"

"I had a letter asking whether I still had any financial interest in the Garcia Ranch."

"From whom?"

There was a rustling sound as if her mother was opening up the letter. "Your law firm. That's why I used this number."

"I didn't send you a letter." Julia frowned. "Who signed it?"

"There is no signature." Lupita paused. "The thing is, what do you want me to do? Should I answer it?"

"No, please don't," Julia said firmly. "I'll find out what's going on, and who sent it."

"I don't believe I have any interest in the ranch. I told your father that if there was anything owed, I'd leave it to you."

"Dad told me he'd left the whole thing to Miguel."

Her mother sighed. "It wouldn't surprise me even though he must know that Miguel is temperamentally unsuitable to be a rancher. But, your father and I never got divorced so I suspect the legal situation might be more complicated than he realizes. If you find out who sent the letter, will you let me know? I don't like loose ends."

"I will." Julia nodded even though her mother couldn't see her. "How's everything else with you?"

"Good, actually. The clinic is busy, but not over-whelmed, and that's just how I like it."

"Anything you need supply-wise?"

Lupita laughed. "You know me, Daughter. I'll take any-thing you've got."

"I'll check out your website and see what I can do," Julia promised. Her mother's clinic survived on gifts and donations from various charities and individuals.

"Okay. I'd better go. Clinic starts in five minutes and there's already a line. Stay well, *querida*. I love you very much."

"And I you. Bye, Mom."

Lupita ended the call and Julia stayed where she was, imagining her mother opening up the doors of her clinic in the bright sunlight and lush greenery. She knew that having made the call, Lupita would immediately put it out of her mind and focus on the thing she loved best: caring for others. Her passion and need to make a difference in the world had taken her a long way from Garcia Ranch. As an adult, Julia was in awe of her determination; as a child she'd wondered why her mother loved other kids more than her.

But who had sent the letter? Julia rose from her seat and went into the outer office where Miley and some of the other team members worked. Everyone looked up as she appeared and stared at her.

"This is going to sound weird, but did any of you recently write a letter to a medical clinic in Guatemala?"

Miley glanced around and then shook her head like everyone else.

"Is something up, boss?"

"Nothing that needs to worry anyone," Julia assured them. She beckoned to Miley to follow her back into her office and close the door.

"The only person I know who has a clinic in Guatemala is your mom," Miley said. "Why would someone be writing to her if they weren't you?"

"That's the million-dollar question." Julia grimaced. "I have my suspicions, but I definitely can't prove them."

"I assume it's got something to do with Blaine?" Miley suggested. "How would he know about your mom?"

Julia shrugged. "He came out to the ranch. Maybe my dad mentioned her or something. But why would he contact her?"

"Maybe he's looking for dirt on you?"

"Like what?" Julia stared at her paralegal. "That I occasionally use the office mailing department to send her stuff without paying the postage?"

"I wouldn't put it past him." Miley tapped her fingers against her mouth. "How about you leave it with me? I'm kind of friends with his admin because she hates his guts? She might be willing to tell me if she wrote that letter for him."

"Would you?" Julia asked. "I'd really appreciate it."

"Sure, and I'll keep it to myself, all right?" Miley nodded and turned to the door. "She's not in today, because Blaine is out. I'll try and talk to her tomorrow."

"Where's Blaine?"

"Good question." Miley stopped walking. "I'll find that out as well."

Julia sat down at her desk again and struggled to get her thoughts in order. She had to write a presentation for Blaine to give to Mr. Bashear at the end of the week summarizing their last quarter. Blaine had explicitly told her to make him look good, but Julia wasn't sure it was possible. He spent most of his time wining and dining clients, and very little either managing his team, or putting in the hard work of actually setting out his legal arguments.

For some reason, Melanie, who was usually tough on all her team, let him get away with it. Unsettled by the call from her mother, Julia walked over to stare out her window at the other tall buildings that surrounded her office. Far below her, in the dark shadows cast by the skyscrapers, the traffic looked sluggish and small—not that San Francisco could rival most cityscapes having way too many earthquakes to build really high.

If she couldn't get herself together she'd have to work late tonight again. With a sigh, she returned to her desk.

She had dinner arranged with the small-town developer she'd liked most from the ones Miley had contacted. They were bringing her a series of plans and suggestions about making the transition from ranchland to housing far less stressful and invasive while being respectful of the land and its heritage. She wasn't sure if Morgan Valley would ever need the information, but she definitely wanted to share it with Silver and Ben for their heritage foundation.

Miley had also secured her a one-on-one breakfast meeting with Mr. Bashear at his hotel so no one at MZB would even know they'd met. The fact that he'd agreed to it had made Julia hope that whatever Melanie and Blaine had been saying about her hadn't impacted his appreciation of her talents.

She opened her laptop and stared at the half-completed document extolling Blaine's talents and pulled out her notes. If there was ever a prize for fiction at her job, she'd be a shoo-in.

Kaiden paused at the kitchen door, his toolbox in his hand, and checked to see who was there before entering. Beth came through the door with an empty tray and smiled when she saw him.

"Hey. I wondered if you'd be coming in today."

"Why wouldn't I?" Kaiden lowered his voice. "Is Miguel still here?"

"He stayed the night. Some guy came and picked him up this morning, and they went out together. He didn't say if he planned to come back, and he hasn't left anything in his bedroom."

Knowing Miguel's secretive habits, Kaiden wasn't surprised by any of that.

"How's it been going?"

Beth started unloading the new dishwasher. "Juan's absolutely thrilled to see him."

"I bet." Kaiden buckled up his tool belt.

"But just before I left yesterday they had some kind of falling-out. I couldn't hear much of what Miguel was saying because he always speaks so quietly, but Juan was angry about something."

"Miguel probably told him he's not coming back to run the ranch."

"That's kind of what I gathered." Beth nodded. "I suppose it's good that Miguel came back to tell him to his face. From what Julia said, I guess he'd been avoiding it."

"That's Miguel for you." Kaiden uncovered the countertop and considered it anew. "He's never been good at facing the consequences of his actions."

"You were friends once, weren't you?"

"Yeah, we were." Kaiden nodded.

"Then maybe you could ask him what's going on?"

Kaiden pictured Miguel's cold eyes and blank expression. Whatever his old friend had been through since he'd left Morgan Valley had only accentuated the ruthless streak buried inside him.

"I'll certainly give it a try," Kaiden said. "Is Juan okay this morning?"

"He's trying to pretend that everything is fine, but I can tell that he's tense. It would've been nice if Miguel had told him whether he was coming back or not."

Kaiden looked out the window. "His rental is still here, so I'd say that was a yes."

"That's good then." Beth shut the dishwasher door. "Would you like some coffee? I just made a pot."

Several hours later, while Beth was in town with Juan at Dr. Tio's, Kaiden heard the sound of a car pulling up on the driveway. He looked out of the window to see Miguel exiting the vehicle. The driver looked slightly familiar. Kaiden craned his neck to get a better look before picking up a random offcut of wood and heading outside.

He pretended not to be interested in the conversation going on between the two men and he headed to his truck whistling loudly. Even as he got level with the car, the driver abruptly put up his tinted window and drove off.

Miguel waited for him to stow the wood in the back of his truck and come back to where he was standing.

"Who was that you were with?" Kaiden asked. "I didn't recognize the car."

"No one you'd know." Miguel turned toward the house. "Are you going to be up here for much longer?"

"Why do you ask?" Kaiden politely held the door open for his companion.

"Because we're paying for a housekeeper. If you're always here Dad doesn't need her."

"I don't have time to do her job and mine," Kaiden said evenly. "And I think Julia's paying Beth's salary, not you."

Miguel took off his sunglasses. "You seem to know an awful lot about what's going on in my family."

"That's what neighbors do. We support each other."

"So it's got nothing to do with the fact that you've always had the hots for my little sister? I thought I'd blown that fricking candle out years ago."

Kaiden shrugged. "You'd have to ask your sister about that. I can't really comment."

"I bet you can't."

"We're not in high school anymore, Mig. Your sister is big enough to decide what she wants to do with her life, and who she wants to see."

"Oh, she told me all about you hanging around." Miguel's smile wasn't pleasant. "Bothering her again. She thought it was pathetic."

Kaiden smiled and leaned back against the countertop. "See, the thing about Julia is, that if she did feel that way, unlike you, she'd tell me to my face." Kaiden stared down at Miguel. "And, weirdly enough, she hasn't, so I'll wait until I hear from her directly, rather than believe you, okay?"

"You need to get off this ranch, Kaiden Miller." Miguel squared up to him. "No one wants you here, sniffing around, making my dad all kinds of promises."

"Promises about what?" Kaiden chuckled. "That the master bath will be finished in three weeks, or that the kitchen will take a bit longer? Give me a break."

"You've always wanted this place, Kai," Miguel said. "Even when you were a kid you'd come around here, desperate for my dad's attention because your old man was a complete bastard. And, you still want it now. You think that you can have Julia, and that my dad will leave you the place instead of me. But it's not going to happen, bro. You don't get to take my inheritance away from me."

"Man, that's some imagination you have there." Kaiden shook his head. "You know all you have to do is stick around and run this place, and it's yours. You've always had that certainty, and you don't want it, you never have. You couldn't wait to get out of this valley."

"That doesn't mean that you get to take it instead," Miguel retorted.

"I never thought it did." Kaiden walked over to his workbench and picked up his tape measure. "If you don't want the ranch, then give it to Julia. Let her put a manager in to run it for you."

"Like she wants it either." Miguel scoffed. "She's definitely changed her mind since she found out how much we can get for it. That's why she put me onto a guy who's a whiz at maximizing profit from land sales. She knows as well as I do that Dad can't run this place, and that he'll want money to fund his health needs in the very near future."

"What guy?" Kaiden tried to look dumb even as his heart plummeted to his boots.

"Blaine Purvis. He came to see me today to talk about selling the place."

"You're going to sell it? Has Juan agreed to that?" Kaiden tried not to sound too shocked.

Miguel shrugged. "He'll come around."

"I doubt it." Kaiden took the pencil out from behind his ear. "If you've finished spouting all your conspiracy theories, can I get on? Despite what you think I have other jobs lined up after this one."

"Actually, I don't doubt you on that at least." Miguel stepped back and assessed the kitchen. "I've got to hand it to you, Kai. This is quality work."

"Thanks." Kaiden returned his attention to his plans. "Juan and Beth should be back any minute now. Maybe you should put some coffee on."

* * *

On the drive home, Kaiden couldn't help but replay his conversation with Miguel over and over in his head. The allegation that he wanted the ranch for himself was stupid, but the other parts . . . He *had* been that needy kid desperate for a father figure Miguel had so cruelly described, but his attraction to Julia had always been separate. He'd just adored her from the get-go.

His fingers tightened on the steering wheel as he allowed himself to face the worst of it. How the hell had Miguel hooked up with Blaine Purvis? He checked the time and made a turn in the road and headed back toward the Gomez Ranch. He needed to talk to someone and he knew Ben and Silver were at their place.

When he pulled up outside the house, he saw Ben riding in on his horse and waved at him.

"Hey, you got a moment?"

"Sure, go into the house," Ben called out to him. "Silver's in the kitchen. I'll be there as soon as I've put Calder away."

"Thanks, Bro."

Kaiden made his way around to the side of the house, left his jacket and boots in the mudroom, and walked through to the large, warm kitchen where Silver was cooking up something on the range. She wore jeans and a crop top and had her back to him.

"Now, don't laugh, Ben, but I asked Matilda for her enchiladas recipe, and I think I've done a really good job this time."

"Sounds great!" Kaiden said. "What time's dinner?"

She jumped like she'd been shot, clutched at her chest,

and spun around to face him brandishing the spoon like a weapon and dripping cheese sauce all over the tiled floor.

"Kaiden!"

He smiled properly for the first time in days. "Yup, sorry if I scared you. Ben told me to come right on in."

"It's fine!" She looked at the spoon. "Let me just—"

"It's okay, I've got it." Kaiden ripped off a few sheets of kitchen roll and dealt with the drips. "The dogs will get the rest of it when they come in."

Silver carefully shut off the gas, poured the sauce over the rolled-up tortillas, and slid the pan into the oven with a relieved sigh.

"I hope it tastes okay. It's Matilda's day off so one of us has to cook, and neither of us are great at it." She glanced at Kaiden. "You're going to stay for dinner, right?"

"With that recommendation, how could I say no? Do you want me to set the table?" Kaiden asked.

"Sure. I think you know where everything is in this kitchen."

"I sure do, seeing as I helped you plan it out."

Kaiden got busy finding glasses, plates, and silverware while Silver worked on a salad and took some garlic bread out of the top oven. He liked the laid-back vibe in his brother's house, which was a good reflection of both Ben's and Silver's personalities.

"When's your next movie coming out?" Kaiden counted out the forks and knives and set them on the table.

"Not for a few months, thank goodness." Silver sliced up the fragrant, crusty bread and put it in a covered basket. "I know Ben is anxious about Jeff, so I'm glad we can be around to keep an eye on his recovery."

She went over to the huge refrigerator and opened the door. "Would you like a beer?"

"Only if you're having one," Kaiden replied.

"Well, duh."

Just as they clinked their bottles together, Ben arrived with his two dogs in tow. He went over to Silver and kissed her right on the mouth.

"Hey, you."

She kissed him back. "Thanks for not telling me Kaiden was coming. I almost threw a pan of cheese sauce at him."

Ben grinned. "I only knew five minutes before you did." He glanced over at Kaiden. "Did you creep up on her or something? Nice." He helped himself to a beer and sat down at the table with a sigh.

"Everything okay on the ranch?" Kaiden asked.

"Yeah, we're doing good. How's it going at home? Is Dad out working yet?"

"I wouldn't know." Kaiden shrugged. "I'm spending most of my time down in Morgantown, or out on the Garcia Ranch finishing Juan's kitchen."

"You and Dad still not talking?" Ben frowned. "It's been weeks."

Kaiden took a sip of his beer as he considered his reply. "I don't have anything I want to say to him right now."

Silver nodded. "I know how that feels. It took me months to want to talk to my dad after he interfered between me and Ben."

"But, it's not like you, Kaiden." Ben sat forward. "You're usually the one we all rely on to fix things with Dad—to make things right."

"Well, maybe I can't fix things for myself," Kaiden

said. "Maybe I'm sick of being that guy." He tried to smile. "Anyways, I didn't come to talk about Dad."

Silver and Ben exchanged a mystified glance.

"What else is up?" Ben asked.

"Miguel Garcia turned up yesterday." Kaiden set his beer on the table.

"Julia's brother?" Silver asked. "The one she thinks doesn't want to run the ranch?"

"The one and only."

"How was he?" Ben regarded Kaiden intently. "You used to be friends."

"Not anymore. He's . . ." Kaiden considered what to say. "Harder, more detached, less easy to read."

Ben shuddered. "He was always a badass, and if you're suggesting he's now worse . . . what does he want?"

"That's the million-dollar question." Kaiden paused. "He brought someone up to the ranch with him—someone he didn't really want me to interact with. He obviously didn't know I'd already met the guy. It was Blaine Purvis, Julia's boss at MZB."

"How does he know Blaine?" Ben asked.

"Miguel said that Julia put him onto Blaine, and that Julia is all in on selling the ranch."

Silver frowned. "Not the Julia I know. She's determined to keep the place for her dad and future generations."

For some reason, hearing Silver say that out loud eased some of the tension in Kaiden's gut.

"That was my take on it too," Kaiden said. "And if Miguel has been left the whole ranch, then what would Julia get out of it anyway?"

"He could have promised her that he'd ensure that Juan

wanted for nothing while he was still alive," Silver mused. "She'd probably go for that."

"But she also knows that Juan doesn't want to sell the place." Kaiden sighed. "I wish I knew what that damn will said. It would really help."

"It's lodged with Henry in town," Ben reminded them. "I wonder if he'd let us take a look at it?"

"Not if he wants to keep practicing law, he won't." Silver frowned at him.

"Then maybe we plan a heist and steal it?"

"Stop it." Silver reached over and slapped Ben's arm. "I normally expect that kind of silly stuff from Kaiden."

"Thanks." Kaiden finished his beer.

"Why don't you ask Julia what's going on?" Silver looked at him inquiringly.

"Because . . ." Kaiden scraped at the label on his beer. "It's complicated."

Ben snorted. "Of course it is. You're a Miller."

"We're kind of not talking to each other right now."

"Why? Did you have a fight?" Silver frowned. "She didn't mention anything to me."

"She tends to keep everything to herself," Kaiden said. "She's had no choice."

"Then why don't you reach out and be the hero of the hour?"

Kaiden crossed his arms over his stomach and leaned back in his chair. "We're trying not to do that kind of thing."

"Why not?" Ben's brow creased. "You're usually the first one to speak up about anything."

"We decided it was for the best for us to just be friends," Kaiden said. It sounded lame even to him.

"So reach out to her as a friend and ask why her brother

who refused to come back to the ranch when she begged him to do so suddenly turns up with her boss!" Silver looked at him like he was a dumbass.

"She knew Miguel was coming back." Kaiden shrugged. "I guess if Juan wants to share what happened between him and her brother then he'll go ahead and do that. It's really not my place."

"I suppose that's true," Silver didn't sound very convinced.

"Maybe it would be better for Kaiden to wait until Julia comes back here so he can ask her face-to-face." Ben, who was watching Kaiden, intently spoke up. "She's coming to the party, right?"

"I assume so." Kaiden hesitated and then decided to just let it out. "But what if she *did* introduce Blaine to Miguel? I can't think of any other way the two of them would have gotten together otherwise. It doesn't look good, does it?"

Ben and Silver looked at him and any last hope that his suspicions weren't valid died.

"I don't get it either." Silver was the first to find her voice. "But I still can't believe Julia has changed that much. Maybe Miguel fooled her into making the introduction, and when she finds out what he's planned she'll be furious? Or it might have been Juan?"

"All the more reason for you to call her right now, Bro," Ben chipped in.

Kaiden shook his head. "I can't do that. I can't afford to make things worse between us than they already are."

"Can't or won't?" Ben picked up the empty bottles and took them over to the sink. "You were on me like a tick when I was being a stubborn ass about Silver, so why won't you take your own advice?"

"Because it's so much easier to give advice than to take it?" Kaiden murmured, and searched for his phone. "I should text Mom and let her know where I am."

"While you've got your phone out you could easily call Julia," Ben said.

Kaiden sent him a death glare and Ben grinned.

"You came here for advice, Bro. If you don't like what you're hearing that's definitely on you."

Chapter Nineteen

"So in conclusion, we've had an excellent year." Blaine smirked at Mr. Bashear. "I truly believe that my taking over the leadership role really improved our standards and morale, which were, in my opinion, getting sloppy."

Julia tried not to roll her eyes as she sat on the sidelines of the conference room in front of the rest of her team watching while Blaine kissed Mr. Bashear's ass. She'd had an excellent and insightful breakfast meeting with Mr. B earlier, and had come out with more hope inside her than she'd had for months.

From the other side of the room, Melanie applauded as Blaine shut his laptop and the lights came up.

"Well done, Blaine." She smiled at Mr. Bashear. "I told you he'd do well, didn't I?"

Blaine was about to rejoin his group when Mr. Bashear stood up.

"I have a couple of questions about your presentation, if I may?"

"Sure!" Blaine swung around. "How can I help you?"

What followed was little short of a massacre. Blaine couldn't answer almost any of the big boss's pointed questions mainly because he'd had no interest in learning anything Julia had tried to teach him. Whenever he tried to deflect or blame her or the rest of the team, Mr. B refused to accept his excuses. He wouldn't even let Melanie answer for him. By the end, even Julia was beginning to feel sorry for her archenemy.

Mr. Bashear turned to her.

"Julia, can you help with any of this?"

"Yes, of course, Mr. Bashear." She gestured to the rest of her team to stand as well. "What do you want to know?"

Julia waited as everyone except she, Melanie, and Blaine filed out of the conference room and Mr. Bashear beckoned them to come forward.

"Melanie, after watching that debacle do you still stand by your decision?"

"Of course I do. I wasn't going to mention it, Edward, but Julia has done nothing but undermine Blaine since the moment I put him in charge." She shot Julia an angry look. "I'm not surprised he didn't have the ability to answer you today. She probably fed him the wrong information."

Mr. B turned to her. "Is that true, Julia?"

"I'm not sure how it could be true, sir, seeing as you asked me exactly the same questions you asked Blaine, and I used the information in the report to answer them." Julia kept her voice and her gaze level.

"That is correct." The big boss nodded. "Blaine was underprepared."

"Because Julia constantly turns my team against me!" Blaine spoke up. "She just wants me to look bad!"

"I think you managed that all by yourself, son," Mr. Bashear said. "I was almost embarrassed by your lack of knowledge." He looked at Melanie. "And I must confess that I was interested enough in your negative reports about Julia, who happens to be one of my protégés, to check out her credentials, and compare them with Blaine's."

Melanie went still.

"Imagine my surprise when I found out that not only did Blaine barely manage to get his law degree, but he happens to be your nephew. Something he didn't declare on his application. Would you like to comment on that, Melanie?"

Julia fought the urge to gawk as Melanie's hand crept to her throat.

"That . . . didn't weigh on my hiring decision, I—"

"I believe it did," Mr. Bashear said gently. "I abhor nepotism. I wouldn't even take my son into this firm until he'd done ten years with a competitor."

He looked over at Julia. "Thank you for your time, Julia, and please thank your team."

"I will, Mr. Bashear." Julia smiled.

Even as she left the room, she wished she could be a fly on the wall. Would Melanie and Blaine manage to keep their jobs, or would Mr. B fire them both? He was quite a stickler for the rules. Whatever happened next, she wouldn't be working with either of them again, which was the best news ever.

In the outer office, Miley came bouncing up to her, braids flying in every direction.

"Hey! We did it! We crushed it!"

Julia accepted the high five and finally smiled. "You were all awesome."

"And we made Blaine look like the dick he is!"

"Apparently," Julia said, lowering her voice, as she was

being indiscreet, but she thought Miley deserved to hear this, "Blaine is Melanie's nephew."

"Get out!" Miley gasped. "No!"

"Yup, but keep it to yourself, okay?" Julia added. "It didn't go down well with Mr. Bashear, I can tell you that."

Miley was still staring at her, totally speechless for once, and Julia took advantage by pulling her friend into an awkward hug.

"Thank you for all you've done to keep my spirits up during this terrible time."

"Right back at you." Miley was grinning like a fool. "We have to go out and celebrate!"

"Let's wait to see what happens to Melanie and Blaine first. But if they are fired, drinks tonight are on me!" Julia promised.

She went back to her office and for once closed the door. She needed time alone to decompress, consider her future, and most importantly do her own little victory dance to celebrate the comeuppance of the obnoxious Blaine.

When she sat down at her desk, she noticed Miley had left a note concerning Mr. Evans's ranch in Bridgeport. Apparently, before they made an offer, the potential buyer wanted her to sound out the town council informally about the chances of them getting a permit to build the guest cabins on the ranch land. Mr. Evans and his family had requested she be the one to handle the matter because of her connection with the town.

Julia checked her calendar. Mr. Bashear was leaving for the East Coast early tomorrow morning, which meant that if he had settled matters with all concerned, she could leave for Morgan Valley and squeeze in a visit to Bridgeport on her way home. The information she'd received from Brooksmiths, the historically sympathetic building company, might go a long way to assuaging Mr. Evans and his family's concerns about selling. And, if he really didn't want to sell to anyone other than a single buyer, or sell at *all*, she would not try to change his mind.

The thought of someone trying to pressure her own father into making that kind of decision made her furious. If the buyers were skeptical, she could always say that despite her best efforts, the council was not willing to allow such a development on the edge of their town. They wouldn't be the first community to make the decision to protect their heritage.

She shut her laptop and checked the time. In just over twenty-four hours she would be home with exciting news about her job and the financial ability to keep her father at the ranch for as long as he wanted. She'd also get to see Kaiden Miller, but what might happen with him was a total unknown. She couldn't stop hoping that there was some way to fix things between them. Three weeks without any communication had been horrible, and she missed him, it was as simple and complicated as that.

Her cell pinged and she checked her messages. Mr. Bashear wanted her to have dinner with him. She accepted the invitation and got back to work. With Blaine hopefully on the way out, she had a lot to clean up.

Julia parked her rental in front of Mr. Evans's front door, patted his dog, and went to knock on the door, only to have it open to reveal a young woman about her own age.

"I do remember you!" the woman exclaimed. "We were on opposing softball teams in high school!"

"Jennifer, correct?" Julia held out her hand. "It's nice to see you again."

"Nice to see you, too. Come on in. I bet you're going to that fancy party at Morgan Ranch tomorrow night, aren't you?"

"Dad and I have been invited." Julia followed Jennifer through to the kitchen where she was offered her choice of coffee or lemonade.

"Well, don't forget to give Kaiden Miller a big kiss on the cheek from me." Jennifer winked. "I guess he's all grown up now."

"Kaiden Miller?" Julia wondered whether she looked as guilty as she felt.

"We dated once. He was such a goofball." Jennifer grinned. "Dad said he'd grown up real nice, and was nothing like his father."

Julia considered Kaiden's abs and nodded. "He sure did."

"Betty, my mom, is sitting with Grandad, so if you just come through to the parlor, we can talk this out, okay?"

"Thank you," Julia said, and followed Jennifer into the sunny parlor where she was introduced to Betty and received a grudging hello from Mr. Evans. She offered him a smile and opened her file.

"Okay, I know you probably don't want to hear about any of these options, Mr. Evans, but I want to give you the full picture." She glanced at the two women. "I talked to the town clerk this morning so I have his opinion as well. I also promise that whatever decision you make, I will report it back faithfully to my potential client and not try to change your minds."

Mr. Evans nodded. He looked way more drawn than he

had four weeks ago. "All right then, missy. Show me what you've got."

"Kaiden?"

"Who else?" Kaiden said into his phone. "What's up, Silver?"

"Can you come over?"

"To your house? Aren't you supposed to be getting ready for some kind of wedding party?" Kaiden folded up the last of his dustsheets and stowed it along with his tools in his truck. He'd finished the Garcia kitchen just in time for Julia to show up, and he wanted to get out of there before she arrived home.

"Yes, we are, but I really wanted to talk to you about something first."

"That urgent, eh?"

"Yes."

Silver sounded uncharacteristically earnest.

"Is everything okay between you and Ben?" Kaiden asked cautiously as he shut the door of his truck.

"Yes! This is just something between you and me, okay?"

"Okay, I'll come over right now. I was just at the Garcias' finishing up so I won't be long."

Beth had taken Juan down to Morgantown so that Kaiden could clean up the kitchen and finish off all the little details so that it looked as good as he could make it. He wanted it to be a surprise for Juan, and for Julia, if he was honest. He'd poured his heart into it over the past few weeks. But, as he wasn't one to stand around waiting to be praised, he'd prefer to get his feedback later.

He drove over to Silver's place and parked beside the

barn. There was no sign of Ben or his truck, which wasn't surprising in the middle of the day. He walked around to the side door and let himself in calling out to Silver.

"I'm in the kitchen!" she shouted back.

He took off his boots and went down the hallway. She was sitting at the table, her elbows on the top and her phone in front of her. Her blond hair was in braids and she didn't look like someone full of party spirit.

"Are you okay?" Kaiden asked.

"Yeah, I'm just . . ." Silver pulled a face. "Not sure what to make of what Julia just told me. I might be misinterpreting what she said, and making everything worse, but I felt like the least I could do was make sure you had all the facts before you saw her."

Kaiden took the seat opposite her. "I have no idea what you're talking about, but I'm sure you'll get to the point in a while."

"Okay." Silver blew out a breath. "You know the Evans Ranch in Bridgeport?"

"Yeah, I took Julia out there a few weeks ago."

"Well, Julia texted me to say she was back out there today."

"And?"

"And she sent me some stuff from a housing development company called Brooksmiths who currently specialize in building . . ." She checked her phone. "Environmentally sympathetic and sustainable resort accommodation and restoration of rural locations."

Kaiden let that mouthful sink in. "Okay."

"She said it's one of the options she put forward to Mr. Evans and his family, and that she thought I might like to know about it too." She looked at him hopefully. "Doesn't that worry you?"

"I'm not sure why it should." Kaiden frowned. "Am I missing something?"

"Last time you were here we talked about why Julia might have changed her mind about selling the Garcia Ranch?" Silver tapped the screen of her phone. "Maybe this is why. Maybe she thinks this really would be the best option for her father, and that she'd still be saving the place even if her father wasn't running it."

"Why would she tell you that?" Kaiden asked slowly. "I know you're friends, but—"

"She didn't."

He rubbed his temples. "I'm getting really confused here, Silver."

"Julia knows that Ben and I are setting up our Morgan Valley Heritage Foundation. She probably thought we'd just like to know about Brooksmiths as a potential collaborator for renovation and renewal projects in our valley."

"Which makes sense." Kaiden nodded.

"The rest of it—the part about her maybe seeing it as a way to justify selling off the Garcia Ranch—is just me making assumptions." Silver held up her finger. "I could be totally wrong, but considering what we talked about, and what Miguel said, I just wanted you to be fully aware of what you might be dealing with."

She sat back and looked at him expectantly.

"You think Julia's getting some cutback from this company to find ranches to build on?" Kaiden asked slowly.

"She might be." Silver shrugged. "It might be tied to her work and she automatically gets a bonus or something if she recommends them."

"I hear what you're saying, Silver, but I just can't see Julia doing any of this."

"I can't either, but there just seemed to be a lot of coincidences, and I thought you should know all the facts before you see her." Silver made a face. "You probably think I'm nuts, and that I've gotten you all worried about nothing now."

"No, I get it," Kaiden reassured her, aware that he wasn't quite as confident as he might appear on the outside. His argument with Julia over the Evans Ranch remained clear in his mind. "It's always better to be prepared for anything."

He got up from the table as did Silver.

"I suppose I'd better go and get ready." Silver came around to give him a hug. "Ben wouldn't let me fly in my makeup artist and hairdresser so I'm doing everything by myself."

"I'm sure you'll look beautiful," Kaiden reassured her even as he hid a grin. "When is your family arriving?"

"Oh, they're already here. Ben's taken them out to see the improvements we've made on the ranch. They should be back any time now."

Kaiden made his way home, mulling over Silver's words. Would Julia really be prepared to ignore her father's wishes and side with Miguel just to get her hands on some money? It didn't seem likely. She already earned a huge salary—enough to keep Juan at the ranch for the remainder of his life.

He reminded himself that Silver loved a good conspiracy theory and sometimes reacted to things like she was living in a soap opera—which to be fair her life did sometimes resemble. The only thing he could do was ask Julia what was going on—which meant he'd have to talk to her—which meant he'd have to pretend she meant nothing to him all over again.

He parked outside the barn and stared at the wooden

slats. He couldn't let Miguel manipulate his father and his sister out of their home. If Julia didn't know that Blaine was working with her brother . . .

"How could she not know? She's the only link between them," Kaiden spoke the words out loud. "None of this makes sense."

He should call her right now. He knew it in his soul, but what if she said it was all true and acted surprised that he was bothered about it? Wasn't it better to wait and ask her to her face? She couldn't hide from him then, and at least he'd have his answer. He checked the time. She might be traveling back. He didn't want to call her if she was driving.

"Coward," Kaiden said as he got out of the truck. "You're just too chicken shit to call her."

He went into the kitchen where his mother, knowing their healthy appetites, had laid out some kind of buffet for them to graze on before they got to the big party later. He helped himself to a plateful of food and some coffee, answered all her questions without really listening, and skedaddled to his room to get ready.

Adam had gone to pick up Lizzie and Roman. Danny and Evan were going with Leanne and Jeff, Daisy was with Jackson, which left Kaiden by himself. These days he preferred it that way because the moment he got in a vehicle with one of his siblings, they started nagging him about his behavior. The only person who wasn't making much of an effort to talk to him was his father, and that suited Kaiden just fine.

He paused as he unbuttoned his shirt. But that wasn't true either, was it? He kind of missed his dad shouting at him. Jeff Miller being quiet and polite for the first time in his life was not as much fun as Kaiden had expected. But deliberately making his dad mad right now was not what Jeff needed to help him recuperate.

Kaiden spent a while ironing his new shirt, brushing his best white Stetson, and polishing his one and only rodeo buckle and belt. As no one else was depending on him for a ride, he could take his own sweet time turning up at the party. As he shaved, he practiced what he was going to say when he saw Julia, but everything sounded false. She knew him well enough not to fall for any of his bullshit.

He studied his face in the mirror. She did know him, probably better than anyone even his own family. Why did he even doubt her? There was no way in hell she'd sell out her own father. How could he be stupid enough to not even try and make things work? If he never asked, he'd never know, and she'd find someone way better.

Decision made, Kaiden got dressed, put on his best pair of boots, and went to confront his future at the party.

Julia walked over to the large picture window in the Morgan Ranch Guest Center and admired the outline of the Sierra Nevadas and the foothills sloping down toward the ranch itself. She hadn't been up to the ranch since Chase and the rest of the family had finally come home and started making changes. After talking to Ruth Morgan she had begun to see why so many new houses were needed in the valley.

The guests of honor, Ben and Silver, hadn't arrived yet. Julia had established Juan in a group of ranchers and left him chatting away in fine form. By the time she'd finished at the Evans place, she'd barely had time to say hi to him before rushing off to get changed. She turned back to survey the room. If she wasn't mistaken, the happy couple had invited everyone in Morgan Valley.

She smoothed down the skirt of her red-and-white-patterned dress and considered how long she would be able to stand upright in her spiked heels before she broke out the flats in her purse. She'd put her hair up and secured it with a large flowered clip on one side of her head. Her father had clapped and said she reminded him of her mother when he'd first met her.

Despite her newly restored confidence in her future career, she couldn't believe how nervous she was about seeing Kaiden again. She had a sense that this time she'd reach him—that together they could make things right between them again.

"Hey."

She'd been so focused on the door, that she jumped when she heard his voice behind her.

"Kaiden!" She spun around like some dizzy rom-com heroine. "I didn't see you come in."

He smiled, but there was a definite hint of watchfulness in his eyes.

"I got here a while ago. I was talking to Blue Morgan about some work he needs doing at his place." His gaze swept down to her feet and back up again. "You look . . . well."

"Thanks, so do you. Is that a new shirt?"

"Yeah."

She nodded, aware that the ease between them had disappeared and frantically wondered how to get it back.

"Was your dad able to come?"

Kaiden jerked a thumb back toward the door. "He's

coming with Mom, Evan, and Danny. They should be here any minute now."

"I heard that you weren't working on the ranch anymore."

"Yeah." He shoved a hand in his pocket and looked out of the window.

Julia repressed a sigh. "Are you okay about that?"

"Why wouldn't I be?"

She waited to see if he was going to say anything else and then slowly nodded, her stupid hopes dying like the wind. "Okay, then. It was nice talking to you, Kaiden. Have a great evening."

She was just about to turn away when he cleared his throat.

"If you can spare me some time after Ben and Silver get here, I'd be grateful."

"Really?" She raised her chin. "Because right now, you look like you can't wait to get away from me."

He shrugged and offered her a faint smile. "Actually, I'm kind of nervous right now, and I don't know how to handle it."

"Nervous about what?"

"Talking to you."

"Right, because I'm so terrifying," Julia said.

"You can be, especially when you're glaring at me like I'm dog meat."

"I am *not*—" She looked him in the eye. "Fine. I'll talk to you later."

She spent the next hour silently worrying while attempting to be pleasant to her neighbors and making sure her father was happy. So much for Kaiden Miller being her soul mate; he was the most exasperating man she'd ever met. If he was planning on asking her to date him, she'd make him beg real hard before she capitulated. She ate food, toasted the happy couple with champagne, and, if asked, would not have been able to name a thing she'd eaten, or even who had made each toast.

Kaiden sat at the top table with his and Silver's families. Julia couldn't help notice that Ben was the only one who was really talking to Kaiden, apart from his mother and Daisy. It appeared that the rift in the Miller family was real. Jeff looked worn to the bone, although he was doing his best to chat with anyone who warily approached him.

After making sure that her dad wouldn't miss her, she walked over to where Kaiden was standing with Daisy. He turned as she approached, excused himself from his sister, and came to her side.

"Do you want to go outside? It's definitely quieter," Julia asked.

"Sure. Do you want your coat?"

"I think I'll be fine. It's still warm out there with the heaters on and the dancing hasn't started yet."

She followed him out of the open French doors and down the shallow steps to the large pavilion where the outdoor weddings were held during the spring and summer. There was a DJ setting up his stuff, but apart from that, the space was almost deserted, which suited Julia just fine. If everything went wrong she'd rather not have an audience to her humiliation.

She walked over to the far end of the pavilion, which looked out over the water meadows, and turned to face Kaiden with what she hoped was a welcoming smile.

"So, what do you want to say to me?"

"Don't rush me." He rubbed a hand over the back of his

neck. "I'm trying to think of how to ask the questions so you won't get mad."

"Knowing you, that's probably impossible." Julia smiled. "How about I start with an easy one. What's going on between you and your family?"

"What's that got to do with anything?" He looked genuinely confused.

"I thought we were supposed to be friends. I thought you might like to talk about it to someone outside the family."

"It's . . . complicated."

Julia simply looked at him until he sighed.

"My dad just got to me and I quit. He thought it over, decided Evan could do a better job than me, and accepted my decision."

"Your dad has always been difficult, what did he do or say to finally push you over the edge?" Julia wasn't satisfied.

"He caught me on a bad day." He grimaced. "Same day I had that fight with you, to be honest."

"Oh." It was her turn to wince. "I'm sorry."

He shrugged. "It was bound to happen at some point. Don't blame yourself. I don't regret it, you know? It gives me way more time to sleep in and do my carpentry."

She didn't believe that for a second, but she let it go.

"Of course everyone has taken Dad's side because he's sick, and apparently I shouldn't be adding to his stress," Kaiden said. "I keep telling them that him not arguing with me all the time is way better for his health, but they don't see it like that."

"I should imagine they are worried about both of you," Julia said gently.

"Nah, why would they worry about me?" Kaiden smiled.

"The third expendable son? The one whose father was quite happy to let go?"

There was a hint of bitterness in his voice that made her reach out and touch his arm.

"Kaiden . . ."

He shook off her hand. "It's okay, I'm not going to turn this into a huge pity party. I'm a big boy. I made my choices. What's up in your world?"

Wanting to give him a moment to regroup, she offered him a cautious smile. The conversation wasn't going at all as she had hoped. Perhaps she needed to be more assertive and persuade him on her own terms.

"Big changes are afoot," Julia said.

"Yeah?"

"Blaine and Melanie were fired."

"Awesome!" He offered her a high five. "You in charge now?"

"Well, I was offered that role, but Mr. Bashear, the B in MZB, asked me if I'd be interested in forming a new team for the company."

"Doing what exactly?"

She took a deep breath. "I'm going to be actively recruiting clients who want to buy land in more rural areas, and develop it in a sympathetic and environmentally sound manner that takes account of the local community's needs and wishes."

"Really?" His smile disappeared and he suddenly looked way too much like his father.

"What's up?" Julia asked. "I thought you'd approve."

"That you're going to be helping your clients screw over ranchers like Mr. Evans?"

"Screw over?" For a second she struggled for words. "Where the hell did that come from?"

He half turned away before swinging around again. "I heard you'd been back to the Evans Ranch with a proposition for them. Is that true?"

"Yes, it's my job to negotiate between buyers and sellers and set the terms." Julia nodded. "Who told you that?"

"It's not important. Did you persuade that frail old man to sell his family land off to a developer?"

A sense of coldness settled low in Julia's gut. "I offered him several options, one of which was a proposal from a developer who specializes in environmentally sympathetic and sustainable resort accommodation and restoration in rural locations. What about it?"

"Brooksmiths?"

"Yes." She frowned. "They are an excellent company, how do you know about them?"

"That's a really interesting question, Julia. Does Blaine know who they are?"

She shrugged. "He might have heard of them, but I doubt he would've been interested in their philosophy. He wasn't the most environmentally aware person I've ever met."

"If he was 'aware' of them, do you think he might have mentioned them to Miguel?" All trace of the usual smiling Kaiden Miller she loved had disappeared, leaving her completely off balance. She'd never seen him lose his temper before. It wasn't a pretty sight.

"*Miguel?*"

He raised his eyebrows. "Are you going to tell me that your father didn't mention that Miguel came to the ranch?"

"I've barely spoken to Dad. I literally got in late from Bridgeport, took a shower, and drove out to Morgan Ranch." Julia pressed a hand to her throat. "Miguel came to see Dad? When?"

"Yeah, with his buddy Blaine Purvis."

"And you didn't think to let me know about that at the time?"

"Miguel said you knew everything, and to be honest, Julia, how else would your brother know Blaine if you hadn't introduced them?" Kaiden wasn't letting up.

"I don't know the answer to that." She had a horrible sense that the whole discussion was veering over a cliff that she hadn't even realized was there, and that Kaiden's current agenda had nothing to do with declaring how much he cared about her. "What else did Miguel say?"

"That you'd both decided to sell the ranch."

"And you *believed* him?"

"Not at first, but I think I have a right to ask you what your intentions are when you've just taken on a job where you'll be encouraging Mr. Evans to give up his ranch to this 'sympathetic' developer, and might think of doing the same to your father." He shook his head. "What the hell is wrong with you, Julia? Mr. Evans trusted you!"

"Actually, I'm not at liberty to discuss Mr. Evans's business decisions with anyone, and you, personally, have no right to ask me anything." Julia's hand curled into fists.

"Okay." He paused and let out a frustrated breath. "I'm trying to understand here. Does Brooksmiths pay you a commission or something? Does Blaine? Is it worth it for you?"

"Wow." Her voice was shaking so hard she could barely control it. "I didn't realize you thought I had no soul."

"I didn't say that—"

She forced herself to meet his gaze. "Everything you just said was so completely wrong that I'm not even going to attempt to defend myself. If you truly think that's what

I'm like, and that's what I'd do, then you really don't know me at all."

He sounded just like her father, assuming that a woman could never be trusted, that she'd always lie, and she was sick of it.

"I'm just trying to get the truth, Julia." Now he sounded almost as wretched as she did, but she wasn't buying it. "I don't want to believe *any* of it."

"But you chose to believe Miguel." She shrugged. "And that's not the first time you've done that, is it?"

He frowned.

"When Miguel told you I would never go out with you, you said all kinds of awful things about me. That's why you fought that last time, because he defended me."

"I fought him to make him shut his damn mouth," Kaiden snapped. "*He* was the one who said foul things about you! He thought I'd be willing to spread disgusting rumors about his own sister! I would *never* have done that."

"Even more reason that you shouldn't have believed him now, then."

"I didn't! I tried to call you—"

"Hogwash." Even after that startling revelation, Julia wasn't about to make things easy for him. "I don't know how Blaine got to Miguel, or what he offered him. Maybe my dad mentioned him. I do know that someone from my law firm contacted my mom and asked her if she had any remaining interest in the ranch."

"Your mother?" Kaiden frowned.

"Yes, I suppose you're going to doubt my word about that as well, aren't you? Because God knows you can't trust a woman to tell the truth." She smiled even though it hurt. "I have to get back to my father. We obviously have a lot to talk about."

"Don't—just walk away from me," Kaiden said urgently. "If I'm wrong about this—I apologize, but can't we talk it out?"

"What reason would I have to talk to a man who leapt to a million wrong conclusions and doesn't trust me?" Julia blinked back tears. "Please don't come to the ranch again, or at least wait until I'm gone."

"Julia . . . this isn't what I want at all." Kaiden attempted to step in her path. "I told you I'd screw up. I wanted to make things right with you."

"Too late." She couldn't bring herself to look at him. "Have a great life, Kaiden. Maybe you should make up with your dad and family because God knows why anyone would want to trust or care about you when you're incapable of reciprocating. Maybe you're far more like your father than you realize."

She pushed past him, headed for the lobby, and went straight to the restrooms. Nancy was just coming out of the door, but she took one look at Julia and reversed course.

"What's happened?"

"Nothing." Julia sat down on one of the chairs in the anteroom and took the tissue Nancy held out to her. "Just my whole life imploding."

Nancy sat beside her and put a comforting arm around her shoulders as Julia finally started to cry.

"I guess Kaiden Miller is being an ass?" Nancy asked eventually.

"When is he not?" Julia swallowed hard.

"That's my girl." Nancy squeezed her shoulder. "Any chance he can grovel sufficiently to make things better?"

"I don't think so."

"Well, that's his loss. He definitely doesn't deserve you."

The door opened and Silver came in wearing a short, pink, shiny dress that would make most women look like Barbie, but somehow worked on the movie star.

"Oh, no!" She sank to her knees on the carpet in front of Julia. "Did he make you cry? I'm so sorry, I thought I was *helping*."

Even though she had no idea what Silver was talking about, Julia automatically tried to think of something comforting to say. "It's fine."

"No, it's not!"

Nancy stood and glanced down at Julia. "I'll go and check on your dad, okay? I'll tell him you're not feeling great and that you might need to go home."

"Thanks," Julia said. "I really mean that."

Nancy blew her a kiss. "That's what friends are for, right? And if I see Kaiden I'll kick him in the nuts for you."

Silver took Nancy's vacated seat, her gaze anxious, her hands clenched together in her lap. "This is all my fault. Ben told me I shouldn't have interfered. I thought that if Kaiden knew about Brooksmiths, then he'd be better prepared to understand what you and Miguel might decide to do."

Julia sucked in a breath. "You told Kaiden I was forcing Mr. Evans to sell his land to a developer who would cut me in on the deal?"

"No!" Silver looked aghast. "Is that what Kaiden said to you?"

"Among other things. I only told you about Brooksmiths because I thought it might be of interest to your foundation." Julia blew her nose one last time. "Look, I appreciate you trying to help, but maybe you could go back to your party? I have to take my father home."

"But I feel terrible . . . I was worried about what Miguel was up to with Blaine, and I added two and two and made five," Silver confessed.

"Kaiden told you about Blaine and Miguel and yet he didn't bother to tell me?" Julia looked up.

"Yes, he didn't know what to do, because—"

"He assumed that the only way Miguel would know Blaine was if I put them in touch." Julia stowed her last tissue in her purse and put on her flat shoes. "I can see why that would've worried him. It's a shame he didn't think to ask me about it rather than you."

"We told him to call you and ask," Silver said earnestly. "But he didn't want to bother you because he really didn't believe you'd do such a thing and he thought your father would've clued you in about everything."

Julia stood and smoothed her skirts. "It's a pity he didn't keep believing that, isn't it?" She smiled even though her face didn't want to. "I need to go."

"I've let you down." Silver met her gaze head-on. "I've let you both down, and I know I can't apologize enough to make it right."

"Go and enjoy your party, Silver," Julia said gently. "When it comes down to it, the only people responsible for this mess are Kaiden and I. So don't beat yourself up about it."

Silver nodded, but there were tears in her eyes as she left. Julia wished she had the energy to be angrier with Kaiden's sister-in-law, but what was the point? The moment Julia had starting speaking, Kaiden had leapt to his own conclusions, and things had gone downhill from there.

She'd had so much to tell him about what had happened at work, and the Evans deal. Now, nothing really mattered because when it came down to it, he couldn't bring himself to trust her.

She forced herself to reapply her lipstick and mascara in the mirror before she ventured into the fray again.

She'd been in love with a mirage, not a man, and that mistake was definitely on her.

Chapter Twenty

Kaiden paced the lobby, his gaze occasionally checking the entrance to the women's restrooms in case Julia re-emerged. Eventually, Nancy came out and headed straight for him. Her hair was in red and white spikes with candy-striped ribbons on them that matched the pattern of her short dress.

She poked him hard in the chest. "You're an idiot."

Before he could answer, she turned around and marched away again.

"Like I didn't know that," Kaiden muttered to himself.

How had everything gone so spectacularly pear shaped? He'd ended up losing his temper, hurting Julia, and getting shit wrong. Now, he'd lost the ability to regroup, and ask all the questions he should have started with before jumping in with both feet and accusing her of selling out her own father. As soon as he'd started talking and seen her horrified expression, he'd known he'd gotten it completely backward.

As his temper took hold of him, he'd merrily kept digging his own grave. He just wasn't good at this serious stuff. It scared him. He always screwed it up because he was afraid of getting too deep and personal, so he self-destructed.

Silver came out of the restroom looking like she was about to burst into tears. She didn't even see Kaiden, but headed straight toward Ben, who immediately wrapped his arms around her and held her close. Kaiden was so busy watching his brother that he almost missed Julia emerging.

She'd definitely seen him, though. At first, she looked like she'd rather talk to a skunk. But he watched as she raised her chin and looked him up and down just like she'd done when he'd first turned up at Garcia Ranch and found she'd come home.

"Julia." He hurried toward her. "Look—l know I'm the last person you want to talk to right now, but I can't leave things like this. I messed up."

"Yes, you did."

"I know you probably won't believe me, but I want to make things right, I need—"

She held up one finger. "Actually, Kaiden, I don't care what you need right now when I'm barely holding myself together. I just want to crawl into my bed and cry myself to sleep, okay? So, why don't you go home and try and work out where you went wrong. Maybe, just maybe, in a couple of years when I've calmed down and rebuilt my shattered heart, I might be ready to speak to you again?"

"Your heart?" Kaiden stuttered as everything suddenly got a thousand times worse.

She blinked and looked away from him. "Yes, I was hoping we could talk about that, but I guess I made a mistake about everything."

He reached out an imploring hand. "You didn't, I should've—"

"Please stop talking."

"I can do that," Kaiden said cautiously.

"Then, can you leave?" She held herself like a queen. "You really suck."

"I know that, too." He nodded. "But—"

Her manicured finger came up again and this time pressed hard into his chest. "No buts right now. I don't have the bandwidth to deal with them."

"Understandable." He blew out a harried breath and looked her right in the eye. "I'm sorry I lost my temper. I fucked up."

"Finally." She inclined her head an icy inch. "That's a way better apology than anything followed by a qualifier." She stepped away from him. "I need to find my father."

He, too, took a step back, even though he didn't want to. "Okay, I'll be in touch."

She gave him her best haughty lawyer's smile. "No, thanks."

"You can bet on it. I'm going to make this right, Julia, I promise you." He refused to give up on her that easily.

"We'll see, won't we?"

He had to watch her walk away knowing that she might never walk back into his arms, or be willing to listen to him ever again. It was the hardest thing he'd ever had to do in his life. He swallowed down a barrel load of emotions. Funny how you only realized what you were losing and what you loved when it was too late.

Kaiden opened the refrigerator door as quietly as he could and got out the milk. After the awfulness of the party he hadn't been able to sleep without reliving Julia's expression the moment he'd accused her of selling out her own father. Even as he beat himself about that, he'd remembered how her father wouldn't trust her because she was a woman, and realized that extra level of hurt he'd created. He should have called and laid it all out for her. He was an idiot.

He found the pan his mom used to boil the milk and retrieved the hot chocolate mix from the pantry. When he reemerged into the kitchen his dad was sitting at the table.

"Make that for two, will you, Son?"

"Sure." Kaiden was way too miserable to argue with his father. He made the drinks in silence, brought them both to the table, and sat opposite his dad.

"Thanks." Jeff took a sip. "That's good."

"You're welcome."

"Your mom thinks this helps me sleep."

"She thinks it makes everyone sleep. It's like her wonder drug." Kaiden wrapped his hands around his mug. "I thought you'd be tired after the party."

"I was, but that doesn't mean I can sleep. I do my best worrying at night."

"Me too."

"We're quite alike in some ways."

"So everyone keeps telling me." Kaiden kept his tone neutral. "I can't say I see it myself."

"That's because you worked much harder than I ever did to control your temper. Getting riled up is fuel for me—it keeps me going. For you it was . . . destructive."

"I don't remember the last time I lost my temper," Kaiden lied. He wasn't stupid enough to tell his father he'd lost it with Julia earlier that night.

"I do." His father blew on his hot chocolate. "You were

in the barn and were supposed to be stacking the hay bales as I sent them up. You and Ben were messing around, and he knocked you flying. You got mad and rushed him, and he almost went over the edge. He probably would've broken his neck at that height if I hadn't reached out, grabbed hold of his shirt, and hauled him back in."

"I don't remember that." Kaiden studied his hands.

"Sure you do." Jeff set his mug down. "You don't want to, but it's the truth. You cried your eyes out and ran off. I had to find you and bring you home. I didn't even bother with a punishment because I thought you'd learned your lesson, and I was right. You never let your temper get out of control now, maybe too much."

"I don't like conflict."

"I know, you'd rather turn it away with a smile and a joke, but sometimes you need to get your mad on, Son. Sometimes you need to dig in and do the hard work."

Like he'd done earlier . . . and that had gone *so* well because he had no idea how to handle his anger. He'd learned to tamp it down and pretend it didn't exist. Kaiden took another slow drink aware that his father might be onto something but unwilling to admit it. "So what's that got to do with anything anyway?"

"Nothing much." Jeff shrugged. "Just passing the time until you have something of interest to tell me."

"Why would I tell you anything?" Kaiden asked.

"Because sometimes you need advice? And, because you are like me, maybe I can help you."

"I screwed up. It's on me. I'm the only person who can fix it," Kaiden said firmly. "I don't need anyone to tell me that. I should have slowed down, I should have listened more before I jumped to any conclusions."

"Story of my life." His father nodded. "But, one thing

I can tell you is that if the other party is willing, then you can make things right."

"I'm not willing to wait twenty years until Julia returns to Morgan Valley, Dad."

"Then do it sooner." Jeff set his mug down on the table with a thump. "You've got no responsibilities here right now, you have a great skill set. You could live anywhere."

"Trying to get rid of me again?" Kaiden sat back.

"I'm trying to make up for keeping you here after Ben flaked out." Jeff grimaced. "I was afraid you'd make the same mistakes so I clipped your wings. That's one of the reasons why I let you go from the ranch. I wanted to give you back your freedom."

Kaiden stared at his father for a long moment. "Do you really think I'm going to buy that crock of shit?"

His father slowly smiled. "Why not? It's the only one I'm selling."

Julia settled her father into bed and walked through to the kitchen to fetch him a glass of water. She snapped on the lights and gasped. The new accessible appliances gleamed softly and the cabinetry . . . was so beautiful, and so Kaiden that she wanted to bawl like a child. She smoothed her hand along the work surface, admiring the line of the grain and the intricately carved edging. She'd wondered if he'd pass the work on to someone else, but she could feel him in every curve.

She took the water back through to her father and lined up the many pills he had to take. There were five for his MS, and two for high blood pressure, a side effect of the other drugs.

"Here you go, Dad. I'm sorry we had to leave so early. I had a really long day, and I was just exhausted."

"To be truthful, I was getting rather tired myself." He patted her hand. "I'm not used to such big crowds."

Julia waited as he took his pills, and tried to think of how to phrase her next question.

"How is Beth working out for you?"

"She is an angel." His smile widened. "I don't know what I would do without her. Even after all the amazing improvements to the place I was beginning to wonder how I'd manage all on my own after you'd left. And Beth is such sunny company. She cheers me up without even trying." He hesitated. "It's been hard to deal with the thought that I'm stuck in this chair for the rest of my life. It made me miserable as hell."

"I'm not surprised." Julia nodded, amazed that her father was actually confiding his feelings in her. "It's a big change for you."

"I've tried to accept it as God's will, but I've still got a long way to go with that." He smiled up at her. "I guess that's why I've been so intent on getting Miguel home where he belongs."

Julia sensed her opportunity. "Dad, is it true that Miguel came here?"

"Yes." Her father's smile disappeared. "He was very pleasant until I refused his request to sell the ranch."

"Did he say who he planned to sell it to?" Julia asked.

"He brought a proposal from that colleague of yours." Juan pointed to an MZB folder in the stack by his bed. "They wanted to build three hundred houses on my land."

"That's awful." Julia shook her head. "Is it okay if I read this?"

"Of course." Juan handed over the file. "Miguel said you agreed with him."

"Did you believe that?" Julia met her father's gaze.

"No, because why would you have spent so much time and money making the ranch a better place if you planned on tearing it down?" He met her gaze. "When I saw the final bills for the remodel I was horrified. It never occurred to me that you would have to keep working to pay for everything. I was too worried about myself, and didn't think about the cost for you."

"That's okay, Dad." Julia swallowed hard.

"I told Miguel that too. He was very unhappy with me."

"I wish you'd called me. I would've set him straight."

"I was too embarrassed to call you." Juan sighed. "You've been telling me that Miguel didn't have my best interests at heart for years and I've refused to believe you. He threatened to have me declared incompetent. He said that Blaine would find a way to do it legally."

"You should have called me immediately." Julia said.

"I was too ashamed to admit that my son, the person I'd wanted to continue our family legacy, had so little regard for me or the place of his birth that he was willing to sell it to strangers."

She reached out to hold his trembling fingers. "You don't need to worry about Blaine anymore, Dad. He's been fired. And, I wouldn't have agreed to let Miguel get power of attorney over you anyway."

"I'm not sure you could have stopped him, my dear." Juan sighed. "I have been very remiss and very unfair to you. I wonder if you would consider meeting with Henry to go over my will? I can't remember what I put in there, and it's worrying me."

"If you like, I'll give Henry a call, and ask if we can speak to him next time I'm home."

"That's an excellent idea." Juan squeezed her hand.

"Speaking of calls, Mom got in touch with me a few days ago," Julia said gently. "She'd been contacted by someone at MZB asking if she still had any financial interest in the ranch. She originally thought it was me, but after Miley did a bit of digging, she found out that the letter originated from Blaine's office."

"Blaine again." Her father shook his head. "Kaiden told me Blaine was snooping around in my bedroom and he did ask me a few personal questions. Maybe he saw my photographs and worked out that if he wanted to buy this land, he'd have to talk to everyone involved. I'm not surprised Miguel fell for it."

"I'll talk to Miguel," Julia reassured him. "And I won't let anyone move you one inch off this ranch unless you want it to happen. I promise."

"Thank you, Daughter." Her father kissed her fingers. "Thank you for everything."

Julia settled him back against his pillows, handed him the novel he was reading, and left the room. She couldn't resist going back to the kitchen to appreciate the gift Kaiden had given them both. He'd mentioned that he always tried to put little references to himself and to the people in the house in his carving. Having seen Ben and Silver's box up close, she already had a sense of how he did that.

It took her a while, but she found a rolled-up scroll with a ribbon in one high corner that she assumed referenced her law degree, two little faces of a cow and its calf for her dad, and a miniature of Domino, Kaiden's horse. Whatever happened between her and Kaiden in the future, she would never forget the beauty he had created with his hands for her and her father.

She took her cell out of her purse and sent a text to Miguel.

Blaine Purvis no longer works at MZB so any scheme you hatched with him to get rich quick at Dad's expense is over.

Seconds later her phone rang.

"What the hell did you do?" Miguel demanded.

"Nothing. My boss's boss fired him for incompetence," Julia said. "Just as a matter of interest, did you contact him, or did he contact you?"

"He contacted me."

"And suggested you plough up your birthright and turn it into three hundred identical boxes which would triple the size of Morgantown overnight?"

"Everyone I talked to in the valley said they needed housing, so I'm not sure what you're whining about. Blaine said he could cut us both in on the deal."

"Blaine is a snake. He would never have followed through," Julia shot back.

"Yeah, he would. I'd make sure of that."

She didn't like the hint of menace in her brother's voice one bit.

"Anyway," she pressed on. "I wouldn't have agreed to the sale, and neither would Dad or Mom so you would've been outvoted."

"Weird because Blaine said you would do as you were told if you wanted to keep your job at MZB, and Mom gave up her share in the place to you. Dad would've come around eventually. I'm his favorite kid."

Julia took a moment to process what her brother was saying before she replied.

"I'm kind of shocked at how easily you were prepared to sell your whole family down the river, Miguel."

"I need the money," he said bluntly. "I don't need it tied up in an old-fashioned ranch that will never make a profit."

Part of her wanted to reason with him, to remind him of all the happy times they'd had at the ranch, and all the love that had surrounded him, but it had never been enough. He'd always found his family and the ranch stifling, and he appeared to have gotten worse.

"I won't let you get power of attorney over Dad, either." Even as she regretted all the words she couldn't say to him, Julia wasn't backing down. "He's of perfectly sound mind and can make his own decisions right now."

"Then it appears we're at an impasse," Miguel said. "But don't get complacent, Sister. I can always find another lawyer. I'm not going to let this go."

He ended the call, leaving her staring out at the moonlit sky, tears crowding her throat. She always felt far closer to the stars on the ranch than in the city, and tonight they were particularly bright. She picked one and wished as hard as she could.

With a sigh, she got herself a glass of milk, turned off the lights, and went to bed. She had to get back to work on Monday and, with all the changes going on, she knew she'd be busy. She could only hope she wouldn't have a moment to think about Kaiden Miller. She'd set him a task. If he really wanted to make things up to her then he knew what to do. Whether it would ever feel right again was still up in the air.

* * *

"Thanks so much for seeing me, Mr. Evans."

Kaiden took the seat opposite his host and set his coffee on the table. He'd called Mr. Evans the day after the party and had driven out to see him after he'd gotten back from church. Julia was planning on leaving town immediately, and, although he desperately wanted to make things right before she left, he knew she wouldn't listen to him right now.

"It's a pleasure, son," Mr. Evans said. "How's old Jeff doing?"

"He's getting there. He's going back to the hospital this week for his final checkup before they pass him over to our local doctor's care. He seems to think he's ready to go back to work."

"Good for him." Mr. Evans shifted restlessly in his chair. He looked like he'd lost even more weight since Kaiden had last seen him, and had an oxygen tube taped to his cheek. "I can barely get out onto the porch these days."

"I'm sorry to hear that, sir," Kaiden said.

"You said you wanted to know what I'd decided to do about the ranch?"

"Yeah, I know it's none of my business, but I wanted to tell you about a new foundation my brother Ben and his wife have set up. One of the things it does is offer advice to people in your situation—legal representation, that kind of thing, to stop you being taken advantage of by predatory builders or lenders."

Technically, Mr. Evans wasn't in Morgan Valley, but Kaiden had asked Silver and Ben if he could use their foundation as a conversation starter. Silver was feeling so guilty about what had happened with Julia that she'd jumped at the chance to help put things right.

"That's a very kind thought, Kaiden, but I received

excellent legal advice from Miss Julia. She laid out all the options to me and my daughters, and promised to follow through on whichever one we picked."

"That's good to hear." Kaiden paused. "She didn't push you to choose one thing over another, then?"

"Not at all. In fact, I think she was surprised at the decision I made." Mr. Evans chuckled, which turned into a dry cough that seemed to go on forever. "She was absolutely determined that no one, not even my girls, would tell me what to do."

"That's great." Kaiden took a sip of his coffee. "So, you're staying put?"

"Nope. I decided to move into town so I'll be closer to my daughter Betty and my grandkids for the short time I have left." He met Kaiden's gaze. "The cancer has spread and it's inoperable. I've only got a few months to live, and I want to be with my family."

"I'm sorry to hear that. And that's . . . totally understandable, sir." Kaiden nodded.

"I had a long talk with the representative from Brooksmiths, and I like what they plan to do with the place. It'll be small cabins built from natural resources for hikers and fishermen to stay in. They'll clean up the river, shore up the banks, and maintain all the wildlife and open spaces. Andy, the guy I spoke with, comes from Lake Tahoe, so he knows this area well, and understands the land management issues we face with the extremes of the weather, flooding, drought, and snowstorms."

Mr. Evans took a long drink of his lemonade while Kaiden let his words sink in.

"Excuse me for asking this, sir, but how do you know

that they'll follow through on their promises?" Kaiden had never known when to keep his mouth shut.

"Because after I'm gone, my daughters and grand-children get to see and approve all the future plans for the ranch. If they object to something, it goes to the whole board of Brooksmiths, and they all get to vote." He reached over to a stack of papers on the table and extracted a folder. "You can read up about it here if you like."

"Thank you." Kaiden took the folder. "This sounds like something my brother's foundation would love to know about as well."

"I think Miss Julia said she was going to mention Brooksmiths to them," Mr. Evans said. "Now, you can't take that away with you because it's the only copy I have, but if you want to sit here and read it while I take my nap, be my guest."

"If you don't object, I can do better than that." Kaiden held up his phone. "I can take photos of the pages."

Mr. Evans shook his head and whistled. "I always forget those things can take pictures. Feel free to go ahead."

After leaving the Evans place, Kaiden drove to Ben and Silver's home and parked behind his brother's truck. Things had been a little awkward when he'd popped in earlier because of what had happened with Julia, but Kaiden was not going to blame Silver for anything she'd said. She'd only been trying to help. What happened after that was totally on him.

As soon as he walked into the kitchen, Silver handed him a mug of coffee. "How did it go?"

"Mr. Evans decided to sell the land to Brooksmiths."

"Really?" Ben, who was sitting at the countertop using

his laptop, looked up. "Did you offer him our foundation's help to deal with their lawyers?"

"He's good with it." Kaiden sat on one of the high-backed chairs at the counter next to his brother. "He wants to be in Bridgeport with his family. He doesn't have much time left. The money he makes will fund his care and leave plenty for his daughters."

"That sucks." Ben grimaced.

"He seemed at peace with it." Kaiden set his mug down. "He had a long chat with Brooksmiths. From what he told me, he approves of their plans for the ranch. He also said that Julia was great, that she made sure no one was pressuring him to make his decision, and promised to follow through with all his demands and concerns."

Silver made a face. "I wish I hadn't said anything even more now if that's possible."

"Hey, if Julia had told me Mr. Evans had sold to Brooksmiths I would still have gotten mad at her." Kaiden sighed. "I guess I was just looking for a reason."

"Why?" Silver asked.

"Because I didn't want to deal with all the other stuff," Kaiden said reluctantly as he studied his mug. "The 'hey I think we've got something real together, and I want to find a way to make it work.'"

It suddenly went very quiet. Eventually, he had to look up.

"What?" Kaiden raised an eyebrow.

"You're in love with her." Ben made it a statement rather than a question.

"Yeah, I suppose I am." Kaiden winced. "Like she's going to go for me now, after I basically accused her of selling out her father's ranch."

"Ouch," Ben said. "That was a dick move."

"We survived worse, Ben. I'm sure Kaiden can fix this." Silver came to stand beside Ben and put her hand on his shoulder. "What are you going to do to make things right?"

"I'm working on that." Kaiden drank more coffee. "Julia said she might talk to me in a couple of years if I get my shit sorted out."

"That's hopeful," Ben commented as he fought a smile.

"I'm thinking if I can show her that I worked out what was going on between Miguel, Blaine, and the rest of the family she might appreciate it."

"She's a lawyer, so yeah." Ben nodded. "Might as well try and do something smart for a change."

Kaiden shot his brother a glare. "Julia mentioned that someone from MZB contacted her mother in Guatemala about her interest in the ranch."

"Her mother?" Silver asked. "I didn't realize Julia was still in contact with her."

"They all are. Lupita and Juan never got divorced, they just separated. Lupita's a doctor. She runs a children's clinic. I'm hoping Juan still has her phone number so I can give her a call. I bet it was Blaine who wrote to her."

"So, your stupid plan is you're going to present Julia with all the facts and ask her to judge you?" Ben asked, the skepticism on his face highly visible.

"Yeah, so she knows I finally get it." Kaiden nodded. "And then, when she forgives me, I'm going to follow up with the whole love thing."

"Good luck, Bro." Ben grinned and reached over to shake his hand. "You're so going to need it.

Chapter Twenty-One

"Julia?" Miley poked her head through the open door of her boss's office. "There's a real-live cowboy at reception asking for you."

"What?"

Julia looked up from her notes. She'd taken over Melanie's old corner suite, and still got a vicarious thrill every time she stepped over the threshold.

"Like a gorgeous, fit, hot hunk of man kind of cowboy," Miley said in tones of reverence and awe. "I'd save a horse any day."

Julia rose from her chair and followed Miley down to the lobby of the MZB offices. Even from the back she knew that particular cowboy way too well. He hadn't seen her yet so she could drink in the angles of his pretty face and spectacular physique without his noticing. With his white Stetson, cowboy boots, and fleece-lined denim jacket, he should've looked out of place in her world, but somehow he looked just like home.

She hadn't heard from him in a month, and had missed him so badly that she'd contemplated breaking her own rules and texting him. She was glad that it hadn't taken him two years to come and find her.

He swung around from his contemplation of the artwork and offered her the full blast of his cocky smile.

"Ms. Garcia."

She found herself smiling back. "Mr. Miller."

He walked toward her and was intercepted by Miley, who stepped in his path and stuck out her hand.

"Hi! I'm Miley. Ms. Garcia's paralegal."

"Hey, Miley." Kaiden shook her hand. "Kaiden Miller. Nice to meet you."

His amused gaze settled on Julia. "I was hoping I could persuade your boss to have lunch with me today."

"Why on earth would she say no?" Miley breathed as she neglected to release Kaiden's hand. "I mean, if she can't make it, I'd be happy to go in her place—like a sacrifice thing, taking one for the team, you know."

Kaiden finally eased his hand free, and Julia stepped forward.

"I think I can make time for lunch." She gestured behind her. "Would you like to come through to my office, Kaiden, or would you prefer to meet me somewhere?"

"I'm happy to wait while you finish up."

As they walked away, behind Kaiden, Miley was giving Julia her impression of a dying swan, complete with an enthusiastic thumbs-up.

She led the way into her office and stood back to let him go past her, getting a lungful of pure Northern California cowboy as he squeezed by.

"Nice view," he commented going straight to the window. "Corner office and everything."

"Thanks." She sat behind her desk and looked expectantly at him. "What brought you into the city today?"

"I had some business to attend to for Ben and Silver's foundation. As they aren't always going to be available in Morgan Valley, I'm going to act as the local liaison point."

"That makes sense." She tried to act like this was a normal business meeting, but her heart was thumping, fit to burst.

"I came to meet with some developers to get a sense of what they can do for us." Kaiden fingered the brim of his hat.

"What kind of developers?" Julia asked.

"Land developers, your kind of people." He studied her carefully. "Like Andy from Brooksmiths."

"Those guys who pay me the big bucks to destroy small ranchers like you and my dad?"

She waited to see how he intended to deal with her deliberate lob.

"Mr. Evans seemed to like them. He truly believes he is leaving his ranch in good hands." He paused. "He made me realize that sometimes, giving the land back to nature, or using it in a different, more sympathetic way can be a valid choice."

"I agree with Mr. Evans. There certainly isn't a one-size-fits-all approach." Julia sat back and crossed her arms over her chest. "You've obviously been doing some homework."

"I tried. Andy's a good guy with an honest heart and a respect for the land. I can only appreciate that." Kaiden took the seat in front of her desk. "I also talked to your parents."

She shut down her laptop and fussed around to avoid his gaze. "Really."

"Yeah, I guess I should've realized that when I caught Blaine in your father's bedroom, he wasn't just admiring the new plumbing, but working out who he had to deal with if he wanted to get possession of your family ranch."

"Correct."

"Except, he didn't want to bring someone like Brooksmiths on board. He was thinking large-scale development, and a huge backhanded payoff for him. When he talked to Miguel and your father, he got the impression that the ranch would go directly to your brother, and that he was the guy to target."

"You should have called me the moment you saw Blaine with Miguel," Julia said.

Kaiden winced. "Yeah, I absolutely should've done that, but seeing as I was in the middle of a big fight with my own family, I didn't think you'd appreciate me getting involved with yours. And I assumed—"

"That I knew because I'd obviously introduced them," Julia cut across him.

"I still should have followed through." He didn't look away. "I told myself it would just make things worse, and that if you already knew about it from your dad, and didn't see a problem, then I'd be opening up a whole new can of worms. I'm shit at confrontation, Julia. It's no excuse but it's the truth."

His willingness to face up to his mistakes didn't take away the hurt, but it did make her feel a little better.

"Blaine also thought he could blackmail me to fall into line if necessary by threatening my job," Julia said.

Kaiden frowned. "I wish that asshole was still employed here so I could pay him a little visit."

"Blaine was just doing what he always does." Julia waved a dismissive hand. "The person who let his family down was Miguel. He didn't have to listen to Blaine, but he wanted the money."

"Yeah, I'm sorry about that." Kaiden's voice softened. "I can't imagine how I'd feel if one of my siblings pulled that crap."

"Miguel isn't interested in the ranch, or its history, or his family." Julia swallowed hard. "Dad asked me to talk to Henry when I come back because he wants to review his will. He wants to make sure Miguel can't get control of everything and sell up."

"You are planning on coming back, then?" Kaiden asked slowly.

"Yes, I am."

"Even with me still living there?"

She met his gaze. "Conceited much?"

His lips twitched. "Even with this promotion?"

"Actually, this promotion makes it easier for me to work from home." Julia took a quick breath. If there was a time to be brave and lay everything out on the table, it was now.

"As I mentioned before I'm officially fronting up a new West Coast initiative within MZB to establish and nurture environmentally responsible partnerships with land developers and builders in historically sensitive areas."

He stared at her for a long moment. "Places like Bridgeport and Morgan Valley."

"Exactly. I'll be traveling more, but I don't have to come into the city every day, which is why I'll be able to come back and see Dad much more often. And, with the salary increase I can afford to pay for a ranch manager."

"That's great."

She frowned. "You don't sound very pleased."

"Well, you've kind of stolen my big pitch." His grin was almost her undoing. He stood, stuck his hand in his pocket, and looked down at his boots. "The thing is. I was going to offer to move here."

"*What*?" Julia might have squeaked.

"I kept telling Adam that he shouldn't expect Lizzie to upend her entire life just for him, and then I realized I was unconsciously doing the same thing to you. I was thinking I had to get you back to Morgan Valley, when it's actually easier for me to uproot and come here. I can bring my business with me, you could continue doing what you do . . ."

He tailed off. "Am I getting ahead of myself?"

"Maybe you are." She waited until he looked her right in the eye. "I am doing all these things for myself, not for you, Kaiden. You might find this difficult to believe, but I am perfectly capable of getting on with my life without you in it."

"I know that." He didn't look away. "I messed up. I didn't listen properly, I jumped to all the wrong conclusions, and worst of all I hurt you."

She nodded and he continued speaking.

"I guess what I'm asking for, is a chance to make things right, because I'm not sure I can live without you in my life." He grimaced. "I should've started with that rather than with what *I* want."

Her breath caught as he approached her desk, took off his hat, and went down on his knees in front of her.

"Yeah, I definitely got this backward," Kaiden said. "I forgot the groveling apology. Would you like me to kiss those fancy shoes of yours—they're hot, by the way—or kiss your fingers, and tell you how much I've missed you, and what an ass I am?"

"I know you are an ass." Julia scrabbled to latch on to something concrete.

He reached for her hand. "Then will you consider forgiving me?" He met her gaze head-on. "I got mad because I panicked. It was easier to believe you were in the wrong than acknowledge all my scary feelings for you and deal with them. And, once I'd gotten mad, I kind of thought that meant it was all over between us."

She considered long enough to make him sweat.

"I don't want you to move here," she said finally.

"Okay." His smile faltered and she hastened to reassure him.

"You're too much a part of Morgan Valley. I'd much rather you were there for me to come home to. I intend to come home a lot."

He shrugged. "We could do both. I could travel with you when I can, and stay to keep an eye on your dad and the ranch when you can't be there."

"I'd love it, but how would Jeff feel about that?" Julia asked cautiously.

"He fired me, I don't work for him anymore, remember?" He smiled up into her eyes. "These plans are all great, Julia, but they don't mean squat unless I also say this." He took a deep breath. "I love you, I want to make this work, and I think we can do it if we both want it."

"Even though you are incredibly annoying, and we

might fight occasionally?" Okay, she was definitely babbling now.

"Yeah, because you *get* me, you allow me to be myself, and that's something I don't get from anyone else in this world."

"I feel the same way," Julia confessed, aware that she was hanging on to his fingers for dear life. "You don't mind me being successful, or decisive, or any of those things some people can't deal with."

"I think you're amazing." His voice deepened. "I love it when you hand me my ass. You taught me that getting mad doesn't have to mean the end of everything—that I'm *safe* with you." He rose on his knees and slipped his hand behind her neck. "I love you, Julia Garcia, and I know we can make this work."

She leaned into him and placed her hand on his shoulder. "I love you, too, and we definitely can."

With a murmured sound, he pressed his lips to hers and she yielded her mouth to him. Their kiss was deep and so profound Julia came close to losing it.

When Kaiden came up for air, he glanced back at the door.

"Does that thing have a lock?"

"Yes."

"Then stay exactly where you are." He rose from his knees, went over to the door, locked it, and checked it twice. "Any other way someone can get into this room?"

"Not unless they come through the window," Julia said demurely. "I've always had this fantasy of being made love to in my office."

"Really?" Kaiden took a professional look at her desk. "Because I think this is sturdy enough to bear your weight."

He patted the wooden top. "If you want to pop up there, I'll test out my theory."

Julia was already standing. "Shall I take my shoes off?" she asked as he lifted her to sit on the front of her desk. Her skirt hitched up displaying a stunning amount of thigh.

"Hell, no." Kaiden stared approvingly at her navy-blue four-inch heels.

He stood between her legs and cupped her face in his hands. "I'm so sorry I lost my temper with you. I just don't do that, I promise—"

"Stop." Julia placed a finger on his lips. "One of the things I like about you is that I can be myself, and I want you to feel the same way. It's okay to get mad occasionally, it doesn't mean that's the end of everything. In some ways it's just a beginning."

He kissed her forehead. "Not Jeff Miller mad, though."

"I did say occasionally." She sighed as he nuzzled her mouth. "Can I just say how much I've missed this?"

"Which particular parts?" He pressed forward until she could feel how much he wanted her. "Because I've been getting some heavy workouts in the shower thinking about you this last month."

"You poor baby." She wriggled her hand between their bodies and stroked the fly of his jeans. "I almost wish I'd been there."

He groaned and kissed her harder. "You're just making it worse for yourself." He removed her hand and cupped her mound. "You're wet for me."

"Yes." She moved against his questing fingers. "So just for once, can we forget the foreplay, and just get to the main event?"

"So bossy," he murmured as he snaked two fingers beneath the lace of her panties and thrust them inside her.

She moaned his name, which did all kinds of things to his heart, and more importantly his dick.

She flung a hand out to the side. "My purse is in the bottom drawer of my desk. I have condoms."

"Yeah?" He eased her panties down, careful not to catch them on the heels of her shoes. "I have one in my back pocket, so we're good."

She opened her eyes wide at him. "You were really sure you'd succeed here?"

He loved the hint of indignation in her voice. "Pretty much." He pressed three fingers deep inside her and thumbed her bud. "Let's be honest, Garcia, you're a complete pushover."

She came so suddenly he could only ride it out with her as he used his free hand to unzip and shove down his jeans and boxers. She helped him with the condom, which was good considering his hands were shaking, and then he was thrusting inside her, and everything was right with his world.

It didn't take long for them to fight their way to a frantic finish as they climaxed together. Kaiden rested his forehead on her shoulder as he struggled to get his breath back.

"I love you, Julia," he whispered as she smoothed his hair like he was a cat.

"I love you, too." She pushed at his chest. "I hate to break the mood, but the desk is creaking really badly. The last thing I need right now is for it to collapse, and for the entire staff at MZB to rush in here, and find us doing . . . *this*."

As he hastily disentangled himself, Kaiden started to

chuckle. One thing was certain. His life would never be boring with Julia Garcia in it.

"I booked a hotel room if you'd like to try this again with a little more privacy?" he offered, as she carefully slid off the desk righting her skirt the second her heels hit the carpet.

"Where are my panties?"

He patted the pocket of his jeans. "I have them safe right here."

She bent to pick up something that had fallen off the surface of her desk giving him way too many ideas, and making zipping his jeans even harder. When she straightened, her cheeks were flushed, and her mouth soft and rosy from his kisses.

"Didn't you promise me lunch or something?" she asked.

"The hotel definitely has room service."

"Fine." She sighed and went to get her purse. "Now, hand over my panties."

"You sure about that?"

She held out her hand and smiled when he complied. "Give me five minutes in the restroom, and I'm all yours."

"Hey." He caught hold of her elbow as she went to go past him. "You good with all this? Splitting our time between Morgan Valley and here? Seeing each other? Loving each other?"

She cupped his cheek. "Yes."

"A woman of few words." He had to kiss her again.

"Which is a good thing because you talk way too much." She gave him a saucy smile. "I'll meet you in reception, okay?"

"Sure, try not to look like you've just been doing what

we've been doing, okay?" he called out as she unlocked the door.

She stuck her tongue out at him and disappeared down the hall. Kaiden took the time to straighten up the place and set himself to rights before putting his Stetson on and strolling down to reception. Whatever happened next, he'd found a woman who was his perfect match. He was fairly certain they'd fight occasionally, but he wasn't worried. She wouldn't walk away from him, and he would try and be worthy of her for the rest of his life.

He grinned like he'd won the PBR world championship. For once in his life, he really had come out on top.

SHAKSHUKA WITH CHICKPEAS AND FETA
FOR KAIDEN

Ingredients:
3 tbs garlic-infused olive oil or add chopped garlic
½ cup chopped green onion stems or 1 chopped
    onion
1 large pepper, chopped
½ chile jalapeño stemmed, seeded and minced
1 tsp (but add to taste) taco seasoning
1 jar marinara sauce (or homemade marinara)
1 can diced tomatoes, drained of juice
1 can chickpeas, drained and rinsed
3 oz cubed/crumbled feta cheese
4 large eggs
¼ cup chopped cilantro, to garnish

Heat oil in a wide pan, add onions, pepper, and chile, sauté until soft.

Stir in the taco seasoning; add marinara sauce, canned drained tomatoes, and chickpeas.

Cover and bring to a simmer, then reduce down for 5 to 10 minutes. Add feta.

With heat on low, make 4 wells, crack an egg into each, spoon sauce over the top, and cover and cook for 5 to 6 minutes until the eggs are set.

Sprinkle with cilantro and serve.

Connect with U_s

Visit us online at
KensingtonBooks.com
to read more from your favorite authors, see books
by series, view reading group guides, and more.

Join us on social media

for sneak peeks, chances to win books and prize packs,
and to share your thoughts with other readers.

facebook.com/kensingtonpublishing
twitter.com/kensingtonbooks

Tell us what you think!

To share your thoughts, submit a review,
or sign up for our eNewsletters, please visit:
KensingtonBooks.com/TellUs.

Books by Bestselling Author
Fern Michaels

___The Jury	0-8217-7878-1	$6.99US/$9.99CAN
___Sweet Revenge	0-8217-7879-X	$6.99US/$9.99CAN
___Lethal Justice	0-8217-7880-3	$6.99US/$9.99CAN
___Free Fall	0-8217-7881-1	$6.99US/$9.99CAN
___Fool Me Once	0-8217-8071-9	$7.99US/$10.99CAN
___Vegas Rich	0-8217-8112-X	$7.99US/$10.99CAN
___Hide and Seek	1-4201-0184-6	$6.99US/$9.99CAN
___Hokus Pokus	1-4201-0185-4	$6.99US/$9.99CAN
___Fast Track	1-4201-0186-2	$6.99US/$9.99CAN
___Collateral Damage	1-4201-0187-0	$6.99US/$9.99CAN
___Final Justice	1-4201-0188-9	$6.99US/$9.99CAN
___Up Close and Personal	0-8217-7956-7	$7.99US/$9.99CAN
___Under the Radar	1-4201-0683-X	$6.99US/$9.99CAN
___Razor Sharp	1-4201-0684-8	$7.99US/$10.99CAN
___Yesterday	1-4201-1494-8	$5.99US/$6.99CAN
___Vanishing Act	1-4201-0685-6	$7.99US/$10.99CAN
___Sara's Song	1-4201-1493-X	$5.99US/$6.99CAN
___Deadly Deals	1-4201-0686-4	$7.99US/$10.99CAN
___Game Over	1-4201-0687-2	$7.99US/$10.99CAN
___Sins of Omission	1-4201-1153-1	$7.99US/$10.99CAN
___Sins of the Flesh	1-4201-1154-X	$7.99US/$10.99CAN
___Cross Roads	1-4201-1192-2	$7.99US/$10.99CAN

More by Bestselling Author
Hannah Howell

Available Wherever Books Are Sold!

Check out our website at
http://www.kensingtonbooks.com